THE
*A*FFAIR

THE
AFFAIR

ANNA
DILLON

POOLBEG

Published 2004
by Poolbeg Press Ltd
123 Grange Hill, Baldoyle
Dublin 13, Ireland
E-mail: poolbeg@poolbeg.com
www.poolbeg.com

© Anna Dillon 2004

Copyright for typesetting, layout, design
© Poolbeg Press Ltd

1 3 5 7 9 10 8 6 4 2

A catalogue record for this book is available from the British Library.

ISBN 1-84223-147-2

Typeset by Patricia Hope in Goudy 11.3/15
Printed by CPD Group, Wales

About the Author

Born and raised in Dublin, Anna Dillon is the author of the Seasons' Trilogy: *Seasons, Another Season* and *Seasons' End* and the novel, *Lies*.

Acknowledgements

Writing is generally considered a solitary occupation and it is, right up to the moment the manuscript is delivered to the publishers. Then it becomes a group discussion. The role of the group is quite simple: to make the work better, much, much better.

I have to thank everyone in the Poolbeg group, especially Paula and Gaye for their support and encouragement and Brona too.

I also need to acknowledge the advice of the many people whose comments I sought and (usually) listened to, especially CS, JC and GW – all of whom wished to remain nameless. I've no idea why!

Dedication: For Michael, without whose help...

BOOK 1

The Wife's Story

Did I suspect?

I've asked myself that question time and again, but if I'm to be perfectly truthful, I didn't.

You see . . . I trusted him. I loved him. Are they one and the same emotion? Trust and love? They are . . . or, at least, I think they are.

But once the doubt entered my mind, then everything he did was suspect. From that moment on, I could not believe a word out of his mouth.

And when I discovered the truth, I hated him.

CHAPTER 1

Thursday 19th December

Kathy Walker signed the Christmas card with a flourish.

Love from Robert, Kathy, Brendan and Theresa.

She turned the card over, pushed it into the red envelope, licked the flap with two quick movements, making a face at the taste of the gum, then picked up her pen. And stopped. What was the address? She looked up from the pile of envelopes and frowned: 21 something-Park, or was it something-Grove?

Kathy stood away from the kitchen table and pressed her hands into the small of her back, working her neck from side to side, hearing muscles pop alarmingly. She had been writing cards for nearly two hours – a chore she hated and always left until the last minute – and she was now stiff and sore, and just a little irritated. It was the same every year: she wrote the cards, she signed for both of them – and, of course, the majority of the cards were going out to Robert's friends and business associates.

Next year would be different, she promised grimly, hunting for her address book. Then she smiled, and for an instant looked younger – much younger than her forty years – remembering that she'd made the same vow last year. And probably the year before that too.

Kathy found her address book under a pile of last year's unused cards. She always bought Christmas cards in boxes of twenty . . . and she always left three or four in the bottom of the box, promising to use them next year. She never did.

Leaning over the table, she flipped the tattered black address book open, hunting for the address of Robert's cousin. She'd met the man at their wedding eighteen years ago, and doubted if she'd recognise him today if he stood in front of her. Also, he never sent a Christmas card. This was the last year she was sending him one: she was going to make a list of those who sent cards and cross-reference it with the list of what she sent out. Next year she'd only send cards to those people who had sent one to them. That was fair.

She smiled again. She was sure she'd made the same promise last year. And she was convinced that she was sending out twice as many cards this year as she had last year.

She glanced at the clock: just after three. She'd make the four o'clock post if she hurried. Then she was going to order in take-away rather than cook: Indian for Robert and herself, Chinese for Brendan and Theresa. If she timed it right, the children would be coming in from school right about the same time the food arrived. It wasn't very Christmassy, she knew, but they'd have their fill of turkey and ham next week.

Only four cards left. All to Robert's business colleagues. She sat down at the table again and turned the cards over in her hands. He should really write these himself. She pushed them into their envelopes, but left the flaps open. She'd address them, so he'd have no excuse. The first was to the head of the little multi-media company he used, on the Quays. The second to the talent agency that supplied extras for crowd scenes. She smiled as she scribbled the address. It wasn't that long ago that she'd delivered these cards by hand, trudging across the city to push them into the letterboxes because they could not afford the stamps.

How quickly things changed.

Robert's struggling independent television-production company had landed one small job, an insert for a documentary on racism. The documentary won a Palm d'Or award and Robert rode the coat-tails of that success. He had new corporate brochures printed up which certainly gave the impression that R&K Productions had won the award themselves. As usual, no-one bothered to check, and the little lie became self-perpetuating. Kathy remembered a dinner where she was introduced as "one half of the company that won the Palm d'Or for that marvellous documentary . . ." She hadn't the nerve to contradict the speaker.

The company flourished and in doing so had taken its toll on them both over the years. Building a business meant that certain things – family relationships, personal time, holidays – went by the wayside. R&K Productions still made innocuous documentaries, but nowadays principally concentrated on corporate videos, training videos, the occasional advertisement, or they shot local-colour pieces – inserts – for foreign videos. She knew Robert finally accepted – and regretted – that he'd never now make huge landmark documentaries for National Geographic, the Discovery Channel or the BBC. Kathy didn't share those regrets: this way the money was regular and with two teens growing up in the house, she'd take regular money over artistic integrity any day.

She looked at the envelope in her hand. "Burst Post-Production Services." She said the words aloud, surprising herself, the sounds loud in the silence of the kitchen. Post-Production – what exactly was that? She'd been married for Robert for eighteen years now and she still hadn't quite worked out the intricacies of his world. She still couldn't tell her Best Boy from her Gaffer or her ADA from her AD.

Kathy riffled through the address book looking for Burst, though she knew it wasn't in it. She guessed this was one of the new companies Robert had only started working with this year: he never wrote the most recent addresses in the old address book. He preferred to store them in his fancy mobile phone.

Kathy wandered out into the hallway. This was their second home and although this would be their sixth Christmas in it, she'd never quite got used to the sense of space, particularly in the hallway. Their first house had a short, dark, narrow hallway that led straight into the kitchen; this one boasted a large circular opening which, to be truthful, she thought just a bit wasteful. She would much rather have had bigger rooms. It was also cold; the ornate marble floor was lovely to look at, but it radiated the chill like a fridge.

"Robert!" She leaned on the blond wood stair-rail and looked upstairs. "Robert!" Tilting her head to one side, she could faintly hear the thrum of the shower in the bedroom.

She tapped the cards in her hand against the banister, then, sighing, she started up the stairs. On the landing her feet sank into the deep pile of the impossible-to-keep-clean cream-coloured carpet. Their bedroom was at one end of the house; the children's rooms were at the other. It afforded both parties a measure of privacy. She pushed into the bedroom, blinking in surprise at the image of the petite woman with the heart-shaped face reflected in the mirrored doors of the wardrobes. She paused for a single moment, assessing herself: she needed to lose at least four inches around her waist, and grey roots were showing through her chestnut-brown hair. She was content to look forty – at least she didn't look fifty! But right after Christmas she was going back to the gym. She'd get an afternoon appointment when all the trim, slim and well-toned young mummies who filled the morning classes were picking up junior from school. Real women, with real figures, went in the afternoons, she'd discovered.

The shower was louder now, and she could see tendrils of steam creeping from beneath the en-suite door. The water would be scalding; she didn't know how he could stand it so hot. Robert was humming something vaguely Christmassy – "Do They Know It's Christmas" she thought, but it would be impossible to tell, because, even though she loved him dearly, she would be the first to admit that he could not hold a tune.

Robert's clothes were scattered across the bed. Automatically, she stooped and lifted a crumpled silk tie off the floor. She'd given it to him as part of his Christmas present last year. She felt a guilty twinge: she'd got him another tie this year. He was impossible to buy for: anything he wanted, he simply bought. Shirts and ties were always a safe bet.

Kathy sat on the edge of the bed and looked around the too-white bedroom – she'd change it this year, she promised. White was too cold, too hard, and the mirrored doors bounced the light back, making her squint, deepening the lines on her forehead and around her mouth. Even the peach-coloured duvet looked pale and washed-out. She'd get some colour charts after Christmas, she promised herself, adding it to the list of things she was going to do "after Christmas". She also knew that the list would not survive into the second week of the New Year.

Kathy spread out the cards on the bedspread and reached into the pocket of Robert's jacket, which was thrown across the end of the bed, and pulled out his mobile phone. The XDA2 was the latest toy and essential for every gadget-freak. Not much thicker than a normal mobile, it was a combination phone and pocket computer, with a large rectangular colour screen. When he first got it, he'd sat up in bed beside her one night and demonstrated all its capabilities, only giving up when she fell asleep.

Kathy eased the little pen off the side of the phone and turned it on. The screen flashed blue, then lit up with tiny coloured icons. She touched the pen to the little address icon at the bottom of the screen and a listing of names and addresses appeared. She started to scroll down the names to the "B's" looking for Burst Post Production.

Bryant, Edward.

Burford, Kenneth

Burroughs, Stephanie.

The name stopped her cold.

Burroughs, Stephanie.

For an instant, a single moment of time, the room shifted, all the colours becoming brighter, sharper, though the sounds were muted. For the space of a single thumping heartbeat her entire concentration was on that name glowing white on blue on the screen.

Stephanie Burroughs.

That was a name she hadn't come across in a long time.

There was a tiny red flag on the screen beside the entry.

The shower changed tempo and then died, Robert's off-key singing becoming louder.

Moving quickly now, fingers fumbling, she turned off the phone and clicked the pen in place. Shoving the phone back into Robert's jacket pocket, she darted from the room.

"Kathy? Were you looking for me?"

Robert's voice trailed her down the stairs. But all she could hear was the thundering of her blood in her ears.

Stephanie Burroughs.

CHAPTER 2

Kathy's heart was hammering so hard in her chest that she could actually feel the flesh tremble beneath her skin. There was a lump in her throat that made breathing difficult and she kept trying to heave in breath.

She stood in the kitchen doorway, breathing the chill December air, her arms locked across her chest. Stray snowflakes spiralled out of the darkness and kissed her cheeks and forehead. She was blinking furiously, but she would not cry. Not yet. Not now.

Stephanie Burroughs.

With a little red flag beside her name.

The conscious part of her brain suggested that it might be nothing. Stephanie Burroughs was in the television production business; Robert was sure to have the names of just about everyone in the business in his phone. Instinct and emotion kept flashing back to the little red flag icon beside the name. You only put a flag beside something important, didn't you? Still, part of her reasoned, it could be perfectly innocent.

But she knew it was not.

Kathy shook her head savagely. She brushed at her eyes with

the palm of her right hand, pushing away the tears which threatened to flood. She could be wrong. She might be wrong. She wanted to be wrong.

But she wasn't.

Not this time. Not now.

Stephanie Burroughs was back.

Six years ago, around about the same time they'd moved into this house, Robert had had an affair with Stephanie Burroughs. Kathy knew he'd had an affair. She'd always been slightly nervous of Stephanie's association with her husband, and then, when a friend – who was no longer a friend – had spotted them together at a concert and gleefully told her, her suspicions had been confirmed. Three months of too many shoddy excuses, too many nights when he would come home later and later, too many weekends and nights away during the week, suddenly made sense. Everything pointed to one inescapable conclusion: her husband was having an affair.

On one terrible midsummer's evening, with the sun low and red in the heavens, she had turned and faced him. He'd been standing over the barbeque in the back garden, head wreathed in fragrant wood-smoke, meat crisping on the grill. Without preamble, she asked him flatly if he was having an affair with his researcher. In that instant when his eyes slid from hers she knew the truth, before he lied and denied it. Flat out denied it, with enough anger and outrage to rattle her convictions. She'd brought out her suspicions, and he'd managed to counter every one of them with a rational excuse. She'd never managed to prove it, and weeks of recriminations and anguish had followed. Then Stephanie had left the company and moved away and with her departure a lot of the heat had gone out of the argument. Things drifted, then settled back into their old routine.

Kathy had almost, but not quite, forgotten about the woman. It had been a long time since Stephanie's name had flitted across her consciousness, though she still felt that little moment of nervousness when she saw her husband looking at a pretty woman at a party, or on the street.

And now this: Stephanie Burroughs' name in his new phone, with a little red flag beside it.

"Hey, what's up – there's a gale blowing through the house!" Robert came up behind her, wrapping his arms across the top of her shoulders, resting his chin on the top of her head. He smelt fresh and clean, of soap and water and a hint of some cologne she didn't recognise.

Kathy pulled away and stepped back into the kitchen. "Just getting a breath of air, the kitchen was stuffy." She closed the door and spun away from him, not looking into his eyes, fearful that he would see something in her face or that she would see something in his: after eighteen years of marriage it was difficult to keep a secret. She began to tidy the last few cards off the kitchen table. "I left a couple of cards on the bed," she began.

"I saw them . . ."

"I don't have addresses and besides they're personal cards – it would be better if you wrote and signed them."

"What's wrong?" he asked quickly.

Kathy glanced sidelong at him. "Nothing."

He'd been twenty-four when she married him, a tall, gangling youth with a shock of black hair that refused to stay combed. The hair had remained more or less intact and he'd filled out some, but in truth he'd aged well. Unlike her, she thought bitterly. He'd matured; she got old.

"Why do you ask?" she added.

Robert smiled, the corners of his lips creasing and he tilted his head to one side, a movement she'd once found endearing, but which now irritated her. "Because you've got the *tone* in your voice."

"Which tone?"

"That tone." His smile deepened. "The tone that tells me that you're pissed off at me."

Kathy sighed.

"Oh, and the sigh is another sure sign."

"Look, I'm tired. I've been writing cards for hours. Mostly your cards, to your friends, and your colleagues. I do it every year. And every year it's last minute and I'm always short of the addresses. You don't help."

She watched the smile tighten on his lips. "I've just come in from a ten-hour day," he said, his voice still light and reasonable. "Traffic was a bitch and I've got a presentation to make in the morning. Let me get a cup of tea, then I'll go through my address book and give you every address you need."

"I've done them all," Kathy said tightly, aware that she was losing this argument before it had even begun. "The four on the bed are all you have to do."

"We're arguing over four cards?" he asked.

"No, we're not arguing over four cards," she snapped. "We're arguing over the one hundred and twenty I've written. Without your help."

Robert nodded and shrugged. "I should have taken some into work with me." Then he glanced up at the clock. "I'll go and get the kids."

Before she could say another word, he turned and strode from the kitchen, across the dining-room and out into the hallway. She could see him snatching his leather jacket off the rack behind the door and then he left, pulling the front door shut quietly behind him.

Kathy, leaning on the kitchen table, listened to the car start up and gently pull away. He'd done it again. Managed to twist and turn her words until suddenly she felt she was in the wrong, that she was arguing about nothing, then he turned and walked away. He was good at that. In all the years she'd known him, he always walked away from an argument.

If that had been her, she'd have slammed out of the hall door and revved off at high speed, spattering gravel against the side of the house. He was always just too damned controlled.

She shoved the Christmas cards into a plastic bag – she'd bring them down to the post office tomorrow and if they didn't arrived before next Wednesday, then tough. She scooped up the blank cards and shoved them unceremoniously into their boxes. She'd sort them out next year.

Kathy turned away from the table, and hit the switch on the side of the kettle, setting it to boil. She had spooned two teaspoons of instant coffee into a cup when she remembered that she was trying to cut down on her caffeine intake. Well, the bottom of the cup was wet: she couldn't pour it back into the jar. She hadn't managed to lose any weight for the various Christmas parties they'd been invited to – and was feeling slightly guilty because she'd avoided going to a couple of business-related events which she knew would be populated by bright young things as thin as sticks, with designer dresses artfully draped on their bones. Robert had gone to the parties on his own; he didn't seem to mind.

The kettle whistled, the sound startling her.

He'd left his phone.

Kathy stopped suddenly. He'd left his phone. Snapping off the kettle, she darted out into the hall and pulled open the front door. The car was gone. She turned and ran up the stairs. As far as she could remember, he hadn't had his phone in his hand when he'd come into the kitchen. She knew he hated carrying it in his trousers pocket: it was just a little too large and he usually wore it clipped to his belt, like a kid wearing a toy gun, or he carried it in his inside jacket pocket like an oversized wallet. She raced into the bedroom.

His jacket was where she'd left it and there, just visible, was the silver edge of the phone.

There was a place deep inside her where she suddenly knew that she now had a choice. She was abruptly conscious that the decision she made in the next couple of seconds was going to have repercussions for the rest of her life.

She could hear her mother's voice now, clear and distinct, the slightly bitter waspish tones managing to irritate her even though the woman had been dead eighteen months.

"Never ask a question unless you're prepared for an answer you don't like."

Kathy had a vague memory that her father, dead for more than seventeen years, had used a similar phrase, and she reckoned her mother had stolen it from him.

Was she prepared for an answer she didn't like?

Kathy Walker sat on the edge of the bed and slid out the XDA2. Somewhere deep inside her, she already knew the answer. All she was looking for now was confirmation.

Proof. She was looking for proof. She wasn't going to make the same mistake she made the last time.

CHAPTER 3

Stephanie Burroughs.

All the lines beside her name in the phone were filled in: an address in the city, a phone number, a mobile number, an email, a note of her birthday. And a little red flag beside her name.

Her fingers felt numb, hands trembling slightly as she used the little silver pen to tap the flag on the screen. The calendar program came up, a series of little rectangles representing the days of the month. Friday last had a little flag on it; the flag on Stephanie's name was linked to it. She tapped the screen, bringing up the day.

Friday had been a busy day for R&K Productions – or at least for the R part of it. There had been breakfast with a client at eight am, then a ten am meeting followed by a session in studio at eleven thirty. Artwork was pencilled in for three o'clock, then nothing.

Except for a red flag at five. No notation.

Kathy frowned. Last Friday . . . Robert had been late home last Friday; he'd been meeting a client he told her. It had been close to midnight when he'd arrived in.

Conscious that time was slipping by, she changed back to the month view and moved to the next red flag. It was for the previous Tuesday. Again, late in the afternoon, the last event of the day, with no appointments scheduled following it. The flag before that was for the previous Friday. She nodded quickly. He'd been late that Friday, but she couldn't remember anything about the Tuesday. Robert was often late home from work: in fact he was late more often than not.

Now she moved forward in the diary. The next red flag was for tomorrow night, Friday night. Red flag at four, with no appointments following it.

She changed back to the Contacts page, and quickly scrolled down through the names. She only came across two other names with red flags, and she recognised both as long-standing clients.

Feeling unaccountably guilty, she went through the other pockets, not entirely sure what she was looking for. He'd taken his wallet with him, and all she found were a couple of Pay & Display stubs, the remains of a packet of mints and a receipt from the Kylemore in Blanchardstown Shopping Centre. Two beverages. She smoothed out the receipt on the bed, trying to decipher the date.

It looked like last Tuesday, at five ten pm. What was Robert doing in Blanchardstown last Tuesday evening? Robert hated shopping, hated shopping centres particularly. Getting out to the shopping centre in afternoon traffic so close to Christmas would have been a nightmare; getting back would be even worse. When Robert wanted to shop, he popped across to the Pavilions in Swords.

Lights suddenly flared against the bedroom window as a car pulled into the driveway. Calmly, Kathy stuffed the Pay & Display receipts and the mints back into his jacket pocket. She stuffed the Kylemore receipt into her own pocket. Then she closed down the XDA and clicked the pen back into its slot, slipped the phone into her husband's jacket pocket and was in the process of descending the stairs when the hall door opened and Robert, followed by

Brendan and Theresa, bundled into the house in a tumult of noise and chill air.

"We got take-away," Brendan called, holding up the brown-paper bags.

Kathy smiled automatically. "Great. I was going to suggest that anyway." She was looking at her husband, at the man she thought she knew and realised she didn't.

Robert caught the quizzical look and tilted his head in a question. "Everything OK?"

"Fine," she lied, "just fine."

CHAPTER 4

"I was thinking," she said suddenly.

"Always dangerous . . ." he quipped.

Kathy could see him through the bathroom door, standing in those ridiculous striped pyjamas bottoms which she absolutely hated, but which he insisted on buying for himself. She was sitting up in bed, supported by a trio of pillows, holding a magazine up in front of her face. Although her head was tilted down, as if she was reading, she was watching him over the top of the page.

"You've been working so hard lately . . ."

The electric toothbrush began to buzz and whine. Robert was paranoid about his teeth. Two years ago, when they'd least been able to afford it, he'd spent nearly two thousand euro having them straightened and bleached. Now he went to the dentist every three months to get them whitened. She thought it made them look terribly artificial, like a set of false teeth. Lately, he'd been talking about having laser surgery on his eyes, even though he only needed glasses for reading or close work on the computer screen.

Kathy waited until the whine of the toothbrush faded away,

then she tried again. "I've been thinking, you've been working so hard lately, I've barely seen you. I thought we should try and have a night out."

"Good idea."

"I was thinking tomorrow night."

And how will you answer, she wondered. Will you say yes to me, and make me feel foolish because I've doubted you, make me feel guilty because I spied on you and doubted you or will you –

"I can't. Not tomorrow night. I'm entertaining a client. Christmas drinks." He came out of the bathroom, patting white toothpaste off his chin, staring directly into her eyes as he smiled at her with those huge brown innocent eyes of his.

"You never said."

"I'm sure I did." He pulled on the pyjama top.

"I'd have remembered."

He shrugged and turned to toss the towel back into the en suite. It missed the rail and slid to the floor, where she would pick it up in the morning. She caught him looking at himself in the mirrored wardrobe doors, just a quick glance, but something about the way he looked, then nodded approvingly . . .

Still keeping her head down, turning the magazine pages slowly, pretending to read, she raised her eyes and looked at her husband. Really looked at him. It's said that you really only see someone when you first meet them, and after that you never really *look* at them again. The picture the brain establishes in that first glance is the one that remains. How long ago was it since she'd looked at him, seen him as a person, an individual, a man?

Was it her imagination, or was he looking a lot more tanned and toned than was natural? He'd always been careful about his weight and was positively obsessive about his hair. Squinting slightly, she stared at his hair, and realised that some of the grey was gone. About a year ago he'd started to develop grey wings – distinguished and handsome, she'd thought – just above his ears. Now she realised that they had faded and almost vanished. Indeed, his hair was lustrous and shining, making her wonder if there wasn't a colour or a tint in it. It looked like he'd lost a little weight too; his stomach seemed flatter and there was the hint – just a hint – of muscle. Even though it was the depths of winter, and they hadn't been on a summer holiday, his skin was an even tan. She couldn't even see a tan mark on his wrist where he habitually wore his watch. The tan looked too perfect to have come from a bottle – there were no streaks, no darker patches: my God, he was going to a tanning salon, she realised.

Kathy turned the page of the magazine. The words were dipping and crawling across the page and she was unable to make sense of them, but she concentrated on moving her head as if she were reading. Who was he tanning for? Not for her, certainly. Suddenly that single thought – not for her – saddened her. When had he stopped trying to impress her? When had she stopped being impressed by him?

"Who are you meeting tomorrow?" she asked casually.

"Jimmy Moran," Robert said without missing a beat. "We're having dinner in Shanahan's on the Green." He threw back the covers and slipped into the bed, sending a wave of chill air radiating through the sheets. "You didn't turn on the blanket," he said, almost accusingly.

"I didn't think it was that cold." Ever since she'd started to put together the pieces, she'd been running hot and cold. She tossed the magazine onto the floor and slid down in the bed, pulling the covers up to her chin.

"Are you not going to read?"

"No, my eyes are watering; I think I've got a bit of eye strain." She reached up and turned off the light over her side of the bed.

"Well, I'll read for a bit, if you don't mind."

She knew even if she did mind, he'd still keep the light on. He reached down to the side of the bed and lifted up the book he was reading, *The Road Less Travelled*.

She waited in silence for a moment, then she heard a page

turn. He was an incredibly slow reader. She could read two books a week; he'd been reading his current book for at least a month, maybe longer. Not looking at him, she asked, "When do you think we might be able to get a night out? Before Christmas?"

There was a pause. She heard another page turn. "We might leave it until after Christmas. It's a nightmare trying to find a place to eat and parking is impossible." He attempted a laugh. "All the restaurants are full of people like me, treating clients like Jimmy to too much wine." She heard the book hit the floor, and then his light snapped off. "After Christmas, we'll find a little time. Maybe even head off for the weekend. What do you think?"

"That would be nice," Kathy said. She was reminded that he'd said the same things about the same time last year. They hadn't gone away; there was never enough time.

CHAPTER 5

Friday 20th December

Rose King rested her elbows on the kitchen table and reached out to take her friend's hands. "But you're not sure."

Kathy Walker shook her head. "No. Yes. No. I don't know."

"You're suspicious."

"I'm suspicious."

"And you've been suspicious before?"

Kathy nodded. "I have."

"I'll bet there's not a woman on this estate who hasn't been suspicious about her husband at least once."

"Have you? Been suspicious, I mean?"

Rose's smile tightened. "I have. More than once."

Rose King was five years older than Kathy and looked five years older than that again, with what looked like a perm that had gone out of fashion in the Seventies, but which was her own hair. No matter what she did to it – had it cut, coloured or straightened – within a matter of weeks it returned to its unruly mop. A short, stout woman, she had raised three children, the youngest of whom had just left home. She'd recently told Kathy that this would be the first Christmas in more than twenty years that she and Tommy, her husband, would be alone. She was dreading it.

Rose and Kathy had formed the unlikeliest of friendships, starting twelve years ago when Brendan, Kathy's eldest, was starting school. Kathy walked past Rose's slightly dishevelled front lawn four times a day. A brief hello had turned into a few words as the weeks went by, which had gradually turned into longer chats. Soon Kathy was stopping for a cup of tea, then Rose was dropping in. On the surface they had nothing in common, besides being neighbours, but they had no secrets from one another. Even when Kathy had moved house, going from one end of Swords to the other, the two women had kept in touch and remained friends.

"What could you suspect your Tommy of?" Even the thought of Tommy – fat, pompous and, when he wasn't wearing a ridiculous wig, as bald as an egg – having an affair, brought a smile to her lips.

Rose shrugged. Then she grinned. "I know what you're thinking. You're thinking that my Tommy isn't going to have much of a chance with the women."

"I didn't say that."

"You didn't have to." Rose reached for the cup of tea, brought it to her lips, then put it down without tasting it. "My Tommy. Fat and bald Tommy. But he wasn't always fat and bald." She shook her head in wonderment. "I know for certain that he's had one relationship that lasted four years. And there's definitely been two other briefer affairs."

Kathy stated at her blankly. She was shocked, but she wasn't sure whether it was at the thought of Tommy having an affair and or by the calm, almost conversational way that Rose announced the news. More to disguise her incredulity, she got up and grabbed the kettle. Turning to the sink, she busied herself filling it. "I never knew . . . you never said."

"It's not the sort of thing you drop into conversation, is it?"

"How long ago . . . I mean, when did you first suspect?" Kathy whirled around. "I'm sorry, I shouldn't have asked. It's none of my business."

"Ten years ago was the first time," Rose continued as if she hadn't heard Kathy. "I don't know her name; I never bothered to find out. She was an old flame, I think, one of his many previous girlfriends. They'd kept in touch on and off, then they started seeing one another for a drink. The drinks turned to meals, the meals turned to . . . well, I don't know what they turned to, but I suspect that they ended up in bed together." Rose delivered the statement in a flat monotone.

Kathy shook her head. Through the kitchen window, she could see out into the grim-looking winter garden, the trees stripped of leaves, the ornamental pond which she hated covered in a scummy layer of brown. Reflected in the glass, she could see Rose's face, staring at her.

She turned back from the sink and sat at the kitchen table again, not sure what to do or how to respond. She had waited until Robert had gone to work and the children had raced to catch the bus before phoning her friend. She thought she would tell Rose her story and get some advice; she certainly hadn't expected to hear something like this. She found herself shaking her head again.

"I know," Rose said. "It's Tommy, isn't it? The thought of him naked is so ridiculous. And let me tell you, it is. But, you know, he can be so charming, so kind. That's what first attracted me to him." She laughed shakily. "He was no oil painting, even in his youth, but he made me laugh. I read somewhere that that's what women go for. Forget your muscles and good looks: most women go for charm and smiles. That's why liars get all the girls."

The kettle started to whistle and Kathy returned to the sink. "I read that too."

"A couple of years after that," Rose continued, "I suspected he was carrying on with yer one from number fifteen."

Kathy snorted, the sound unexpected. "The big one with the . . .?"

Reflected in the kitchen glass, Rose nodded. "The very same.

He started doing the accounts for her after the business folded. Remember, her husband ran the little electrical store just off the main street. He had the grand closing-down sale, everything must go, all items dirt-cheap. Well, he made a fortune that day, then did a runner with the takings, the contents of their bank account and the little scrawny bit who served behind the till."

"I remember now. I bought a vacuum cleaner there."

"I got a deep-fat fryer. Well, my Tommy started popping over once a week. Then it was twice. Then . . . well, I don't know. It finished when she moved out."

Kathy made a fresh pot of tea and brought it back to the table. "You said there were three occasions . . ." she gently prompted Rose.

"About two years ago, I suspected something was going on. He started acting strange. That's when he started getting really conscious about the hair, and got the wig."

"I remember." The wig was the talk of the estate. It was a confection of hair that seemed to balance precariously atop Tommy's head, and it never moved, not even in gale-force winds.

"You know, he thinks no-one has noticed the wig," Rose said "because no-one ever asked about it."

"It's a bit difficult to slip it into a conversation. 'Nice rug. Where did you get that wig? How's the wig?' I know if I was to ever mention it, I'd burst out laughing in his face."

Rose started to laugh. She had a deep masculine chuckle and suddenly Kathy was laughing with her, the two women giggling and chuckling together, and for an instant it was just like one of hundreds of other shared mornings, when all was right with the world. Then Kathy abruptly sobered. Things had not been perfect those other mornings: Rose had been living with the fact that she believed her husband was having an affair.

"Did you ever ask him?"

"About the wig?"

"About the affairs."

Rose concentrated on pouring tea, then adding a tiny touch of low-fat milk. She reached for the sugar until she remembered that she was trying to give it up, and pushed it away. "The first time I discovered he was playing away, I thought about it," she said eventually. "I thought about it long and hard, and then I asked myself what I'd do if he answered yes."

Kathy nodded. She'd thought the same thing.

"This was before divorce came into the country, remember. What was I going to do if he said yes? I could ask him to leave, but we still had eight years to pay on the mortgage. What happened if he left? Who would pay that?" She shrugged awkwardly. "I know it sounds like an incredibly practical, maybe even cynical thing to think about, but it's what crossed my mind in the situation. And then I wondered, what would happen if I asked him to leave and he said no? I couldn't stay with him, could I? So I'd have to go, to leave my home and go . . . go where? Ten years ago, I was forty. I'd no qualifications and my nearest relative – an aunt – was in Cork, and she wasn't going to take me in. Nor was I going to ask her. And then, of course, the big question: what would happen to the children? They were doing exams or studying for exams: how would this trauma affect them?"

Kathy took a deep breath. The same thoughts had been milling around in her head all night. She wondered if every woman, faced with the same situation, would have the same concerns. She reckoned they would.

"So what did you do in the end?"

Rose looked Kathy directly in the eye. "I did nothing."

"Nothing." The word hung flat and compromising between them.

"Nothing. I decided he was having some sort of mid-life crisis, and I let it go. I said nothing, did nothing. I was hoping he'd realise he had much more to lose if he left me. I was gambling that he would come to his senses And he did. Eventually."

"You did nothing."

"Sometimes doing nothing is a decision too," Rose said gently.

"Are you saying I should do nothing?"

"No, I'm not saying that. I'm telling you that's what I did."

"I don't think I could do that."

"Before you make any decision, you've got to be sure of your facts. At this moment, right now, you don't know for sure."

Kathy nodded. "I'm almost sure."

"You were almost sure before."

"And I was right then. I know I was. I just had no proof."

"Then you need proof before you confront him," Rose said simply. "And even then, even when you are one hundred per cent sure, you've got to be prepared for the consequences of making the accusation."

Kathy shook her head from side to side and suddenly there were tears in her eyes, but, for the first time since the ugly suspicion had been planted in her mind, they were tears of anger. "If I knew he was having an affair, and I didn't confront him, I couldn't live with myself."

Rose reached over and caught both of Kathy's hands in hers. "That's what I thought in the beginning. Then I realised that Tommy still came home to me every night. These other women were just a distraction, nothing more. If I'd tackled him, I would have destroyed our marriage but I knew if I was patient I would win out."

"I can't do that."

"I know you can't. Not right now. But think about it. Have it at the back of your mind as an option."

Rose released her hands and picked up her teacup. Not looking at Kathy, she asked, "In bed – in the bedroom – how are things? Are they all right?"

Kathy opened her mouth to make a quick response, then stopped. Things in the bedroom . . . were different. They had never been an especially passionate couple and, once they'd got past the first infatuation of their youthful days, their lovemaking became sporadic. After the children came along, it slipped into an irregular Saturday or Sunday morning routine. Then even that pattern shifted and drifted away. In recent months it had died away to nothing. She couldn't remember the last time they had made love. She'd once admired that in Robert: he'd never forced himself on her. On the occasions when he had reached out for her and she'd turned her back on him, he hadn't pursued it, hadn't forced the issue, just kissed the back of her head and rolled away. It had been like that for years now.

She felt a suddenly twinge of conscience. Had her lack of interest in sex been one of the things which had driven him from her?

But no, a marriage wasn't just about sex, a marriage was –

"What?" Rose asked, seeing the expression on the younger woman's face.

"Something struck me. Something important, something I've never thought about before." Kathy licked suddenly dry lips. "What is a marriage? What makes a marriage?" Rose opened her mouth to respond, but Kathy raised her hand. "Is it living together, is it the commitment, the sex, the shared experiences, the trust, the truth? Love? What is it?"

"When I was younger," Rose said, very quietly, "I would have said all of those things. Now," she shrugged, "now, I think it might just be habit."

CHAPTER 6

Rose's parting words had been, "Don't make a decision until you've got your evidence. And be sure this time, Kathy. And if you are sure, then be prepared for the consequences. Not just the immediate consequences, but long term."

Kathy had stood at the hall door and watched Rose make her way down the path. Her friend stopped at the gate and raised her hand and smiled, then turned to the right and headed back home. Kathy watched her. It was just like countless other mornings and it would be so easy to pretend that nothing had changed . . . and yet everything had altered.

She now saw Rose differently.

She hadn't exactly lost respect for her friend, but . . . something was different and she knew that things would never be the same between them ever again, though at that precise moment, she was unsure why.

She could hear her mother's words again: *Never ask a question unless you're prepared for an answer you don't like.*

Isn't that how most affairs started: because one partner never asked the questions? Where have you been, why are you late, who were you with? But you couldn't do that. Even asking the questions would destroy a relationship. A relationship was built on trust; if you trusted someone, you didn't have to ask the questions.

Kathy closed the door and put her back against the solid wood. She shook her head. She suddenly knew why things would never be the same between Rose and her again. When Rose admitted that she'd known her husband had been having an affair – *affairs* – and had chosen to do nothing, in that moment Kathy had lost her respect for her.

You had to do something.

You were supposed to do something.

She just didn't know what you were supposed to do.

Kathy wandered around the house, moving from room to room, looking at them again, seeing them with new eyes. Somewhere at the back of her mind she was wondering what she would take with her if she chose to leave . . . or what Robert would take with him if he left.

Would he leave?

Would she ask him?

The Walkers lived in a large solid four-bedroom in an old estate in what had once been the rural part of Swords, but Swords was practically a suburb of Dublin now. When they first moved into Swords eighteen years ago, she thought they were living in the heart of the country, but there had been a huge explosion of housing estates in and around the North County Dublin area which eroded the rural feel from the environment. The price of their first home had pushed them to the very limit of what they could afford then, and for a couple of years after that. There had been months when they had lived on beans and toast just to make sure they had enough to pay the mortgage. But they had been happy times. They had laughed a lot then. More then they ever did now.

Six years ago, they moved into this house. It was less than two miles from their first home, but it was larger and was surrounded by a green belt. They bought the house for exactly a quarter of what it was worth now. Robert said it would be a fabulous investment: he was right then. He was right most of the time.

She had once loved that about him, loved his absolute confidence and self-assurance. She didn't think she had ever once heard him express any doubts about what he was doing and the direction he was taking their lives. But what she once accepted as confidence, she now knew to be arrogance.

There was nothing of his in the sitting-room. It was rarely used, a habit she'd picked up from her mother: a room kept aside as a "good room" for visitors where the children never ventured. A chunky black leather suite dominated the room and made it seem smaller than it was. She'd never wanted the suite, and would have preferred something lighter and brighter. But when they'd bought it, Robert was still entertaining at home, and he thought the leather suite gave the right impression, one of prosperity and success. The china cabinet against one wall had been her mother's, and was filled with a mismatched assortment of Waterford, Cavan, Galway and Dublin crystal. She never got around to completing any of the sets and doubted if she ever would now. There was no television in the room – in fact, it was probably the only room in the house with the exception of the bathroom which had no TV set in it.

The dining-room, which led directly into the kitchen, was very much the family room. To the left of the black marble fireplace, an enormous thirty-six-inch flat-screen television took up one corner, along with the DVD player, the video player and Brendan's X-Box. Speakers connected to a surround-sound system trailed around the floor. Videos and DVDs were scattered on the floor alongside the television. Robert would want some of those, though she was sure he had not watched any of them, and probably never would. He was always buying DVDs and books for "a rainy day" or for when he got a few hours of free time. Lately he'd had no free time, or if he had he was too busy and she wondered now . . .

She veered away from that thought. She didn't want to know what he was busy with.

Or whom.

The suite here was older, the seats slightly bellied from years of wear, though she had had it re-upholstered recently. When she'd had it recovered, it had looked brand new for about a week. She'd been promising she'd get rid of it for months now and had a vague idea about looking for a new suite in the January sales.

On top of the fireplace was the hideous 1930's clock that Robert had inherited from his grandfather. Kathy hated it, with its yellow, nicotine-stained paper face and a mechanism that whirred and clicked just before it stuck the hour, reminding her of an old man grinding his teeth. Robert would want that and, if he didn't want it, he was going to take it away with him, because she wasn't going to tolerate it in her house.

Kathy stopped and pressed both hands flat against her suddenly churning stomach.

Her house.

Her home.

Hers.

She was the one who spent the time in it, day in and day out. She cleaned it, cared for it, turned an empty shell of a house into a loving home for Robert and her children. Sometimes a whole week went by and the only time she left the house was when she popped out to the shops for a carton of milk, or dropped the children down to school, or picked them up. She knew every nook and cranny, every squeaky floorboard, every curling strip of wallpaper; she knew where the cobwebs gathered, the taps which dripped, and which windows stuck. This was her home. She wasn't going to give it up. If it came to it, she would fight for it.

She shivered suddenly, chill air trickling down the back of her neck: it frightened her that she was thinking like this. But as she began to examine the past and try to establish a future, she was forced to look at words like "separation" and "divorce". And that meant looking at works like "his" and "hers", words which she'd never considered before. It had always been "theirs" even during those terrible days all those years ago when she'd accused him of having an affair with Stephanie. She'd never once thought of divorce then.

Kathy took a deep breath. Rose was right. Before she even started to look down that road, she was going to need evidence. Strong, incontrovertible evidence.

The dining-table and six chairs, one of them mismatched from the time Robert had accidentally sawed through the original and they'd been forced to replace it with the closest match, took up the rest of the dining-room. The family ate there on special occasions, but there had been few of those of late. It had last been used the previous Christmas and would be used again next Wednesday. Now it was covered with the remnants of Theresa's hand-made Christmas cards.

Kathy wandered back into the kitchen and automatically cleared the cups from the kitchen table. She stood by the sink and ran them under the tap, rather than pop them into the dishwasher. She wanted – needed – to be doing something with her hands.

She glanced at the clock and wondered what time Robert would get home tonight. Then she remembered that he was going to be late: he was meeting a client. Or at least that's what he told her. She stopped, frowning. He said he was taking . . . who? Taking Jimmy. Jimmy Moran to Shanahan's on the Green.

"Directory Enquiries."

"Yes, Shanahan's on the Green. It's a restaurant." Her voice surprised her; it sounded strong and confident, loud in the silence of the kitchen. She hadn't realised she was going to make the call until she found the phone in her hand, her fingers tapping out the number for Directory Enquiries.

Isn't this what suspicious wives the world over do, she thought bitterly. Don't they check up on their husbands?

"Yes, put me through, please."

Didn't his lie spill out into everyone else's lives? Friends would lie for him, colleagues would lie, and now here she was, about to add to the fabric of lies that surrounded his affair.

"Hello, good morning. I'm just calling to confirm a reservation. Robert Walker for this evening, seven thirty." It was her best secretarial voice, efficient, slightly bored. She'd played the part often enough in the early days when Robert was setting up the production company, pretending to be his secretary in an effort to convince clients that it was more than a one-man operation.

"Yes, I'm absolutely sure it's for this evening."

Her lips were dry and her mouth was filled with cotton. At the corner of her right eye, a muscle began to twitch uncontrollably. "Perhaps the reservation was made in the company name: try R&K Productions." Once you discovered the first lie, she thought bitterly, the rest followed easily enough. "Well, thank you for trying. Let me get back to my boss. I'm sure there's a simple explanation."

There was no reservation for Shanahan's on the Green. She hadn't expected that there would be. It could be a simple mistake on Robert's part – but Robert rarely made mistakes – maybe it was a different restaurant.

Or he'd lied to her.

And he was meeting his mistress. As he had on every other red flag day.

CHAPTER 7

Kathy Walker stood outside the door to her husband's study. She rested her hand gently on the doorknob, but hesitated, reluctant to turn the handle and step into his domain.

The events of the past few hours had moved so swiftly that it had left her little time for contemplation. Less than twenty-four hours ago, she'd seen the red flag against that woman's name on her husband's phone and she'd jumped to a conclusion. Maybe she was wrong. Her head desperately tried to convince her that maybe it was entirely innocent.

Her heart told her it wasn't.

She had known, because she had suspected for a long time that something was amiss. And once you suspected, wasn't that the first indication that something really was wrong? Wasn't that what all the agony aunts advised? If you knew – truly knew, without question, without hesitation, without doubt – that your partner truly loved you, you would never suspect him of having an affair. But Kathy wasn't convinced that Robert loved her any more. Liked her probably, was used to her certainly, but loved her . . . she didn't think so.

When she had seen that red flag, lots of little things, lots of half-formed questions, slight curious incidents had shifted and settled into a convincing truth. And now, for her own peace of mind, for her sanity's sake, she needed proof. More proof, convincing, positive proof.

But once she stepped into his room looking for proof, things were forever altered. This was a step she could not go back from. Even if she found nothing inside, even if she discovered evidence that completely exonerated him, and even though he would never know that she had been searching, things could never be the same between them again.

He'd betrayed her once.

The thought crept, icy and bitter, into the back of her mind. Betrayed her with the same woman. Or so she believed. She'd had no proof then, no concrete evidence, just fears and suppositions.

She needed to know. She had to know.

Kathy Walker pushed open the door and stepped into her husband's study.

It was originally the second largest bedroom in the house and at one stage they'd planned on giving it to Brendan when he got older. Robert had taken it over when they'd first moved into the house, set up his computer and his files, his bookshelves and his computer editing suite, and even back then she had known that Brendan would never get the room.

The room was a perfect square, a large double window facing the door, looking out over the back garden. That was another reason it was so perfect for Robert: it was quiet. A row of filing cabinets took up the left wall, while a draughtsman's desk was placed directly in front of the window. Robert preferred to sketch out the scenes for his scripts, whether it was for a documentary or an ad, before actually shooting them. A long blond wood table to the right of the window held all the office equipment: printers, faxes, scanners, a large desktop computer and a space where the shiny laptop usually sat, alongside the digital editing suite, where he spliced images, dialogue and music into the advertisements that were R&K's bread and butter. When they first set up the business all those years ago, they sent everything out for editing. Now, with the advances in technology, it was possible to do all of it in-house on a powerful home computer.

She rarely came into this room, it was very much Robert's domain, but she was always struck by how incredibly neat it was. It was an aspect of his personality which she found contrasted sharply with the real man. In his daily life and his personal appearance, Robert was always slightly dishevelled, slightly scattered at all times. She'd once thought it was part of his charm. He'd turned up on a date more than once wearing odd socks and he still had the boyhood habit of buttoning up his jacket incorrectly. Lately however – even before she'd become suspicious – she'd been aware that he'd started taking care of his appearance. She'd noticed some new shirts with strong vertical stripes on the rail in the wardrobe along with a couple of new silk ties in bright primary colours to match them. A sharply styled new suit in a dark Italian wool-silk mix had appeared at the back of the wardrobe. And he'd started getting regular haircuts. It wasn't that long ago that he'd sat on the edge of the bath while she trimmed his hair with her sewing scissors.

But when it came to business, he was incredibly organised. A different aspect of his nature surfaced: efficient, cold and ruthless in many ways.

Kathy stood in the centre of the room and looked around. She was looking for something. She just didn't know *what* she was looking for. But she'd know it when she saw it: it would be another red flag item.

She started with the papers on his desk. A neat pile was stacked in a wire basket to the left of his computer. She knew from experience that he would know if she left anything out of place, so she'd have to take care to leave everything exactly as she found it. She turned the basket upside-down, emptying all the papers onto the desk, face down. Then, she went through them, one by one, replacing them in the wire basket, right side up.

Invitation to a product launch . . . letter from a client . . . art student looking for a job . . . VISA bill . . . invoice from a secretarial agency . . . speeding ticket . . .

Kathy stopped. Robert had said nothing to her about getting a speeding ticket. It was a fixed penalty ticket, two points on his licence, for driving 36 miles per hour in a 30-mile stretch of road in Ballymun last October 31, at 11.12pm. She sighed as she put the ticket back into the basket, wondering if the two points on the licence would affect their insurance. She knew why he had said nothing to her about it. Like most men. he was incredibly vain about his driving and probably felt embarrassed.

The next sheet of paper was a complaint from Tony O'Connor. She remembered Tony. He'd been one of their first clients. He had a number of small carpet and tile shops scattered across the country and employed R&K to do his deliberately cheesy advertisements. He always complained, even when he'd signed off and approved an ad. Some things never changed. Shaking her head, she put it in the basket on top of the speeding ticket.

And stopped.

Something cold settled into the pit of her stomach.

October thirty-first was Halloween. She remembered last Halloween because there had been some trouble on the estate. A group of older lads had got some unbelievably powerful fireworks and had let them off into the early hours of the morning. She clearly recalled sitting on the bed with Brendan and Theresa on either side of her, watching the colourful explosions of light on the other side of the green. The noise was incredible – a mixture of what sounded like gunfire, crackles, hisses and tremendous explosions. A bonfire blazed in the distance and showers of sparks were spiralling high into the heavens and, even in the bedroom behind the closed windows, the air tasted of burnt rubber tyres. At one stage a spent rocket had fallen on the roof, then rolled and clattered off the tiles. The three of them had jumped in unison, thinking the roof was coming in.

But Robert had not been there. She'd remembered being almost grateful. He would probably have wanted to go out and argue with the boys, and God knows how that would have ended up. That night he was in Belfast having dinner with a client; he'd stayed over and come back the following morning.

But how then could he get a ticket in Ballymun at 11.12pm?

Because – *stupid* – he was not in Belfast.

Because – *stupid* – he was driving through Ballymun.

She quickly riffled through the rest of the paper. Something else had bothered her. Yes. There was a VISA bill. How had it got up here? She took care of the bills. In the early years of their marriage, Robert had looked after all the bills, and they'd ended up paying interest on more than one occasion because he'd forgotten to pay on time. Now, she paid all the bills and utilities. They had two Gold Cards, one with AIB and one with BOI. They ran all the house expenses on AIB, and the business expenses on the BOI card.

Kathy turned over the VISA bill again. It was for an MBNA Platinum card. She frowned at the bill; she didn't know they had an MBNA account, and why had she never seen it before? Then she realised it had been sent to Mount Street, which was the office address in the city. It seemed to be entirely for internet purchases: books, CDs, computer stuff. Kathy didn't know Robert bought anything online except for the occasional book from Amazon, and they tended to be work-related titles. There was nothing unusual in it . . . until she turned the page. There were three items listed on the second page of the bill. A sterling purchase from QVC – the satellite TV shopping channel – which came to one hundred and eighty euro. A bouquet of flowers had been ordered online from Interflora. That came to seventy euro. The most recent entry was for the White Orchid Restaurant in the city for sixty-two euro, and that expense had been incurred just over two weeks ago, on Tuesday, the third of December. Last night, looking at her husband's phone, she'd noted that last Tuesday was a red flag day.

She looked at the few pieces of information her cursory search had revealed. He had a credit card he'd told her nothing about, he had purchased a meal in a Chinese restaurant Tuesday two weeks ago when he'd supposedly been working, and – most damning of all – she had him in Dublin last October, when had told her he was in Belfast. And, she also knew for a fact that he was not having dinner in Shanahan's this evening.

What more evidence did she need that he was having an affair?

She hurried through the rest of the documents. But there was nothing of any interest in them. Robert was, by nature, a cautious man, and she was more than surprised that he'd left the incriminating papers on his desk. Kathy started to get angry: he was obviously counting on her docility and stupidity, or else he had so little respect for her that he thought that even if she did come into his room, she wouldn't notice. She had a sudden temptation to rip every file out of the cabinets, shred them, then pile them up in the centre of the floor and let him come home to an unholy mess. She wanted to pin the speeding ticket and the Visa bill to the notice board above the computer.

She wanted to pick up the phone now and scream at him.

But not yet.

Not yet.

She would tackle him, but in her own time and on her own terms. The last time she'd raised the subject of his relationship with Stephanie Burroughs, he had managed to convince her that she was obviously going out of her mind. She'd had no real evidence last time, only a woman's intuition that something was amiss. She would not make that mistake again.

It gave her a certain small pleasure to use the photocopier – his photocopier – to make duplicates of the speeding ticket and the VISA bill. When she did confront him this time, she would have the evidence in her hands.

Kathy carefully replaced the papers in their wire basket and turned to the desktop computer. Robert loved his technology. If he was conducting a relationship with anyone she would certainly find the evidence in his computer. The only problem was, it was password-protected. "In case it was ever stolen," he told her, "or the kids get into it." She realised now that he'd never volunteered the password.

Kathy remembered the last time she'd watched Robert turn on the machine. She had been standing against the filing cabinet looking for a copy of the most recent letter they had sent out to their accountant. The Revenue Commissioners were claiming they never received a tax return for the previous year. Robert had sworn he'd written to the accountant and then sat down at his desk and booted up his computer.

Kathy now crossed the room to stand against the filing cabinet, in the same position she'd held when she'd spoken to him. She closed her eyes, remembering. Robert had been sitting directly in front of her, facing his computer screen. The blue log-on screen had appeared and his fingers rattled in the password. Except . . . except only the fingers on his right hand had moved and they had been positioned at the extreme right of the keyboard.

Kathy stepped up the computer and looked at the keyboard. He must have been using the numeric keypad.

Pulling out his chair, she sat at his desk and looked around for a combination of letters or numbers, just in case he had left the password Blu-tacked or scribbled somewhere. But there was nothing.

She closed her eyes and concentrated again, remembering. She hadn't really been looking at him . . . but she had heard eight distinct taps, hard and definite. She opened her eyes and grinned. She'd bet it was the same code as the burglar alarm. Most people used combinations of letters or figures that were familiar to them. She'd lay money that this was Robert's date of birth.

Kathy brought the machine to whirring life and then waited while the screen flickered, blinked and then cleared again.

Please Enter Password

She hesitated, wondering whether, if she were wrong, the machine would lock up and Robert would somehow know that she'd been into it. Then she discovered that she simply didn't care too much what he thought.

Please Enter Password

Robert's birthday was the tenth of October, 1962. She tapped the digits in carefully, 10101962, then hesitated a moment before hitting *Enter*. Kathy nodded. She was right, she knew she was. Her little finger brushed the *Enter* key.

A light on the front panel of the computer flickered yellow, indicating that the hard disk was working, then the machine chimed musically and opened up to a desktop of icons.

She was in.

CHAPTER 8

Two hours later, Kathy stepped away from the computer. There was an iron bar across her shoulders and her eyes felt gritty and tired. She had been convinced – absolutely certain – that she would find evidence of Robert's affair on the machine.

She hadn't found what she'd set out to find, but what she had discovered had disturbed her. Frightened her even.

She'd gone for the *My Documents* folder first, painstakingly and systematically going through folder after folder, reading letters and memos all to do with business. It left her feeling depressed and a little guilty: she hadn't quite realised that Robert was working so hard. Nor had she realised how precarious R&K's situation was. He'd said nothing to her about the state of the company, but from what she was seeing, while they were not exactly in trouble at the moment, they were certainly heading that way. There seemed to be less business out there, and the independent production companies were constantly undercutting one another simply to get the jobs. He was taking on more and more advertising work, most of it funnelled through one of the large agencies in the city. She came across one letter to a record label where Robert had been forced to cut nearly three thousand euro off the quote for a job simply to get the work. She noted that he'd sent out the email at two o'clock in the morning. She discovered other emails sent out at two thirty, two forty-five, even three ten in the morning.

Robert worked late, both in the office and at home. She'd grown used to it over the years. He worked on into the night, claiming that he got his best work done when the house was quiet and the phones and faxes had stopped ringing.

Last night, lying in bed, with that red flag still pulsing in throbbing time to the migraine headache behind her eyes, she'd imagined him conducting his affairs by email and phone late at night. Her fears shifted and drifted into fragments of dreams in which she stood outside Robert's door, her ear pressed against the cool wood and heard whispers of intimate conversations, the muted chatter of phone sex and then the frantic tapping of his fingers across the keyboard as he sent out erotic emails.

There was nothing; she found no evidence of a single untoward letter.

She'd gone through his *Outlook* program. She'd read every email he received and sent. She'd checked his deleted files and his archive folders. And she'd found absolutely no evidence of anything illicit going on. On the contrary, all the evidence pointed to a hardworking and conscientious man. If he was sending emails to Stephanie Burroughs, he was obviously using another email account, but she had no way of checking that. She turned to look at the empty space on the table. Unless he kept that data on the laptop. Robert carried the laptop into the office with him every morning and brought it home again every night: maybe it would contain the evidence she was looking for.

Maybe there was no evidence, the rational side of her brain insisted. Maybe the few scraps of paper she had collected so far were all that were available. Maybe there were even reasonable explanations for all of them. Too many maybes.

She clicked onto the *Contacts* section of *Outlook* and quickly scrolled through the hundreds of names until she came to the "B's" and then slowed.

Stephanie Burroughs.

There was a little red flag pinned to the name. She double-clicked on the name and Stephanie Burroughs' details opened up. Her name, address, phone number, mobile, faxes, email . . . and a little photograph of the woman. Kathy stared long and hard at the photograph. It had been six years since she'd last set eyes on her, and if this was a recent photograph – and she suspected that it was – then those years had been kind. A round face was dominated by huge dark eyes and framed by deep brown, almost black hair. Kathy knew she was around thirty-five, five years younger than herself. She imagined that she would still be slim and elegant.

But what struck her now – as it struck her all those years ago, when Robert had first introduced them – was how much they resembled one another. They might have been sisters. She always thought that Stephanie Burroughs was a younger, prettier version of herself.

She clicked on the *Details* tab. It was another page of contact details, including Stephanie's birthday. The sixth of November.

Kathy hit the print button and the little laser printer whirred to life, and almost immediately the page of Stephanie's details hissed out of the machine. She added it to the rest of her evidence.

She went to the *Calendar* page. It was a mirror of the calendar she had seen on his phone and realised that the programs on the computer and in his phone were probably synchronised. The same flags appeared on the same days. She scrolled back to the month of November, looking for the sixth, Stephanie's birthday. There was a little red flag pinned to the day, and a single notation: *Galway.*

Galway.

Kathy remembered the day now: Robert had driven over to Galway to meet with a potential client. He'd been due back that night, but had phoned late in the evening to say that he'd had a few drinks and wasn't going to risk driving across country. The following day, which was a Thursday, he'd phoned to say that he was going golfing with the client and would not be back until Friday morning. He finally arrived home late Friday evening.

Kathy sat back in the creaking chair and stared at the screen, remembering. There had been a lot of meetings over the years. A lot of overnights, in lots of cities. She'd never thought about it before, but she couldn't remember if any of those client meetings had ever resulted in a new client signing up with R&K Productions.

Which meant?

Which meant that either Robert was a very poor salesman indeed or perhaps this affair had been going on far longer than she thought. The last she'd heard about Stephanie was that she'd moved away and was working in the States. Or had she? Kathy realised that she couldn't even believe that any more. Had Stephanie left, or had Robert just told her that to lull her into a false sense of security? Had he been seeing her all these years, sneaking off to cities and towns dotted around Ireland to conduct his sordid affair, meeting his mistress in places where they would be least likely to be recognised? Or had he simple been heading off to . . . she checked the address on the sheet of paper . . . to an apartment on the Grand Canal where Burroughs lived?

She had no way of knowing. Circumstantial evidence certainly, but no proof.

Kathy wrapped her arms around her body, feeling sick and chilled. She realised now that she could not believe a single word her husband had told her. And the doubts, the questions, the confusion was tearing her apart.

CHAPTER 9

"You're leaving it a bit late."

Kathy moved the phone away from her mouth and took a deep breath. Sometimes her older sister's schoolmarmish tone set her teeth on edge. "I know, I know. Can you do it?"

"Well, Brendan is seventeen and Theresa is fifteen, I really don't think they need a baby-sitter –" Julia Taylor began.

"Fine," Kathy said, a little more sharply than she'd intended, "I'll ask Sheila." Sheila was Julia and Kathy's younger sister, and Kathy knew that Julia was always a little envious of the amount of time Sheila spent with the children.

"I didn't say I wouldn't do it," Julia said hurriedly. "I was just saying that I thought they were old enough."

"I know they are, but at least if you're here they'll both study for their last few exams, instead of vegging out in front of the TV all night."

"I suppose Robert is out."

"He's entertaining a client," Kathy said smoothly, the words tasting bitter and flat in her mouth.

"And you're left to do the Christmas shopping, I suppose." Julia never made any secret of her dislike for Robert.

"Can you do it?" Kathy allowed a little of the terrible bubbling anger that seemed to be caught in the pit of her stomach to come to the surface. "Yes or no. I don't need the lecture."

"Yes, I'll do it." There was a long pause, then Julia added, "Are you all right? You sound on edge."

"I'm just tired. It's too close to Christmas and I've too little done. I guess I'm just panicking a little. All the shops are open late, and if I get a good run at them, I'll be happier."

"No problem. What time would you like me to come around?"

"As early as you can."

"Aw Mam, not Julia!" Brendan was halfway through buttering what looked like an entire sliced pan. He was making himself a quick snack. "I'm seventeen!"

Kathy gathering up the ironing and dumped it into the cracked plastic basket. Brendan was a younger version of his father and looked and sounded enough like him to disconcert her on occasion.

Theresa burst into the kitchen in a billow of icy air. She too had inherited her father's looks, but not his height. "The bus was late," she announced and snatched a slice of buttered bread from the pile Brendan was busily creating. Normally it would have instigated an argument.

"We've got Julia baby-sitting us tonight," Brendan said glumly.

"Mam!" Theresa turned the single word into an accusation.

"I know, I know," Kathy snapped. "You're fifteen and your brother is seventeen. And I'm the one who's disappointed that I still have to get you a baby-sitter at your age."

The two children read the warning signals and kept quiet.

"It would be lovely to be able to go out and trust you both to get your homework and studying done. But I can't. That's why I've got to get your Aunt Julia to mind you. Trust me, I like it even less than you do. I'm the one who had to listen to her lecture me." Hugging the basket of ironing like a shield, she hurried from the kitchen before she said anything else.

Kathy thumped up the stairs, angry with herself for getting annoyed with the children. It wasn't their fault. She'd spent the day trying to make sense of what she'd discovered upstairs. All the bits and pieces went round and around in her head, a hideous jigsaw of untruths, suppositions and lies. By the time the children had come in from school, there was a sick headache sitting behind her eyes and a ball of acid indigestion lodged in her stomach. Even watching Brendan buttering the bread was enough to make her stomach roil and twist.

Balancing the ironing basket on her hip, she pulled open the door to the airing cupboard and began to sort through the clothes, the simple mundane task distracting her. Theresa's socks – every one a different shade – Brendan's school tee-shirts, all of them stained yellow beneath the arms, Robert's boxer shorts. She stopped and held them in her hands. The material was still warm from the iron. When had he started wearing boxers?

It was another question. Suddenly, she had nothing but questions. She's been married to Robert for eighteen years, and had known him for three years before that. Twenty-one years. She knew a lot about him – she thought she knew everything. But now it was becoming apparent that she knew damn little about the man she'd married. She shook her head suddenly, the savage movement setting off the pain behind her eyes. This wasn't the man she married. The Robert she married would not have lied to her. The Robert she married respected her. Loved her.

She wondered when that had changed.

When they'd first married, he wore jockey shorts. Same pattern, same baggy shape, plain white. She frowned, trying to remember when that had changed. A year, no, two years ago. About the time he'd started going to the gym.

He'd taken up going to a gym just off the M50. He told her the year's membership came courtesy of a client. Then one day he came home with a packet of boxer shorts which he'd bought in Dunnes in Blanchardstown. All the lads in the gym were wearing them, he told her; he felt a bit out of place wearing jockeys.

Wadding the boxer shorts into a ball, she flung them into the back of the airing cupboard. Was it a lie? Was it the truth? Nothing made sense any more.

Kathy stepped into the bedroom and did something she rarely did: she turned the key in the lock. She stood with her back against the wood and stared at herself in the mirrored wardrobes. There were black circles under her eyes, and her hair needed a colour and a comb, but she wasn't ugly, wasn't too much overweight and when she made an effort she could look pretty.

Stepping away from the door, she approached the mirrors. She saw a forty-year old woman who looked older. There were lines around her eyes, etched into the corners of her mouth, tiny vertical strips on her top lip. The bags under her eyes looked bruised and the whites of her eyes were threaded with burst veins from crying. She saw someone who looked like her late mother.

Was that what Robert saw?

Her lips moved, shaping the next question: what do you see when you look at me? She didn't know, because he never told her. She frowned, and the lines etched across her forehead deepened and a trilogy of vertical lines appeared between her eyebrows.

When was the last time he told her that he loved her?

When was the last time she told him that she loved him? The question blindsided her, catching her unawares.

"I always tell him," she said aloud. Reflected in the mirror, she could see the lie in her eyes. She didn't always tell him.

"He knows I love him." How does he know, the niggling voice asked.

"I do everything for him, wash, cook, clean, rear the children." And he works long and hard so that you want for nothing. That makes you even.

Kathy turned away from the mirror, unhappy with what she

saw reflected there. She slid open the wardrobe and began hunting out clothing. Was it something she'd done? Had she driven him away, into the arms and bed of another woman? It was a question she didn't want to tackle, didn't even want to examine, because she was afraid of the answer.

When was the last time he told her that he loved her . . . and meant it? There was a time he said it every morning before he went out to work. "I love you." Then again, last thing at night. In the early years of their marriage she was a voracious reader. She'd often sit up half the night reading. When Robert got into bed he would snuggle down beside her, head almost lost beneath the duvet, arm draped across her stomach. When he heard her light click off, he would mumble, "Love you." And then his breathing would settle and he would fall asleep almost immediately. Last thing at night and first thing in the morning. That simple sentence bracketing her day. It gave her extraordinary pleasure.

Kathy dressed hurriedly, pulling on a pair of thick woollen trousers and fishing out her heavy Aran jumper. The temperature had been falling steadily and the forecasters were suggesting that there might be a white Christmas. The bookies had cut the odds from one hundred to one right down to ten to one. She found her fur-lined boots in the back of the wardrobe. Robert had given them to her as part of her Christmas present two years ago. They were hardly the sexiest of presents, but they were practical. She pushed her left foot into a boot and tried to remember what he'd given her last year. Something very ordinary, she knew that, something . . .

Kathy shook her head. She couldn't remember.

Last year, amongst other things, she'd given him a state-of-the-art digital camera. When he opened the box, his only comment was that he hoped she'd kept the receipt so they could claim the VAT back on it.

What had he given her last year? That was going to bother her for the rest of the night.

Kathy hooked her leather jacket out of the wardrobe, then pushed the mirrored door closed and examined her reflection. Bundled up, she looked frumpy, she decided.

"I'll be gone a couple of hours," she announced to Brendan and Theresa. They were sitting in the kitchen, which now stank of burnt toast.

The two children nodded. They were watching the small TV set high on the wall. Anne Robinson was telling a C-list celeb that he was "The weakest link. Goodbye."

Kathy pulled the kitchen door closed, then opened it again. "Can either of you remember what your father got me last Christmas?"

"The new Maeve Binchy and perfume," Theresa said quickly, without taking her eyes off the screen.

"That's it. See you later. Be good for your Aunt Julia." She pulled the door closed and headed out to the garage. A book and perfume. She remembered now. The book had been great, but the perfume was not even her brand. She remembered he hadn't even taken off the price-stickers. He'd picked up both in the Stephen's Green shopping centre. How much thought had gone into that present?

Kathy wondered what he'd got his girlfriend.

CHAPTER 10

Kathy passed her sister's SUV at the bottom of the road.   Julia
didn't see her: she was clutching the wheel of the big vehicle with
white-knuckle intensity, staring straight ahead. Kathy knew her
sister hated driving the SUV because of its size, but she drove it
because she thought it was a status symbol. She was so shallow.

But at least her husband was not having an affair.

The thought, icy as the winter weather, insinuated itself into
her consciousness. Julia and Ben, her husband, had been married
for twenty-seven years and there'd never been any doubts that
they loved one another. You just had to look at them together to
realise that. Kathy wondered what someone looking in on her
relationship with Robert would think. Would they imagine that
after eighteen years of marriage, everything was fine between them,
that they were still in love, or would they be able to tell that
something was desperately wrong? What were the signals that
something was amiss with a relationship?

Kathy flicked her headlights on to full beam. They picked up
stray chips of ice and snowflakes spiralling out of the heavens,
making it look as if she was falling into the snow. She dipped the
lights and dropped her speed.

This was madness.

No, this was not madness. This was necessary.

She was heading into Dublin a week before Christmas, right into rush-hour traffic with what looked like a snowstorm coming in. She thought about heading back and, for a single moment, considered it seriously. But if she went back she knew she would have lost momentum. Tomorrow was a day closer to Christmas and, for some reason that date – that significant family-orientated date – was assuming a huge importance. She had to know for certain before Christmas. Perhaps it was simply that she did not want to go into the New Year knowing – or not knowing – that she was living a lie. That her marriage, her relationship, her love was compromised, that her future was uncertain and her past unknown.

She pushed the Skoda's heater up to full – it made little difference to the temperature as far as she could see. At the bottom of the road she turned to the right, which by-passed Swords main street. She could see that it was solid with cars, no doubt drawn to the shopping centre. She cut down a narrow side street, which took her out at the end of the main street and allowed her out onto the main Swords Road. Traffic was heavy, but most of it was heading out of the city.

Kathy eased onto the main road, trying to remember the last time she had driven herself into the city at night. Whenever they went out at night, Robert drove them there. If he had a few too many to drink, she would drive them home however. She suddenly smiled, realising that she was holding the steering wheel in the same white-knuckled grip as her sister. The smile faded. If – and it was still only an if – it turned out that Robert was, indeed, having an affair, she was not looking forward to telling either of her sisters, but especially Julia. Julia had the perfect marriage, the perfect family, the perfect home. She knew that Julia would sympathise, though she suspected that secretly her sister would be thrilled. Her opinion of Robert would be vindicated; she would be able to say "I told you so," and would insist on dispensing advice, whether Kathy asked for it or not. Sheila, her younger, unmarried sister, would be genuinely sympathetic. Kathy resolved to speak to her first.

Deep in the folds of her coat, her mobile phone chirruped and buzzed. Keeping her eyes on the road, she fished into the pocket, pulled out the phone and hit the button which turned it into a speaker phone; at least that way she would not have to hold it up to her face.

"Kathy?" Robert's voice was tinny and brittle. "Where are you?"

"In the car," she said, knowing it was an answer he hated. He knew she was in the car – he wanted to know where she and the car were.

"I've just phoned home; the kids tell me you're heading into the city to go shopping."

She could hear the incredulity in his voice.

"Yes," she said, keeping her voice carefully neutral.

"I don't think this is a good idea. Traffic is shite, and the weather is closing in. Forecasters are promising snow and maybe black ice this evening."

"I need to get a few things. I thought I'd head into Stephen's Green." Then she smiled bitterly. "If there's a problem with the weather, I might drop down to Shanahan's, meet you there. We can drive home in your car and I'll come in with you in the morning to pick up my car."

There was a long pause. She was determined not to break into it.

"Have I lost you?" came his voice at last.

"I'm still here," she said shortly. She was coming up to the airport roundabout. Would she head down the carriageway or take the old airport road, maybe head in via Ballymun? If she took the carriageway, she'd end up getting caught at the tunnel works in Whitehall. The lights were green in her favour and she indicated right to get onto the roundabout, then immediately left to get off again. The old airport road was deserted. "Where are you?" she eventually asked.

"Still at the office. Jimmy's coming here around seven or so." There was a hiss of static. " . . . I really don't think it's a good idea to head into the city tonight. And if I have a few drinks with Jimmy I might have to leave the car myself. That'll be two cars in town. I was half thinking I might even stay overnight in the city. He says I can kip down in his apartment. He's got a place in Temple Bar."

There was another long pause. Robert obviously expected Kathy to fill the silence, but she said nothing. She turned right off the airport road and headed down the long road that ran parallel to the airport runways. On her left, the hard shoulder was dotted with cars, the die-hard airplane spotters muffled against the chill standing alongside their vehicles, binoculars pressed to their faces. There were other cars in the shadows, showing no signs of movement, but their windows were fogged up. When she'd first been going out with Robert, they'd come up here to neck and make out.

"Kathy –"

"I'm at the back of the airport. Signal is patchy."

"Can you not get what you're looking for in the Pavilions in Swords?"

"No," she said truthfully. "I'll see you in Shanahan's later . . ."

"No, not Shanahan's . . ."

Kathy slowed down. She kept her eyes fixed firmly on the road, refusing to glance down at the phone's amber screen. She took a breath before responding, careful to pitch her voice just right. "I thought you said last night you were going to Shanahan's . . ."

"I know, but there was a cock-up. I phoned earlier to confirm and they'd no record of the booking."

Kathy Walker frowned. She knew this to be the truth. So maybe everything else was explicable also. Maybe all her suppositions had a rational explanation. She shook her head: they didn't. "So where are you going to go?"

"Don't know yet."

"Well look, ring me when you find a place, and I'll drop by. I haven't seen Jimmy for ages. How is Angela?"

"Ah, best not to mention Angela. They've separated. He wants a divorce. She says no."

Kathy turned left and headed down a narrow two-lane road. Frost sparkled in the verges. The lights of Ballymun burned amber and white in the distance, bouncing back off the low clouds. The towers were dark and empty – some had been torn down already, the rest were scheduled to be demolished shortly – but the six cranes over the towers were all decorated with festive lights. "I've got to go. I think I can see a police check-point ahead," she lied, and stabbed a finger to terminate the call.

If Robert wanted a divorce would she say no?

Kathy shook her head. She'd say, "Go".

If he didn't want her, if he'd chosen some tart over her, she would certainly would not want him hanging around. But if he was going, she would make sure she'd keep everything that was rightfully hers.

It took forty minutes to get down to Christchurch, and another sixty to get around to the Green. Operation Freeflow was in full swing and street parking was at an absolute premium. The huge LCD screens displaying the available parking spaces around the city were indicating that everywhere was full, but Kathy wasn't looking for a parking space. She drove across the city, down Nassau Street, heading for Merrion Square. Kathy turned right at the maternity hospital, then took the first left into Mount Street, heading straight for the Peppercannister Church. She slowed, hunting for a parking space, but even this far out of the city centre the street was lined with cars on both sides of the street. She was not going to be able to park.

For years Kathy and Robert had run R&K Productions out of their home. About ten years ago, when the company started making some money, they decided that they needed a legitimate address. It had to be close enough to the city centre to impress clients, yet not too close that it was going to cost a fortune. They'd eventually taken a single room on the second floor of a slightly shabby Georgian mews directly across from the Peppercannister Church. When a second room had become available, they'd taken that. Now R&K Productions occupied a suite of four ground-floor rooms, an outer office, a large conference room, tiny kitchen and bathroom. Kathy always thought it was an outrageously extravagant expense; Robert claimed it was good for business.

Kathy slowed and drove around the church. She could see the offices: they were in total darkness. Kathy glanced at the clock on the dashboard. The amber digits said it was six forty-five. She drove around the church again, craning her neck to look down the dark alleyway. There was no sign of Robert's car either.

She was . . . disappointed.

What had she been expecting? To see Robert's car outside the office and then the door opening and Robert and his mistress come out arm in arm? And if she had seen his car outside, what would she have done? Gone in, or skulked outside in the shadows, watching like some shabby detective in a cheap novel?

Kathy drove around the church again, and headed on to the canal. She had another destination.

She found Stephanie Burroughs' address easily enough. It was in a new complex of apartments tucked away behind a pair of electronic gates. With the printout she'd taken from Robert's machine in her hand, she approached the gates and peered in, trying to make sense of the numbering.

"Can I help you?" The voice was querulous, suspicious. A tiny figure materialised out of the shadows.

"Yes . . . no . . . possibly." She tried her best smile.

"Well, make your mind up," the old lady snapped.

"I'm supposed to deliver a Christmas hamper to a Miss . . ." she deliberately consulted the sheet of paper, ". . . a Miss Burroughs. I think she lives here."

"Number 28." The old woman turned and pointed across the cobbled yard towards a brightly lit door. A fully-lit miniature Christmas tree twinkled behind the bubbled glass.

"Oh, so I do have the right address!"

"You do. But there's no point in calling now. She's just gone out."

Kathy tried her winning smile again. "I don't suppose you know where she was going?"

Now the old lady looked at her suspiciously. "Why? You make personal deliveries?"

"Well, this is a very special delivery. I'm under strict instructions to place it directly into her hands. If you do see her, would you mind not saying anything about the hamper? It's supposed to be a surprise."

"I'm the soul of discretion, young woman. The soul of discretion."

"Thank you so much. Happy Christmas."

"You have a Happy Christmas too."

CHAPTER 11

It was after nine by the time she got back, and everyone – Julia, Brendan and Theresa – was in a foul mood. Robert hadn't come home yet.

Julia started putting on her coat the moment Kathy turned her key in the lock. "I thought you'd be back ages ago," she snapped.

"I was as quick as I could be," Kathy said. She opened her mouth to say more, but closed it quickly again. She knew she had a tendency to talk too much, especially when she was nervous, and she was terrified she was going to blurt out her fears to her sister. "Were the children all right?"

"They were fine, I suppose, though they insisted on phoning for take-away food. I don't agree with that take-away rubbish, Kathy, you know that. You never know what you're eating."

"We've never had any problems with the local –"

"It's unhealthy. Fully of salts and sugars and monosodium glutamate."

"They only have a take-away once in a blue moon as a treat."

"They seemed very familiar with the menu," Julia said suspiciously.

"Will you have some tea?" Kathy asked, moving past her, heading into the kitchen. She knew Julia would refuse.

"No, no, I'd best be going. Ben will be wondering where I am."

Kathy moved back down the hall and gave her sister a quick peck on the cheek. Julia smelled of lavender powder, the same talc their mother had worn. Kathy wondered if it was by accident or by design. As she'd got older Julia had come to physically resemble their late mother; she had her hair cut and styled in a slightly more modern version of their mother's cut, and even her clothes were starting to resemble those the late Margaret Childs always wore: cardigans and sensible skirts.

Julia stood in the door, wrapping her coat tightly around her. "You'll be coming down on Stephen's Day." Julia turned the question into a statement.

"I haven't mentioned it to Robert yet," Kathy said truthfully. "But I'm sure we'll be there."

"Have you seen Sheila?"

"Not recently."

"Is there a new boyfriend?"

"I've no idea," Kathy said, which was not entirely true. There was a new man in their younger sister's life, someone Sheila was excited about, but being equally secretive about at the moment.

"She needs to settle down," Julia said and sniffed. "She's getting a little too old for all this running around."

"She's thirty-six. That's hardly ancient."

"I was married with two children by that age. So were you," Julia added. "I'd best be off." She turned to kiss her sister quickly on the cheek, the slightest brushing of her lips, then she rubbed her thumb under Kathy's right eye. "You look exhausted. You've got bags under your eyes. I'll bring you some eye-soothing gel next time I'm over." She turned away and hurried down the path, her footsteps crunching slightly on the frost.

Kathy stood in the door, arms wrapped tightly around her chest, and waited while her sister slowly and carefully backed the big SUV out of the drive. Only when Julia straightened the car on the road and revved away, wheels spinning on icy patches, did she step back and close the door. The hallway was so cold she could see her breath frosting in front of her face.

Brendan and Theresa were in the sitting-room, sprawled in that peculiarly loose-limbed way that only young children and teens can manage, watching TV. Channel Four was running a *Big Brother* Christmas Special.

"Did you get your homework done?"

They both grunted.

"Any word from your father?"

"He phoned earlier," Brendan volunteered, "but said he'd try you on the mobile."

"I spoke to him."

"I hope he gets home soon," Theresa said. "There'll be snow tonight."

"He did say if the weather closed in, he might stay in the city," Kathy said, more to reassure her daughter than to repeat the lie he'd told her.

Theresa nodded without looking up. "Good. That'd be better. Safer."

Kathy wandered into the kitchen and began to clear up the take-away bags and foil containers. Robert was a good father, she had to admit. The children wanted for nothing . . . except perhaps a father. Much of the rearing had been left to her. He was so rarely home in the early years of their marriage; he'd often gone to work in the morning before the children awoke, and returned late in the evening when they were in bed and asleep. They only got to see him at the weekend. And even then he was invariably working. Kathy gathered up the plates and opened the dishwasher. They had a good relationship with him now though . . .

She stopped and straightened. Had they? Had they a good relationship? What constituted a good relationship, she wondered.

He bought them everything they wanted. Christmas was no

longer special because he gave them presents out of season, and often came home with toys and games, books and clothes, little items of jewellery for Theresa, software for Brendan. They both idolised him; how were they going to react when . . . no, not *when*, just *if*. At the moment, it was still *if*.

But how much time did he give them?

She began to slot the plates into the dishwasher. She couldn't remember the last time he'd spent time with them, when he'd simply taken them out with him for the sheer pleasure of their company. The last movie they'd been to see as a family had been . . . She shook her head: she couldn't remember. He'd missed Brendan's football matches and Theresa's school recitals because he'd been working.

Or had he?

Again, the poisonous, insidious thought curled around the question. Had he been genuinely working, or had he been with his mistress? Every excuse he'd ever given her was now suspect.

On impulse, she picked up her phone where she had tossed it on the table and dialled his mobile phone. The call was diverted directly to his message machine; he must have it turned off. She went back to her handbag and pulled out the sheet of paper with Stephanie Burroughs' details on it. Then she picked up the phone and was just about to dial the number when she realised that her number would show up on Burroughs' screen. Sitting at the kitchen table, she spent ten minutes trawling through the phone's menus looking to switch off *Send own number*. When she'd set it, she phoned the house and checked the caller ID. *Private Number*, showed on the screen. Then she phoned Stephanie Burroughs' number. It rang and rang. She was just about to hang up when it was answered.

"Hello."

The voice was crisp, professional, brusque even. There was the tinkling of a piano in the background, the hum of conversation, a clinking of glass. A bar or a restaurant.

"Hello?"

"Hello. Is that Becky?"

"No, you have the wrong number."

"Sorry –" Kathy began, but the phone went dead. Stephanie had killed the call. "Now what exactly did that achieve?" she asked aloud.

"Mum, you're talking to yourself again." Theresa padded into the kitchen. She went straight to the cupboard and pulled out a box of cornflakes.

"I thought you had take-away."

"I did. But that was hours ago. I'm famished." Theresa filled a bowl to the brim with cornflakes, then added almost half a pint of milk. She glanced sidelong at her mother. "Did you get everything you were looking for in town?"

"Not everything," Kathy said truthfully. "I made a start." She turned to look at her daughter. "Have you given any thought to what you'd like for Christmas?"

"I gave my list to Dad."

"I haven't seen it yet."

Theresa concentrated on her cereal.

"Would that be because I might have a problem with some of the items on the list?" Kathy asked.

Theresa shrugged, a mere shifting of the shoulders.

"But you know your dad will get them for you."

"It's just one or two small things," Theresa said defensively.

"You mean one or two pages of small things. I'll talk to your father about them."

"He said he'd get them for me."

"I'll have a look first."

"Don't be mean, Mam. Dad said he'd get them; he'd no problem with the list!" She gathered up her bowl and padded back into the dining-room, ignoring the no-food-in-the-dining-room rule. Kathy was too tired, too drained to argue. She could hear Theresa speaking urgently to her brother, no doubt explaining how mean their mother was going to be over the Christmas presents.

They had this battle every year. Theresa would produce a list of just about everything she had seen on TV, found in a magazine, or that her friends had. Kathy would then edit the list down to one or two big presents, plus some small stocking-fillers. The trick was always to try and make sure both children were opening approximately the same number of presents on Christmas morning. More recently however, Theresa, who was absolutely her father's pet, had discovered that if she asked him directly for something, he would more often than not just get it for her. Last year there had been a major upset on Christmas Eve, when Kathy discovered that Robert had bought Theresa just about everything on her list. She'd had sixteen presents to unwrap. Brendan had eight.

Robert had promised her that it would be different this year. Obviously he'd forgotten.

Kathy tidied up the kitchen and filled the kettle for the morning. He'd started to forget lots of things: points on his licence, a new credit-card account . . . and the fact that she was still his wife.

"Time for bed."

"Mam!"

"Aw, Mam!"

Kathy crossed the floor in two quick strides and snapped the TV off. "Bed. You'll be on holidays soon. You can stay up late then." She picked cushions off the floor and tossed them back on the chairs. "And Theresa, when I call you in the morning, get up. I'll not call you again, and if you miss the bus I am not driving you down to school."

Theresa uncoiled from the chair and marched out of the room, leaving her cereal bowl on the floor. Kathy was going to call after her, but Brendan hopped up and grabbed the bowl and spoon. "I'll get it."

"Thanks."

"Is everything all right, Mam?"

She glanced up, struck by the note of concern in his voice. He looked so like his father. She'd first met Robert when he was in his early twenties and had worked for him on and off before they had started dating. He'd been handsome then – still was, she supposed – and Brendan had inherited his father's dark good looks. He was seventeen now, and had several on-and-off-again girlfriends. She'd discouraged them, trying to get him to concentrate on his studies. The problem was that Robert had already promised him a place in the company when he left school. Brendan then decided that there was little point in breaking his back studying, inasmuch as he already had a job to go to. Since then, his exam results had slackened off. Too many C's, lots of D's. Before he'd talked to his father it had been mainly B's and a few A's.

"Mam?" Brendan asked again.

"I'm fine. Tired. Lots to do with Christmas coming."

Brendan nodded, though he didn't look convinced. "When's Dad getting back?"

Kathy shrugged. "Who knows? I don't." Something in her voice betrayed her. She caught the frown that appeared on her son's face, and added quickly, "It's a busy time for him, wining and dining clients. So much of the business he gets comes from personal contacts. He could be home at any time."

Brendan nodded. But she could tell that something was disturbing him. She opened her mouth to ask, then shut it again. She didn't want to run the risk of upsetting her son, and maybe have him go to Robert.

"You get off to bed now. I'll lock up down here."

"Good night."

"Good night, and no reading. It's late enough."

She waited until she heard Brendan's door click shut, before she moved around the house, turning off lights, and locking doors. She flicked on the porch light, then stood in the hall watching isolated flakes of snow drift past the cone of light. She wondered if her husband was on the way home to her, or was he going to spend the night with his mistress.

CHAPTER 12

It was close to two thirty when Robert finally returned home.

Kathy wasn't asleep. She'd tried reading for a little while – the new Patricia Cornwell – but the words had shifted and swum on the page and she gave it up when she discovered that she'd read the same paragraph at least half a dozen times and it still didn't make any sense. Dropping the book on the floor by the side of the bed, she'd flicked off the light, then climbed out of bed, pulled back the heavy curtains and stood by the window, staring down the road. Watching. Waiting. Though she was not entirely sure what she was watching or waiting for.

For the first few years of their marriage, she never went to bed until Robert returned home. As the clock ticked on beyond midnight, she'd feel her tension increase as she began to imagine the worst: a drunk driver, a car accident, a mugging. She couldn't remember when she stopped waiting up for him. When he started staying out regularly, she supposed, when it became the norm rather than the exception.

Finally, chilled through to the bone, she climbed back into bed and lay on her back, staring at the patterns cast by the streetlights on the ceiling. She was trying to make sense of the last two days: but she couldn't.

It kept coming back to questions, with one question dominating all others: why?

Why would Robert have an affair?

Was it something she'd done? Something she hadn't done? Why?

Kathy dozed off with the question buzzing in and out of her consciousness.

The dream was formless, incidents from eighteen years of marriage running and rolling together into an endless sequence. In the dream she was always alone, alone in the house, alone with the children, shopping alone, taking them to school alone, cooking, washing, cleaning . . . alone, alone, alone. Weekends alone, holidays alone, bank holidays alone. Alone, alone, alone.

Kathy came awake, suddenly, cleanly snapping from disturbing images to consciousness.

Even fully asleep she'd heard a key turn in the lock. She was out of bed and at the window before she realised what she was doing. A curious mixture of emotions – relief and disappointment – flooded through her when she saw Robert's car in the driveway. Then she slipped back into the warm bed and pulled the blankets up to her chin.

Alone.

Listening to Robert moving about downstairs, trying and failing to be silent, she realised that the abiding emotion of the dream had remained with her. She felt lonely.

Where had the boyfriend she'd married gone? What had happened to the man she'd shared everything with? Where was the man she'd loved?

A suddenly flush of emotion brought tears to her eyes and she blinked them away furiously, then brushed her fingers roughly across her face, wiping away the moisture.

She was lonely.

Suddenly she recognised that empty feeling she'd been living with for the past number of years, that emptiness, that hollow interior. She had the children to keep her busy, she had a few friends and there were neighbours she was friendly with, she had family close by, she kept busy, she did classes, but that didn't fill the emptiness.

She heard Robert start up the stairs.

And then she realised that if he left in the morning, she would miss him certainly – miss his presence about the house, but probably not much else. He'd withdrawn from her a long time ago, little by little. She was only realising it now.

Would his departure make any real differences to her life?

Very little. And that response disturbed her more than any other.

"I wasn't sure if you were coming home tonight."

"I didn't mean to wake you."

"You didn't wake me."

She watched the vague outline of him pull off his tie and fling it in the general direction of the dressing-table chair. She heard the silk hiss as it slid to the floor.

"I only had a couple of drinks and the roads weren't too bad." He pulled off his suit jacket and folded it over the chair and began to unbutton his shirt.

"I phoned earlier."

"I didn't get a call."

"It went straight to your machine."

"We went to the Market Bar off George's Street – the stone walls probably killed the signal."

Didn't kill your girlfriend's signal, she wanted to add, but didn't. Instead she asked, "How is Jimmy?"

"Jimmy is fine. He sends his love."

"I'm surprised he remembered me."

"Of course he remembered you."

"So you didn't get into Shanahan's?"

Robert's white shirt reflected brightly in the streetlights. He peeled it off and dropped it on top of his jacket. "I'm going to phone and complain in the morning. I'm sure Maureen booked, but they said they'd no record of the booking."

"What does Maureen say?" Maureen had manned the front desk of R&K from the very beginning and Robert always said employing her was the best decision he had ever made. She'd started out in RTE as a production assistant, and had spent twenty-five years with the national broadcaster before she went freelance. She knew just about everyone in the business.

"Maureen's out sick at the moment."

"You never said."

"Oh, I'm sure I did."

She allowed a snap of anger in her voice. "You did not! I most certainly would have remembered. I worked with Maureen, remember?" For a long time Maureen was their entire staff, and the two women had worked closely together. When Kathy's mother had died suddenly and unexpectedly eighteen months previously, leaving the three sisters distraught, Maureen had made all the funeral arrangements. "How long has she been out sick?"

"Three weeks . . . four," Robert mumbled.

"And you never told me!" Her voice rose and she lowered it again with a deliberate effort. "You never told me. I would have called her, visited her."

"I've been busy. I must have forgotten."

"What's wrong with her?"

"Chest infection or something. Doctor's note says she won't be back till next year. And it's the busiest time," he added almost petulantly.

"You make it sound as if she went sick deliberately. I can't remember the last time she was ill. Can you?" she accused.

Robert didn't answer. Naked, he stepped into the en suite,

pulled the door closed and clicked on the light. The edges of the door were picked out with light. She heard the buzz of his electric toothbrush. That was another of his tricks: when he was confronted with a question or situation where he knew he was in the wrong, he simply would fail to answer or he'd change the subject.

"Who's on reception now?" Kathy asked, when he came out of the en suite, flooding the room with light, temporarily blinding her.

"A temp. Illona. Russian, I think. I got her from an agency. She's very good."

Kathy had used the few moments while Robert was in the bathroom to cool her temper. She realised she'd been very close to losing it when she'd learned that her friend Maureen was out sick. For a moment there the conversation had threatened to drift and she needed to keep it on track.

"Perhaps Illona made the reservation?" she suggested.

Robert pulled out a fresh pair of pyjamas and tugged on the bottoms. "Maybe. But it was about four weeks ago; I'm sure Maureen was still around then. I'll still complain to the restaurant in the morning, if I get a minute."

"Do you want me to do it for you?" she asked, expecting him to say no.

He shrugged into the top. "If you get a chance – yes, that would be great. Table for two, Friday night, 7:30, in either my name or Jimmy Moran's. I used his name too just in case he arrived first."

Robert got into bed, wafting icy air under the sheets. He leaned across and kissed her perfunctorily on the cheek, and she caught a hint of alcohol on his breath. Nothing else. No perfume, no scents of soap or shampoo which would indicate that he'd recently had a shower.

"Night," she muttered and rolled over, utterly confused now. Was she completely wrong: had he really been having dinner with

Jimmy Moran tonight? He'd hardly allow her to phone the restaurant and complain if he hadn't. And, of course, he wasn't to know that she'd already phoned them.

But if she was wrong about him meeting his mistress, if he'd really been meeting Jimmy, then her suspicions were unfounded, and if she was wrong about that, what else was she wrong about?

Robert's breathing settled into a gentle rhythm.

Had she wrongly suspected him? Was there a reasonable, rational explanation for all the evidence she'd accumulated – the few scraps, she corrected herself. Was she being nothing more than the paranoid, mistrusting, insecure wife of a handsome man?

It was half past four before she finally fell into a fitful disturbed sleep. It seemed like less than five minutes later when the alarm crackled and pinged.

CHAPTER 13

Saturday 21st December

Kathy sat in the car facing Glasnevin Cemetery and stared through the windscreen at the round tower outlined against an eggshell-blue sky. She was chilled through to the bone, but it had nothing to do with the icy December air: it was this place.

Her mother and father were buried there, sharing a grave in the heart of the old cemetery. Scattered in other graves – some marked, others without a marker – were various aunts and uncles and assorted cousins. Kathy hated the place, always had. She possessed a vivid imagination, and it was easy for her, too easy, to imagine the bodies in the ground, some still clothed in flesh, others nothing more than bones. In her imagination, they always had eyes – which snapped open to look at her. She hated the finality of the place, the huge headstones, the carved angels, the great slabs of decorated concrete placed over the graves.

When she and her sisters were children, it was a Sunday family ritual to come and visit Glasnevin just about every week. And every week, as they walked through the gates, her father would make the same joke, the "dead-centre-of-Dublin" joke and every week she, and her two sisters, would groan aloud in unison. It became part of the ritual.

They would start with the graves of her grandparents and gradually work their way, Sunday after Sunday, to the graves of all their dead relatives, cleaning them up, plucking out weeds, washing down the headstones with soapy water from lemonade bottles. She knew all the names by heart, all the dates and even though she never met any of the people, she felt she knew them intimately. She knew that Aunty Mae had fought with Cousin Tony and they didn't speak for nearly thirty years, she knew that Cousin Jessie – who wasn't really a cousin at all – was left at the altar by Tim, who later went on to marry Aunt Rita, and that Uncle Fitz had a special coffin made because he was so big. It was only later, much later, she realised that was how her father had kept alive their family history – even if he hadn't realised it at the time. Even now, all these years later, she would be able to find each and every one of those graves. She knew for a fact that her own children would not be able to find their grandparents' graves, and knew precious little about her side of the family, and even less about Robert's.

Shortly after her mother died, and she'd stood and watched the polished coffin slowly lowered into the hole in the ground, she had gone to her solicitors and added a letter of instructions to be opened upon her death. It directed that she was to be cremated and her ashes scattered out to sea. She didn't want to be put in the ground and a stone slab raised over her head.

The clock just inside the gate clicked onto eleven and Kathy checked her watch. She'd wait another couple of minutes.

The cemetery was busy and the woman selling flowers outside the gates had a huge display of Christmas wreaths and those bright red flowers that only seemed to appear in December. She thought they might be poinsettias, but she wasn't sure. Kathy glanced over her shoulder at the back seat. She'd brought a small bouquet of flowers, and suddenly it seemed too small, too inconsequential to mark her parents' grave. She'd get a wreath, she decided.

It had been six months since she'd last visited the grave. She could come up with any number of excuses, but the truth was simpler: she didn't want to. This was not how she wished to remember her mother and father, cold and dead in a rotting wooden box in the ground. To her, they would both always be alive and vital. She remembered a quote she'd read somewhere: *Nothing ever truly dies while it remains alive in the memory.*

Except love. Love can die.

She didn't want to think about that just now. She opened up her handbag and fished out the two small memoriam cards she carried tucked into the front pocket. Holding one in each hand she looked at the fuzzy, slightly out-of-focus photographs of her mother and father. Her father's card was cracked and faded, the paper slightly yellow; her mother's still looked new. Margaret Childs had died eighteen months ago. There was no reason, no illness. She simply went to bed and never woke up. Jimmy, her father, died seventeen years ago, a year after she'd married Robert. Jimmy had been a smoker all his life and a third heart attack had finally taken him.

A tap on the window made her scream and physically jump.

Kathy rolled down the window. "Jesus Christ, you nearly gave me a heart attack!"

"Well, you're in the right place for it." Smiling brightly, Sheila Childs, her younger sister, leaned into the car to kiss her sister's cheek, filling the car with cold air and a slightly bitter citrus perfume. Then she saw the cards in her sister's hand and the smile faded. She lifted Jimmy Child's card from her sister's palm and tilted it to the light. "I was thinking about him only the other day. I couldn't find my card." She handed the card back to Kathy.

Kathy shoved both cards into her handbag, rolled up the window and climbed out of the car. "I think about him a lot," she said. She reached into the back seat to lift out the small bouquet.

The two sisters linked arms and darted across the road. They could not have been more dissimilar. Sheila Childs stood at least three inches taller than her older sister, and was thin to the point

78

of emaciation. The colour of her hair tended to change with the seasons, but lately she'd been going back to her natural deep red, adding gold highlights to emphasise her pale flawless complexion. Whereas Kathy was dressed in a three-quarter length black leather coat, black trousers and low-heeled black boots, Sheila was elegant in a cream-coloured belted mac and impossibly high-heeled ankle boots.

They were through the cemetery's tall wrought-iron gates before Kathy remembered her intention to buy a wreath. Suddenly it didn't seem to matter.

The cemetery was deserted and they had the narrow pathways to themselves. The air was crystal clear and although the winter sun was without heat, it painted the tumbled stones and ancient trees in sharp relief, making them look almost artificial. Frost and frozen snow glittered in the shadows and dusted the tops and crevices of some of the more ornate headstones.

The two women walked in silence, turning right down an avenue of evergreens, heading into the heart of the old cemetery. A robin darted into the middle of the path, cocked its head at them, then twisted away. Sheila turned her head to follow its path through the trees. "It's so peaceful here," she said. "I love it."

Kathy looked at her in surprise. "You love it?"

"Always have. Remember those Sundays when we were younger, when Mam and Dad would take us here to clean all the graves."

"I was thinking about that in the car. I hated those trips."

"I loved them. I loved the peace and tranquillity of this place. I seem to remember that no matter how hot it was, it was always cooler here." She gripped her sister's arm and stopped. "Listen."

Kathy stopped. "What for? I can't hear anything."

"Exactly," Sheila smiled. "That's what I love about this place. It's like a cocoon."

"You always were weird." Kathy squeezed her younger sister's arm to take the sting from the words.

The two women wound their way past the crypts and turned left, long shadows dancing ahead of them. The graves in this section were old, most no longer tended and forgotten, but dotted amongst them, like strange blooms, were newly opened graves, a profusion of coloured wreaths and cards amidst the withered grass.

"Are you going to tell me what you wanted to see me about?" Sheila asked finally. "It's not every Saturday morning I get a call from my favourite sister."

"I'm glad you said favourite sister. Your big sister was asking after you last night."

"How is she?"

"Wants to know if you have a boyfriend yet."

"Tell her if she wants to know she can pick up the phone and ask me," Sheila snapped. "She's not my mother." Then she smiled. "She just thinks she is."

"If it's any consolation, she treats me the same. Will you go down to her place on Stephen's Day?"

"I might. I haven't decided yet."

"You could shock her and bring your young man with you."

"That would shock her. But even if I do go – and I'm not decided yet – I'll not be bringing Allen with me."

"So that's his name. Allen."

"I'd told you that."

"You had not! You've been very secretive about him. I was beginning to wonder what was wrong with him."

"There's nothing wrong with him. He's perfect."

"The last one was perfect. And the one before that. Even the one with the funny eye was perfect," Kathy reminded her.

Sheila laughed, the sound loud and startling in the silence of the graveyard. A pair of crows rose complaining into the eggshell-blue sky. "Maybe *he* wasn't perfect. But he was very rich and that compensated for a lot of his other failings"

"Sheila!" Kathy was genuinely shocked.

"But this isn't why you asked me here this morning, is it, to

80

talk about my taste in men? I can't remember the last time you suggested that we visit our parents' grave. You've got something on your mind."

Kathy walked a dozen steps in silence. "I have," she said finally. "And I need some advice."

"This is a first. You've never asked me for advice before in my life."

"Well, this is an area you are an expert in: men."

Sheila started to smile. "I'm not sure that was meant as a compliment."

The two sisters turned left onto a narrow pathway. Their parents' grave was about halfway up on the right-hand side, a simple white headstone with a white surround, with the surface of the grave covered in fine white pebbles. A single black pot stood in the centre of the grave. What looked like wilted and withered carnations drooped from the vase.

"Julia was here," Kathy muttered.

"But not recently," Sheila added.

The two sisters moved silently around the grave. Kathy emptied the dead flowers and carried them off to the nearby bin. When she got back, Sheila had arranged Kathy's bouquet in the bowl, and was rubbing down the surface of the stone with a tissue. They stood side-by-side and stared at the stone.

"A *loving father. Sadly missed*," Kathy read aloud. "We should have added a line when Mam went down. Something similar."

"It's funny, I know he's gone longer, but I remember him more clearly than Mam," Sheila said.

"I have better memories of him. Fonder memories," Kathy agreed.

In the last five years of her life Margaret Childs had become increasingly bitter and disillusioned with life and living. She found fault with everything and it had reached the stage that the grandchildren – and indeed her own daughters – found it difficult to visit with her. Family occasions were a nightmare, and she'd ruined Julia and Ben's twenty-fifth wedding anniversary celebration with her bickering and fault-finding.

"When I go, don't put me down here. I've told Robert and I've written it in a letter that goes with my Will. I want to be cremated. Remind them, will you?"

Sheila shrugged. "I don't care what you do with me when I'm gone. Have a party. I'd like that."

"You're the youngest. You'll see us all down."

"Maybe," Sheila smiled, but it was the slightest twisting of her lips and her eyes remained distant. Then she turned to look at her sister. "So, tell me . . ."

Kathy took a deep breath. Still staring at the stone carved with her parents' names, telling them too she realised, she said aloud. "I think Robert is having an affair." Her breath steamed on the air, giving the words a form. "I don't know what to do about it." In the chill December air, it sounded so cold, so matter-of-fact, so unbelievable. She glanced sidelong at Sheila. "Do you believe me?"

Her younger sister looked shocked. She finally took a deep breath. "Of course, I believe you." She paused and added. "Are you sure?"

"Nearly positive."

"Nearly positive doesn't sound too sure," Sheila said quietly. She took her tissue and rubbed it absently over the top of the headstone, not looking at her older sister. "Tell me."

Kathy sat down, perching on the edge of the stone surround. The stone was cold and hard beneath her, but in a strange way she welcomed the chill. The last couple of days were so unreal, dream-like almost. This was real: sitting here, now, on the icy stone in the deserted cemetery. She could take nothing for granted anymore. She'd been forced to look at possibilities that in the early part of the week would have been completely alien to her. Her safe secure world had been shattered. Maybe the last week had not been the dream, maybe the weeks and months and maybe years preceding it had been the dream. And now she'd woken up.

"Six years ago . . ."

"This started six years ago?" Sheila was shocked.

"Yes, in a way it did." Kathy ran her gloved hand over the pebbles on the grave. "Six years ago, I first suspected that Robert was having an affair. A woman called Stephanie Burroughs joined the company as a researcher on a project, a documentary if I remember correctly about Route 66 in America. Young, about your age, pretty, bright. They spent a lot of time together. It was about that time he started staying out later and later in the evenings. Her name kept cropping up in conversation. Eventually, it got too much for me, I tackled him and accused him of having a relationship with her."

"With what evidence?" Sheila wondered.

"Well, that was my mistake. I'd nothing but suppositions and feelings."

"But no hard evidence."

Kathy lifted her head to stare into her sister's dark eyes. "I had my intuition."

"I wonder how many marriages that has ruined?" Sheila asked softly, then waved Kathy on before she could comment.

"I tackled him. He denied it. Naturally."

"But you got over it. You must have; you're still together."

"We got over it. It was difficult. We'd just moved house, there was a lot going on. It was easy enough to concentrate on other things and let it slide. I discovered that Ms Burroughs had moved away, gone to America I think. Robert stopped talking about her – in fact, from the night I tackled him, he never mentioned her name again."

Sheila wrapped her arms around her chest and sank down on her haunches beside the headstone. "But now something has changed."

"The day before yesterday I came across her name – Stephanie

Burroughs' name – in his mobile phone." Even as she was saying it, it sounded flat to her ears.

Sheila looked at her blankly, obviously expecting more. "And?"

"Her name was in his phone, with a little red flag alongside it."

Sheila dug in her pocket and pulled out her own phone. She flipped it open with a twist of her wrist and handed it across to her sister. "Scroll down through this. I'm sure you'll find the names of the last four men I've dated on it. That doesn't mean I'm still seeing them."

"But her name is on Robert's new phone. He only got it a couple of months ago."

Sheila snapped her phone closed. "I got this less than a month ago. All that happens is that the names are stored on the card in the phone. When you pop the card into a new phone, all your contact details are there."

"There was a red flag beside her name."

Sheila stared at her sister, saying nothing.

"I know, I know. It sounds weak, doesn't it?" She straightened suddenly. "Look, I'm sorry for dragging you out here. Maybe I'm losing my mind."

"No, you're not. Maybe you're just reading too much into a situation."

Kathy dusted down her coat. She faced the grave, crossed herself automatically then turned away and headed back down the narrow path. Sheila hesitated a moment, then followed her. They walked a few yards in silence together.

"I searched his room," Kathy said suddenly. "I discovered he had a credit-card account I knew nothing about. He'd bought flowers, some stuff from a shopping channel, and a meal in a Chinese restaurant in Dublin. I discovered a speeding fine for a time when he was supposed to be in Belfast." Spoken aloud, in the cold light of day, she realised again just how weak her accusations were. "He spends a lot of time away from home. He works late," she added. Now that sounded petty, she thought.

"So what are you asking me?" Sheila said.

"Do you think he's having an affair?"

"Do you really want my advice and opinion or do you want me to support you," Sheila asked, "because they are not the same thing. If you want me to support you, I will do that. But I don't think you want my advice."

"You don't believe me?"

"I didn't say that."

"You don't have to. How can you explain the evidence?"

"What evidence?"

"The credit card," Kathy snapped.

Sheila reached into her pocket and lifted out a black leather wallet. She snapped it open. There were four credit cards in little plastic windows. Tucked into folds behind them were at least another half dozen plastic cards, store cards or affinity cards. "At home, I get an offer of a credit card at least once a day. Gold cards, platinum cards, American Express, Visa, MasterCard, Bank of Ireland, MBNA, Allied Irish Bank. Maybe he simply took up the offer of a good rate."

Kathy rounded on her sister. "What about the speeding ticket? He got it in Ballymun on Halloween night. The same night he was supposed to be in Belfast."

"Did he drive or take the train to Belfast?"

Kathy opened her mouth to reply, then closed it again, suddenly feeling ill. Had Robert taken the train that time? He sometimes did. Particularly if he was going to be away overnight – he felt nervous bringing a Dublin-registered car over the border. He'd taken the train recently when the BBC were holding a conference in the Europa. "But how would that explain the car?"

Sheila shrugged. "Ask him. Did he lend it to someone? Was it in the garage?" She turned and caught her sister by both arms. "You've got to be so careful, so sure of your facts. You've already made one accusation you could not back up. Some men would have walked away at that point. Now you're about to make another accusation. Be sure. Be very sure this time."

"Whose side are you on?" Kathy asked shakily.

"Yours. Always yours." They reached the gates of the cemetery. Sheila stopped and held her sister's hands. "I've been there, but from the other side. I was once stopped in the street by a woman I'd never met. She accused me of having an affair with her husband. I knew the man, I'd worked with him on a couple of occasions, but I most certainly was not having a relationship with him. Turned out he hadn't been having an affair with anyone. The couple broke up not too long after that. He couldn't live with the mistrust. Don't make that mistake. Don't throw away eighteen years of marriage. Don't find an affair if there's none to find." She kissed her sister quickly. "I'll see you over Christmas. Phone me if you need anything."

CHAPTER 14

At least he hadn't changed the locks.

Kathy Walker pushed open the door of R&K Productions and stepped into the office. A blast of warm air hit her and she frowned. He'd left the heating on over the weekend. If Maureen was there, she would never have allowed that to happen.

Then the alarm began to blip.

Had he changed the code? Kathy shoved the door closed and pulled open the little box on the wall behind it. ENTER CODE was flashing in bright green digital letters. She entered #32 – the number of the premises – and the blipping stopped. When they first moved into the offices, she had chosen #32 because Robert had managed to forget every other combination of numbers.

The office was more or less as she remembered it, though she hadn't stood in it in nearly six months. When she was more involved in the business, she called in every day. There were a few new framed posters on the wall, stills from advertisements or brochures that R&K had worked on, and the computer on the receptionist's desk looked new. Otherwise, it was the same: black leather and chrome furniture, looking a little tired now, and the same combination television and video in the corner, though she noted that a DVD player had been added. Just inside the door, a dispenser for Ballygowan water sat alongside the coffee pot. The ceramic mugs that usually sat alongside it had been replaced by disposable cups. She was tempted for a moment to make a cup, but she didn't want to leave any evidence that she'd been in the office.

She still wasn't sure why she had come to R&K's offices. The drive from Glasnevin across the city had taken her nearly two hours and parking was impossible even this far out from the city centre. She'd eventually found a space on the far side of the canal. Maybe it was her sister's parting words, "Don't find an affair if there's none to find", that had sent her here. Is that what she was doing – looking for an affair, looking for an excuse?

An excuse to do what? Leave Robert? Throw him out?

What was she looking for? When she'd first suspected that he was having an affair, she'd known instantly what she would do if she found out that he was involved with another woman: she would ask him to leave. No, not ask – *demand*. That had seemed so clear the day before yesterday. Today, she was less certain. She was beginning to realise that Rose's advice was probably good advice: let things be, let them sort themselves out.

But she still had to know. For her own peace or mind, if nothing else, she had to know. However, on the long drive across the city, she had come to a decision: if she found nothing concrete in the office, then she would forget about it. She would try to push it from her mind, and make a conscious effort to pay more attention to Robert and the business. If her fears about an affair had forced her to do nothing else, it had made her evaluate her own behaviour over the past few years. And she wasn't too pleased with what she had discovered. Yes, it was all too easy to say that they had drifted apart. Easier still to blame him, and the pressures of work. But what had she done? Or not done? As she became more absorbed in the children and the new house, she'd certainly taken him and the work he was doing for granted. Reading his emails yesterday, realising that he was still working into the early hours of the morning, struggling to keep the business afloat, had made her feel ashamed.

Kathy stepped around behind the receptionist's desk. It was pristine – not a paperclip, not a pencil out of place. The new receptionist was certainly neater than Maureen, she thought. She pulled open the drawers looking for a diary or notepad: all receptionists usually had a scratch-pad where they jotted down the names of the incoming calls. However, even the drawers were neatly organised; even though she'd never met the new receptionist, she wasn't sure she liked her.

Kathy finally found a pad under a well-thumbed version of the *Oxford English Dictionary* in the bottom drawer. It was a red and black spiral-bound notebook. Across the top of each page was a date and below it the times and names of all the phone calls into the office. Kathy carried the notepad to the window and tilted it to the light. She didn't want to risk turning on any of the interior lights and drawing attention to the premises. Most of the names and numbers were incomprehensible, a few were familiar to her from the days she's worked the desk. She ran her finger down the calls for the previous day.

There was no Stephanie Burroughs listed.

Kathy fished out the sheet of paper with Stephanie's details on it and checked the number against the incoming calls. Nothing.

Before she returned the notepad to the bottom drawer, Kathy looked back over the previous week's calls, but, as far as she could see no phonecalls had come in from Burroughs on the office line.

Maybe she was using the mobile, a little malicious voice argued. Maybe she wasn't phoning at all, an even smaller inner voice countered.

Kathy pushed open the door and stepped into Robert's office. It was exactly as she remembered it. The only change was the scattering of Christmas cards on the drinks cabinet and a real Christmas tree in the corner, scenting the air with pine. The miniature tree was decorated with winking white lights which had been left on and the Waterford Crystal Christmas tree ornaments her parents had given them for their first Christmas together. Kathy and Robert decided that they were too good to use at home and would make a much better impression in the office. She ran a fingernail down one of the hand-blown pieces, vaguely touched that he'd kept them for all these years, and was still using them.

The room was a long rectangle. There was a circular conference table at one end of the room, while Robert's desk occupied the other. The conference table was scattered with papers, which looked as if they had been left in a hurry. She touched a page, spinning it towards her. It was a headshot of an incredibly handsome young man. She quickly looked over the pages. They all related to DaBoyz, a boy band she'd never heard of. It looked as if Robert was pitching to shoot their next music video. She knew he knew nothing about music videos, but she guessed that the band didn't know that.

She crossed the office to stand before Robert's desk. It felt strange to be here, sneaking in like a thief into her own company. Because she did own half the company: fifty per cent of the shares were in her name. What would happen if they broke up, she wondered. Would the company have to be sold or broken up, or would he have to buy out her share? And what happened then to his share of the house; would she have to buy him out in turn?

Kathy deliberately drifted away from that thought.

As Sheila had reminded her, she had to be sure of her facts before she went off making wild accusations.

She moved around Robert's desk and sat in the heavy leather chair. It sighed and hissed beneath her weight. She'd bought him this chair shortly after they moved into this office. Like his office at home, the desk was clean and bare except for an ornamental biro and fountain-pen set which was placed at an angle off to one side, alongside a modern desk lamp. Mirroring it, on the left-hand side of the desk was a silver photo-frame in three panels. Kathy reached for it, then stopped, unwilling to touch and possible move it. She turned on the light, flooding the desk in warm yellow light. The frame held three photos: Brendan in the left frame, Theresa in the right, and Robert and Kathy in the middle frame: it was an old photograph taken in New York just before they were married, with the Empire State Building in the background. She'd almost forgotten about the photo. That had been a fabulous holiday, just the two of them, madly in love, engaged to be married, with the world full of possibilities and hope.

If Robert was having an affair, he was hardly likely to keep a photo of his wife and children on his desk, was he?

She tried the drawers. They were locked. So this trip had been for nothing. No, not for nothing. At least it had gone a long way to confirming that Robert was not seeing Stephanie, she wasn't phoning him every day, and there was a family photo on the desk, which at least suggested that his mistress was not visiting him in the office.

Placing her elbows on the table-top and cradling her head in her hands, she squeezed her eyes shut. She felt sick, and yet curiously elated. She'd overreacted. She was tired, exhausted, stressed out by the season. Next year they would go away for Christmas.

Well, at least she'd had a wake-up call. If the last couple of days had done nothing else, they'd highlighted some problems in her marriage, but problems that could be solved. After Christmas, the pair of them would go away for a weekend, and talk. It had been a long time since they talked, really talked about stuff that mattered. With the constant pressures of modern life, it was so easy to lose touch with what was really important.

Thank God, she hadn't said anything . . .

She was leaving the office when she saw the filing cabinet behind the door. She'd not noticed it when she first came in. On impulse, she pulled at the top drawer, expecting to find it locked. It clicked and slid open easily. The files were all neatly tabbed and colour-coded and she saw the hand of the new secretary in it.

The top drawer seemed to be mainly brochures, letters to and from other production companies, pitches for projects, briefs for commissioning rounds.

The second drawer was full of invoices and bills. She hesitated, then lifted out the file marked Eircom. All of Robert's mobile-phone bills were nearly arranged in chronological order. She lifted the most recent bill.

Robert Walker phoned Stephanie Burroughs seven or eight times a day. The first call of the day and the last call at night from his cell phone were either to her home phone or her mobile. Calls ranged in duration from a couple of minutes to an hour.

Every day.

Seven days a week.

Hundreds of calls.

Kathy barely made it to the toilets before she threw up.

CHAPTER 15

"Kathy!"

"Hello, Maureen."

Kathy stood on Maureen Ryan's doorstep, a bunch of flowers held awkwardly under one arm, a bottle of wine in a brown-paper bag under the other.

"Come in, come in. I wasn't expecting you. I'd kiss you, but I don't want to give you whatever I have." Maureen stepped back and allowed Kathy to squeeze past her. "Go straight through into the kitchen."

Maureen lived just off the old Finglas Road, in a two-up, two-down terrace house in the design beloved of Dublin Corporation in the 1950's. She'd been born in the house, and she always said she would like to die there also.

"I should have phoned, I know," Kathy said slightly breathlessly, walking down the narrow hallway and into the kitchen-cum-dining-room. She stopped, shocked. From the outside she had been expecting dark and gloomy Formica and lino, instead she was blinking in brilliant light, looking at the latest in Swedish kitchen design, polished blond wood and cool chrome. The rear window, kitchen door and a section of the wall had been removed and replaced with patio doors which led down into a circular conservatory that was bright and fragrant with Christmas blooms. "This is fabulous," she said.

"Isn't it lovely?" Maureen said, voice wheezing a little as she came up behind her. "We did a pilot for a DIY show a couple of years ago. It never got off the ground, but I volunteered my house for the makeover. I got a new kitchen, a patio and a conservatory and they even paid me to do it."

Kathy turned to look at the older woman. She handed her the flowers and the wine. "I only learned last night that you were sick. Robert forgot to tell me. He insisted he had, but he hadn't."

"I'm sure he's had a lot on his mind lately," Maureen said. She turned away, set the flowers and wine down on the counter and started to fill the kettle. "Sit down. Go out into the conservatory. That's my favourite part of the house."

Maureen Ryan was twenty years older than Kathy, a tall, masculine-looking woman, with strong, sharp features, almost translucent eyes and a shock of snow-white hair which she wore in a single tight braid that hung to the small of her back. When Kathy had first met her, she'd worn half-moon glasses, but she'd thrown them away in favour of contact lenses, claiming that the glasses made her look old. She never married, but throughout her life had been romantically linked in the gossip pages with several minor politicians and one equally minor movie star. Maureen liked to say that the stories were only half true: it had been a dozen minor politicians and two minor movie stars. Normally she dressed in what might best be called smart-casual and was still slim and svelte enough to get away with jeans and boots. Today however, she was in a plum-coloured track suit and incredibly ratty slippers.

Kathy stepped down into the conservatory. The air was perfumed with the scent of the flowers and the musky odour of a fat candle burning on an ornamental stand. Two enormous fan-backed white wicker chairs were placed on either side of a circular glass table. A Stephen King paperback, his book *On Writing*, was open on the table. Kathy remembered that Maureen had always talked about writing a novel based upon her experiences of forty years working in and around the entertainment business.

"How are you feeling?" she asked aloud.

"I'm fine. Getting better." Maureen's voice echoed down from the kitchen. "I picked up a cold, which turned into a chest infection. Inflammation of the plurum, the doctors called it. I wanted to continue working, but there was a danger that it would turn into pneumonia, so, for once in my life I took some good advice and stayed home."

"You should have let me know. I've have come around sooner."

"I thought Robert might mention it to you, but I suppose I should have guessed he'd forget," Maureen said, stepping out into the conservatory. She was carrying a wicker tray, which held a hand-painted teapot and two matching cups. "Aren't these fun; I got them in Aya Napa."

"Isn't that the place where all the young people go for raves?"

"Yes," Maureen said, looking at her blankly, then she grinned. "I like to think of myself as one of those young people."

"You're the youngest person I know. I hope I've still got your energy when I'm . . ." she allowed the sentence to trail off.

"When you're my age, you mean," Maureen grinned.

"Something like that." Kathy sank in the creaking wicker chair and watched Maureen pour tea. "What keeps you so young?"

Maureen lifted her head and grinned, showing perfectly white teeth. "I used to say 'regular holidays and Spanish waiters', but lately I've been saying *Attitude*. I picked an age and stuck at it."

Despite the sick headache throbbing at the back of her skull, Kathy smiled. "What age?"

"Twenty-two."

"I thought most people choose eighteen."

"I knew nothing at eighteen. I knew it all by the time I was twenty-two. By the time I turned twenty-three I knew too much."

95

Maureen passed the cup to Kathy, then waited while she added milk. "I don't think I'm old, therefore I'm not. That's why I hate this bloody chest infection: reminds me that I'm not as resilient as I once was."

The two women drank their tea in silence, looking out over the tiny rectangle of garden.

"This conservatory must make you the envy of your neighbours," Kathy said eventually.

"I did start a trend. There are three similar conservatories in this block alone. It was a pity we couldn't get the DIY show off the ground. I had plans to have the whole house transformed." She sipped her tea. "I must come out and see what you've done with the house. How long are you there now – five, six years?"

"Six, and we've done nothing with it. Somehow there never seemed to be the time. The children are just shooting up and now that they're both in secondary school, they seem to be coming and going at all hours of the day. But next year, I've plans to get in and make some changes . . ." Realising that she was babbling, Kathy abruptly shut up.

"And how is Robert?" Maureen asked.

Kathy blinked at her in surprise.

"I haven't seen him in nearly six weeks," Maureen added.

Kathy shook her head in disgust. "He said you'd been gone for three or four weeks."

"I went out sick early in November. I've not spoken to him since."

"Has he not called?" Kathy asked, getting angry now. R&K's growth and success owed much to this woman. But more than that, she was a friend.

"He called for the first few days, usually when he wanted something, or had lost something, or couldn't find a file. I wasn't really expecting him to keep in touch. This is a busy time of year for him. I expect he's run off his feet."

"I certainly don't get to see a lot of him," Kathy admitted. "Let me apologise for him –"

"Don't," Maureen said quickly, raising a hand. "I've worked with him for a long time. I know what he's like."

"And he hasn't . . . hasn't done anything stupid, has he, like stopping your wages, or anything like that?"

Maureen laughed and then wheezed a rasping cough. "No, nothing like that. He's terrified he'd lose me to one of his rivals. He knows Mason Media have been chasing me."

"Good. Good." Unsure what to say next, Kathy concentrated on her tea.

Maureen sat back into the wicker chair, then lifted up both legs and tucked them beneath her. "I get the impression that this may be more than a social call," she said gently.

Kathy stared miserably into the dregs of her tea. She nodded. "I really did discover you were sick last night. Late last night. Two thirty. Robert was out with Jimmy Moran. Or at least, he said he was out with Jimmy Moran," she added softly.

"That's a curious thing to say," Maureen said, putting down her cup. "You sound as if you don't believe him."

Kathy put down her own cup and looked Maureen in the eye. "I've recently discovered that a lot of what Robert's been telling me was untrue." She breathed deeply. "I believe Robert is having an affair with Stephanie Burroughs. What do you think?"

And she knew, even before Maureen answered, what the answer was going to be. It suddenly seemed colder in the conservatory.

The older woman nodded. "I suspected that for a long time."

"When did you know for certain?"

"About a year ago. I was suspicious for a little while before that."

"A year! A year and you didn't think to tell me!" Kathy bit back the wave of anger.

"I thought about it often enough. There were times when you were in and out of the office regularly that I wanted to say it to you . . . but there never seemed to be the right time. And then when your mother died, you had enough on your plate. I just didn't want to hurt you."

"You should have told me!" Kathy's voice rose as she surged to her feet. "I had a right to know!"

"Have you a right to be angry with me?" Maureen asked quietly. "I'm not the one you should be angry with."

Kathy sank back into the chair and put her head in her hands.

"If the roles were reversed, would you have told me?"

Kathy opened her mouth to snap a "yes" but closed it again without replying. Would she, could she, put another woman through the agony, the self-doubt, the self-loathing, the fear, the anger she'd experienced over the past two days? She wasn't sure any more. Wasn't sure of anything.

"I've just come from the office. I went looking for something – something to tell me that he was having an affair, but hoping to find nothing. I'd almost walked out the door when I discovered his mobile-phone records."

The older woman smiled bitterly. "That's how I discovered the truth too. I was doing an analysis of the bills, looking to make some savings when I discovered he kept phoning the same number. I initially thought it was your mobile, then I realised he was phoning it last thing at night when he should be home with you. Once the suspicion was there, it was relatively easy to put the rest of it together."

"Tell me what you know," Kathy said fiercely. "Tell me everything."

"You really don't need to know. Deal with what you know now."

"I want to know. I have a right to know. I have to know," she said desperately.

Maureen stood. Wrapping her arms tightly across her chest, she turned her back on Kathy and stared out at the empty December garden. "I think they've been having a relationship for about eighteen months. Maybe a little bit longer, I'm not sure.

They were certainly friends and colleagues before that. But I don't think anything was going on then."

"A year and a half," Kathy said numbly. "He knew her a long time before that. I suspected them of having an affair six years ago when she worked for us as a researcher."

Maureen frowned. "I know they worked closely together, but I don't think they were having a relationship then."

"But you've known for a year and a half, eighteen months. Why didn't you tell me, Maureen?"

"It's complicated."

"Complicated," Kathy whispered. "What does that mean? I've just discovered my husband of eighteen years is having an affair for the past year and a half, maybe longer, and you say you couldn't tell me because it's complicated! What's so complicated about that?"

"Stephanie Burroughs puts a lot of business our way." Maureen turned to look at Kathy, her face hard and expressionless, but her big eyes were brimming with tears. "That's one of the reasons I didn't tell you. Stephanie is the account manager with one of the largest advertising agencies in the city – she got us a lot of work. Without her, we would probably have gone under this past year."

Kathy stood and backed away from the older woman. "You let my husband continue his affair because you didn't want to lose your job?"

"His affair was none of my business," Maureen snapped. "His affair is between you and him. No-one else. That's why I didn't tell you. I'm not one of those women who goes running to their friends with news that they've seen their husband with another woman. Don't blame me for this. This has nothing to do with losing my job. If R&K go under, I'll lose my job sure, but I'll get another. But you'll lose your house and at forty-two, Robert's not going to be getting another job any time soon. People like him are ten-a-penny. If I had told you, you'd have either tackled her or him and then what? We'd all have lost, you and Robert most of all."

Kathy licked dry lips. Her tongue felt swollen in her mouth. "You're saying he slept with her to save the business."

"I'm saying nothing of the sort."

"But that's what you're implying."

"No, I'm not implying anything. I'm simply telling you the truth of the matter."

"Then what are you saying?"

"Kathy –"

"Tell me," Kathy demanded, voice rising to a scream. "Why is he sleeping with her?"

Maureen sighed. "I've seen them together. I think they're in love with one another."

CHAPTER 16

Saturday 21st/Sunday 22nd December

The remainder of Saturday passed in a blur and Kathy had no memory of driving back from Maureen's house. She'd kept out of Robert's way, busying herself around the house with the Christmas preparations. Robert had gone out in the morning with the children to buy the Christmas tree, so by the time she got back the house smelled of pine and echoed to Theresa's squeals as she decorated the tree. A trail of pine needles led from the backdoor, through the kitchen and into the dining-room.

Maureen's words had frightened her, confused her. She could almost accept that Robert was having an affair with another woman, but that was sex, wasn't it, nothing more? Maureen said she thought they were in love with one another, which implied . . .

She wasn't sure what it implied.

Kathy went to bed early, claiming a headache, which was true, and lay in the darkness, listening to the sounds of the TV from the room below and the noise of the regular weekend argument coming through the walls from next door. Her neighbours did everything together, golf, tennis, walked and were generally considered to be perfectly matched. Only Kathy knew that they had screaming matches usually about this time every Friday or Saturday night when one or the other – or both – had a little too much to drink. In the six years she'd lived in this house, she'd learned the entire details of their unhappy lives. But when they stepped out on the streets neighbours only saw a perfect couple . . .

When people looked at her and Robert, what did they see? A happily married couple, with the required two children, nice house, two cars? Or could they see the distance that had appeared between them?

The thought shifted and twisted and she suddenly wondered how many other people knew about Robert's affair. She felt her heart begin to thump and a panicked tightness squeeze across her chest at the thought. Dublin was a small city; someone must have seen Robert and his mistress together. If they had, would they have made the connection and assumed the couple were in a relationship? She hated the thought that people knew and were pointing fingers as she drove past or walked down the street, whispering behind her back. The only consolation she had was that if anyone knew, they would have told her. People loved to be the bearers of bad news. Robert and Stephanie were colleagues in the same line of work; it would be natural for them to have meetings and lunches together; maybe no-one suspected.

She hadn't.

Kathy fell into a fitful sleep, only snapping awake again when Robert crept into the bedroom. He undressed in the dark and slid in beside her, sighing with contentment as his head hit the pillow. She had not intended speaking to him – afraid that she might blurt out something, or rage or scream at him, but she needed to say something. The rhythm of his breathing was changing, slowing, as he drifted towards sleep.

"I went to see Maureen today."

There was a long pause and, for a moment, she thought Robert had fallen asleep. There was movement in the bed as he shifted to look at her. In the reflected streetlights, she could see the sparkling whites of his eyes.

"How is she?"

"Getting better. But she won't be back till the New Year."

"Didn't think so," he mumbled.

"She's not as young as she pretends to be."

"I know that." He shifted again, rolling onto his back. "This new girl, the Russian . . ."

"Illona?"

"Yes, Illona. She's very good. Does what she's told, gives no cheek, is in on time, takes exactly an hour for lunch. Maureen does it her way, treats me like a boy and has no concept of a one-hour lunch."

"You're not thinking about sacking her, are you?"

"I've been thinking about it," he admitted.

"I'll not have it!" Kathy snapped. "I forbid it."

"Forbid it?" There was something in his voice she didn't like: sarcasm or contempt. "You forbid it?"

"I still own half the company, remember. Maybe it's time I reminded you of that. Maybe it's time I started to take a more active interest in it." She sat up in bed and snapped on the light.

Robert groaned and shielded his eyes. "It's after one, for Christ's sake. Can we talk about this in the morning?"

Kathy ignored him. "Now that the children are older, I'm thinking in the New Year I might start coming in with you three or four times a week. Even when Maureen comes back she's not going to be able to work full time. I can go back to doing what I used to do: help you run the company. Put the K back into R&K Productions."

"Where are you going to find the time?"

"I'll make the time. I'll concentrate on getting new business; you concentrate on making the material."

"Yea, that would be great, I'm sure," he said, sounding less than enthusiastic. "Let's talk about it in the morning."

"Maureen suggested that things were not going too well for the company."

Robert shuffled up in the bed. "Can we talk about it in the morning?"

"We rarely get a chance to talk any more, Robert, have you realised that? We're running in opposite directions."

"It's only temporarily, and it's Christmas. That always brings its own madness."

"No, it's not temporarily and it's not just Christmas. We've been doing it for months, maybe longer. I rarely see you any more. You're home late four nights out of five, you go in at the weekends, and when you are home, you're locked in your room, working."

Robert shrugged. "It's been busy. I'll admit that."

"Put my mind at ease: tell me the business is going well."

Robert sighed deeply. "We've gone through a rough patch, but I've landed a few new accounts. We're OK again. Next year will be good."

And Kathy knew where those new accounts had come from.

"Does that mean you'll end up working all the hours God sends next year too?"

"While the work is there, I'll do it. I don't have an option. It's one of the joys of being self-employed, you know that."

"Then I'm even more determined to help you. Starting in the New Year, you've got a new employee: me. You can give your Russian girl notice."

Robert made a face and shook his head.

"What's wrong?"

"Nothing is wrong. Here's what will happen. You'll come to work with me for a week, maybe two, then you'll have to take time off to be home here for some reason. Then you'll take more and more time off, and soon enough, you'll be back to the way we are now. Except I'll have to go looking for a secretary again."

"You sound as if you don't want me to work with you."

"I didn't say that. I'd love you to be more interested in the business." He lifted the clock off the bedside locker and held it up before her face. "Look at the time – can we please continue this in the morning?"

"OK," she agreed, turning off her light and sliding down beneath the covers. "But we will continue it," she promised.

"Absolutely," he said.

Lying in the dark, listening to her husband's breathing deepen beside her, Kathy realised that the conversation had gone exactly as she expected. There was no way he could allow her to be around the business; not if he was using it as a base for his affair.

When Kathy awoke, crisp December sunlight was golden on the window and she groaned, knowing that she'd overslept. Robert's side of the bed was empty and there was a single sheet of notepaper on his pillow.

Gone into the office to finish off some work. Will be home later. Love R.

CHAPTER 17

Monday 23rd December

"Are you free tonight?" Kathy tucked the phone under her ear as she went through her clothes in the wardrobe. "I hate to ask . . ."

"I can free things up. What do you need me for?" Sheila's voice was breathless and Kathy could hear music and a cheery voice in the background.

"I'm sorry, I didn't realise you had company."

"Some company. It's a fitness video. Power skipping. Really burns calories." Each sentence came in short bursts.

"Like you need to burn calories," Kathy said, unable to keep the touch of envy out of her voice. "I was wondering if you could sit on the children. I asked Julia the other night and I don't want to ask her again."

"Sure. Where are you off to?" There was a silence and Kathy heard the snap of the skipping rope off the floor. "This is something to do with Robert, isn't it?" Sheila's voice came more evenly now and she'd obviously stopped skipping.

"Yes, it is."

"What are you going to do?"

Kathy pulled out a black polo-neck and tossed it onto the bed.

"I went to see Maureen Ryan on Saturday. You remember Maureen, the office manager at R&K?"

"Of course, I remember her."

"She knew about the affair, Sheila. She knew about it and she didn't tell me."

"I'm not that surprised," Sheila said softly.

Kathy blinked in surprise. "Would you, if you had known? Would you have told me?"

"Honestly?"

"Of course."

"If I knew for certain, I would have tackled Robert first before I spoke to you. What did Maureen say?"

"She says it's been going on for over a year now. They meet every Monday night at the health club just off the M50, and then usually go out for dinner afterwards."

Sheila's voice was deadly serious. "What are you going to do?"

Kathy pushed the wardrobe door closed. She didn't entirely recognise the woman who stared back at her in the mirror. Four days ago, she knew this woman, knew her place in the world, knew what her world looked like. Now, it was like looking at a stranger.

"I want to see them together. That's all. Nothing else. I promise."

"I'm coming with you," Sheila said immediately.

"But the children . . ."

"Are big enough to look after themselves for a couple of hours. Brendan will be eighteen next birthday. He's practically a man."

"Look, thank you for the offer, but I really want to do this on my own . . ."

"And what happens if Robert sees your car and recognises it? We can go in mine. What happens if you have a crash on the way home because you're upset at something you see? No, I'm coming with you. You've got to let me."

"Do I have a choice?"

"Of course, you do. You could ask Julia to go with you."

Kathy laughed, a short barking sound that was completely without humour.

"You really didn't have to do this," Kathy said.

"I wanted to," Sheila answered.

The two sisters were sitting in Sheila's car in the carpark of the health studio and gymnasium just off the M50. The entire glass front of the modern building blazed with lights and the front was strung with Christmas lights. Through the tall windows they could see people working out on the gleaming gym equipment.

The sisters had cruised around the carpark twice before they finally spotted Robert's Audi tucked away close to the hedge in a puddle of shadow. There was a silver BMW parked alongside it, but plenty of empty spaces on either side. Kathy leaned forward, squinting through the windscreen at the car. Was that Burroughs' car?

"This is a good spot." Sheila tucked the car into a darkened corner of the park that afforded a good view of the front entrance to the building to the left and Robert's car to the right. She turned off the engine and the heater cut out. Almost immediately, chilly air began to invade the car.

"Maureen said they usually leave about eight."

Sheila leaned forward to look at the centre. "No matter how fanatical I was about my fitness, I'm not sure I'd be spending the night before Christmas Eve working out."

"No, instead you're sitting in a car with your hysterical sister spying on a philandering husband. I'm sure you could have found better ways to spend your twenty-third of December. Did you not have something planned with your young man?"

Sheila Childs didn't answer immediately. She hit a switch and the windscreen wipers hissed across the screen, wiping away stray flakes of snow. "I'd something planned, but nothing that couldn't be cancelled." She smiled, a flash of white teeth. "Doesn't do any harm to keep them guessing, keeps them on their toes."

"Is that where I went wrong, do you think? He stopped guessing about me; I became too predictable, too ordinary."

"You didn't go wrong. You've done nothing wrong. You've raised two wonderful children and kept the house going, gave Robert the freedom from worry and care which allowed him to grow the business. That's called a partnership."

Sitting in the darkness, staring out at the lights, Kathy put voice to the questions that had been troubling her from the moment she had first seen Stephanie Burroughs' name and known – *absolutely known* – that Robert was involved with her. "I keep asking myself what I could have done differently, how I could have kept him."

"Do you want to keep him?"

Kathy sucked in a deep ragged breath. "I'm not sure any more. Everything has just come at me so quickly. When I try to think logically about it, I get lost in issues like the house and the business and the children . . ."

"And what about what you want? Leave aside the house and business and children. What do you want?"

"I don't know," Kathy whispered. "I'm not sure. Or at least I was sure before I spoke to Maureen. She told me she thought they were in love with one another. And in that moment I hated him. Hated him. And I wanted him back. I wanted to take him away from her. The woman who had stolen him from me." She shook her head. "I can't think straight. Sometimes I feel as if I'm going to burst."

"You're saying it was easier when you thought it was just sex?"

"Yes. Having sex with someone . . . that's one thing. But loving them. Giving yourself emotionally to them. That was the deeper betrayal."

The windscreen wipers worked again, squeaking slightly on the glass. Sheila lifted a bottle of water, twisted off the cap and sipped. She offered it to Kathy who refused. "Allen is married," she said softly.

It took a long moment for the sentence to sink in.

"Allen, the man you're seeing? That Allen? He's married."

"Five years older than me, married for twenty years with three children." Sheila's voice was a monotone.

"Sheila! How could you? Didn't you know? What were you thinking of?" Kathy found herself moving away from her sister, pushing against the door. She stared at her in horror.

Sheila turned her head slightly to look at Kathy. Reflected Christmas lights ran red and white down her face. "Do I love him? No. But does he love me: yes, he does. And that's the problem."

Kathy reached out with a trembling hand and lifted the bottle of water from Sheila's fingers. She swallowed quickly, feeling the cold water move through her system to settle in her stomach.

"I didn't know he was married when I first met him and he tried to hide it from me for a while, but it's easy enough to find out. The married ones never have that endless free time the single ones do. Weekends were out of bounds, Bank Holidays were impossible. It's easy to spot. But he was fun. I enjoyed his company. He made me laugh. And I wanted a man, not a boy. I wanted someone mature, someone who would look after me, respect me."

"But a married man!"

"Yes, well, that was a problem. But you know something, I never wanted him as a husband, I never wanted to take him away from his wife. I enjoyed my freedom too much. I was happy being the mistress. We had great holidays, weekend breaks, great meals, good sex. It was like being twenty again . . . except this time we had the money and the credit cards to enjoy it."

"Does his wife know?"

"I'm not sure. She may suspect."

"Dear God, Sheila, if you knew what I've been through, you would never put another woman through it."

"It was all going fine," Sheila continued as if she hadn't heard her sister, "until he fell in love with me. Now he's talking about leaving his wife and children. He's talking about a divorce. He wants to marry me." Her voice was suddenly shaky. "Can you imagine it: me, married."

"You don't love him?"

"I do not," Sheila said emphatically. "Like him yes, love him no. I was going to see him tonight, talk to him, try and break it off with him, before he tells his wife and does something dramatic. Recently, he started talking about separations and divorce and good dates to marry. I may not be the brightest in the world, but that's when the alarm bells starting ringing for me."

Kathy was shivering, and not with the cold. She couldn't believe what she was hearing. Her sister, Sheila, her baby sister was a married man's mistress. But her sister wasn't a bad person, not an evil person. She hadn't deliberately set out to trap a married man, in fact it looked as if she was doing everything in her power to ensure that he remained with his wife.

"You're going to tell me that I should never have taken up with him in the first place, and you're right of course. But I'm a big girl, I went into this with my eyes open. And when I discovered that he was married, I didn't walk away, did I?"

"Why . . . why did you stay with him?"

Sheila shrugged. "Who knows? We always want what we can't have."

"You've no regrets about his wife . . ."

"No. If she had been looking after him, been interested in him, he would never have wandered in my direction."

Kathy looked away. Is that what had happened: had Robert drifted away because she was no longer interested in him?

"Here they are," Sheila said, pointing.

This was the man you married.

This was the man who had linked you down the aisle, who had

carried you over the threshold, who had made love to you, got you pregnant, stood in the hospital and held your hand while you gave birth.

This was the man whose flesh you knew, whose clothes you washed, whose hand you held, whose lips you kissed.

This was the man you loved and trusted.

This was your husband.

And he was holding the hand of another woman.

Kathy Walker watched Robert stride out from the main entrance of the gym. There was a woman by his side, an ordinary-looking woman, pretty, slim, bright-eyed, smiling. She still looked like a younger version of herself, Kathy thought.

Neither was wearing gloves, and their hands were wrapped together, fingers interlinked. They moved easily alongside one another, confidently, their steps in rhythm. Glance at them quickly and you'd see just another happy couple.

They were both laughing.

Kathy didn't remember the last time she and Robert had laughed together, didn't remember the last time they had held hands so easily, so intimately.

The couple strolled over to the two cars. Both sets of lights flashed in unison as they hit their remotes simultaneously and they laughed again, the sound high and brittle on the chill December air.

Robert opened the door of Stephanie's silver BMW. The interior light popped on. The woman threw her gym bag onto the passenger seat, then turned to Robert. She wrapped her arms around his neck, pressed the palm of her right hand against the back of his skull to bring his head down to a level with hers. Then she kissed him. Robert responded by dropping his gym bag to the ground and pulling her close.

The kiss went on for a long time.

Finally the couple broke apart and Stephanie climbed into the car. She waved once and drove away. Robert picked up his bag and moved around the front of his car.

Kathy pulled out her mobile phone and hit a speed dial.

"What are you doing?" Sheila hissed, snatching for the phone. It was too late. The call connected.

"Hi, it's me," Kathy's voice was level, remarkably controlled.

Across the carpark, less than a hundred yards away, Robert stood with his phone pressed against his ear.

"I'm just wondering what time you'll be home?"

Kathy and Sheila saw Robert lift his left arm to look at his watch. "I'm just leaving the office. I should be there in about forty minutes."

Kathy's hands were trembling so hard that Sheila had to take the phone out of her hand and switch it off.

"Now what?" Sheila asked, when Robert's car pulled out of the carpark.

"I'm going to see Stephanie Burroughs tomorrow," Kathy said, her voice growing firm and cold with resolution. "I have to talk to her."

Book 2

The Husband's Story

At first, I didn't know what I was doing.

That's not an excuse. Simply a statement of fact. But I swear I didn't set out to have an affair. It just happened.

And then things got out of control. They got complicated.

By the time I knew what I was doing, it was too late. I was in too deep.

I was in love with her.

Chapter 18

Thursday 19th December

Robert Walker sighed as the hot spray hit his body. There was an iron bar of tension stretched across his shoulders and what felt like a red-hot coal in the base of his spine from sitting in traffic.

He hated Christmas.

Hated everything that it stood for: its falseness, artificiality, pressure to spend and traffic – especially the traffic. One year, just one year, he would love to take off in early December and return around the middle of January and give the entire Christmas and New Year's nonsense a miss.

Robert touched the dial, inching up the hot water. He dipped his head and turned, allowed the water to play across his neck.

Also, this year R&K Productions had shot a Christmas advertisement in June – when finding a Christmas tree had been next to impossible – and early in November had shot a segment for a docu-drama which was set in the middle of August. Inasmuch as finding sunshine in Dublin in the middle of December was an impossibility, and the budget wouldn't stretch to moving cast and crew to a sunny locale, they had ended up lighting the sets in such a way as to suggest brilliant weather. It meant that his entire year was topsy-turvy.

But it was the traffic he hated. Dublin city traffic multiplied to the power of ten because it was Christmas. Add lousy weather, Operation Freeflow, the port-tunnel works and now Luas into the mix, and the city was practically at a standstill.

Robert tilted his face to the water. He ran his long fingers through his hair, pulling it back off his forehead. Then he grimaced and opened his eyes; strands had come away in his hands, entangling his fingers. He was losing his hair. There was a time when it would not have bothered him; he didn't like to think of himself as vain, but things had changed.

There was a time when experience counted in his business, and no-one really cared what you looked like. But with the impossibility of getting real work – or what he called real work, proper television documentary commissions – he had been forced to take on more advertising and commercial work. He had discovered that in this business looks were everything. He was in the running to shoot the pop video for a boy band at the moment, trying to convince them that he was the right man to create something dark and cutting-edge to match their song. There was no way they were going to give that gig to someone who looked like their father, was there?

He squeezed some shampoo in his hands and began to hum as he rubbed it gently into his scalp. Maybe it was time to look at some of the treatments that were supposed to restore hair. He saw ads in the papers all the time, special shampoos, electric caps, brushes which massaged the scalp . . . maybe there was a documentary in it. He grinned; he could get to try out all the treatments and charge it to the company as research. Maybe not though; with the way his luck was running, he'd probably go bald. Tilting his head back, he allowed the shower to rinse away the soap, then turned off the tap and stood for a moment, dripping, before pushing open the shower stall and standing out onto the bath-rug.

When the new power shower was installed, he'd used the opportunity to re-do the en-suite. It was clean and white – he knew Kathy thought it was too cool and clinical – and one wall was completely covered in mirrored tiles. He felt that it gave the otherwise small room a great sense of space; she told him she hated the reflections which allowed her to see all her imperfections at the same time.

He looked at his reflection in the glass. He was forty-two years of age and probably looked a couple of years older than that. The age showed in the set of his jaw, the lines on his face and around his neck. But he was still in relatively good shape for a man of his years, and although his waist had thickened a little, there was still no hint of a paunch. He worked out regularly, and paid particular attention to his stomach and chest. He'd had a couple of sessions on a sun-bed – the new turbo kind, which you stood up in – and he was really pleased with the results. Now, if only he could save his hair.

Robert stepped up to the mirror and patted his hair dry with a towel. He'd done a piece for a hair company a couple of years ago, and he remembered they advised that patting and gently rubbing were better than briskly scrubbing the hair with a towel. That damaged the delicate follicles. He tilted his head to one side. Earlier in the year, he'd noted the first real and dramatic signs of grey appearing. However, he'd got himself a hair-colouring foam that blended it away before anyone noticed.

Well, Kathy hadn't noticed anyway.

Stephanie had.

She'd spotted it immediately. She preferred his silver wings; she thought they made him look distinguished. He thought they aged him, and blended them away despite her objections.

Wrapping a towel around his waist, Robert reached for the aftershave. He thought he heard a sound in the bedroom outside and popped his head around the door. "Kathy?"

There was no one there, but a depression on the bedcovers was gradually filling in, and there were a few red Christmas envelopes on the bedcovers alongside his clothes, where he'd left them when he'd stripped off before climbing into the shower.

"Kathy?" He stepped out of the en-suite and pulled open the bedroom door. He was in time to hear the kitchen door click. He picked up one of the Christmas cards, leaving damp fingerprints on the envelope, and glanced at it. Then he tossed the card back on the bed again: he knew what this was all about. Every year, Kathy would fight with him about Christmas-card addresses. She never seemed to have them, even though she'd have sent out cards to the same address the previous year. He simply didn't have the time to write dozens of cards. She did. What did she do all day, anyway? And since she'd distanced herself from the company, it was the least she could do.

His XDA was sticking out of the pocket of his jacket and he picked it up, automatically checking the screen for any missed calls: there were none. Then he noticed that the little stylus was lying on the bed covers. It must have fallen out when he picked it up. Frowning, he slotted the little pen back into its holder. It settled with a click; he'd noticed in the past that if it didn't click solidly into place it had a habit of slipping free.

He splashed on some of the new cologne that Stephanie had bought him, wrinkling his nose at the musky smell. He wasn't sure about it at first, it slowly grew on him, and then he realised that it would also serve to mask the heavy musky perfume that she sometimes wore when they went out at night.

He dressed quickly in jeans and a polo neck and hurried down the stairs. The house was still and silent . . . and cold, he realised. There was a chill to the air. He trailed fingertips along the tops of the radiators, but they were scalding hot.

When he pushed open the kitchen door, he discovered the cause of the chill: the back door was wide open and Kathy was standing on the step.

"Hey, what's up – there's a gale blowing through the house."

He came up behind his wife, wrapped his arms around her shoulders and rested his chin on the top of her head. He felt her stiffen and knew immediately that she was going to draw away from him.

Kathy stepped back into the kitchen, forcing him to release her. "Just getting a breath of air, the kitchen was stuffy."

He watched as she pulled the door closed and moved to the table to tidy the cards. "I left a couple of cards on the bed," she began. "I saw them . . ."

"I don't have addresses and besides they're personal cards – it would be better if you wrote and signed them."

After eighteen years of marriage, he'd come to know that something was amiss. He could tell from the set of her shoulders, by the way she refused to meet his gaze. "What's wrong?" he asked quickly.

Kathy glanced sidelong at him. "Nothing. Why do you ask?"

He smiled and took a deep breath, guessing that tonight was going to be one of *those* nights – a cold-shoulder night, he called them, when no matter what he said or did it would be the wrong thing. "Because you've got that *tone* in your voice."

"Which tone?

"That tone." He attempted a smile to lighten the situation. He was too tired, too bone-tired and fed-up for an argument. "The tone that tells me you're pissed off at me."

Kathy sighed slowly and deliberately.

"Oh, and the sigh is another sure sign that you're pissed at me."

She shot him an angry look, and in that instant he caught a glimpse of his late, unlamented mother-in-law, the terminally depressed Margaret Childs. Physically, Kathy resembled her late father, short and round, but about her eyes and thin lips, she favoured her mother.

"Look, I'm tired," she snapped. "I've been writing cards for hours. Mostly your cards, to your friends, and your colleagues. I do it every year. And every year it's last minute and I'm always short some of the addresses. You don't help."

Robert bit back a response. He was going to say, you've had weeks to do it, but you always leave it to the last minute and you always blame me. You could have been doing these a few at a time instead of sitting on your arse watching repeats of *Emmerdale* and *Judge Judy*. But the last thing he wanted was an argument. "I've just come in from a ten-hour day," he said, keeping his voice light and reasonable. "Traffic is a bitch and I've got a presentation to make in the morning. Let me get a cup of tea, then I'll go through my address book and give you every address you need."

"I've done them all," Kathy said tightly. "There are just four on the bed for you to do."

"We're arguing over four cards?" he asked.

"No, we're not arguing over four cards," she snapped, "we're arguing over the one hundred and twenty I've already written. Without your help."

Robert nodded and shrugged. "I should have taken some into work with me," he said. Then he glanced up at the clock. "I'll go and get the kids." He turned and hurried from the kitchen before he said something he regretted. The same argument every year. They probably even used the same words. He snatched his leather coat off the rack behind the door and left, resisting the temptation to slam the front door.

He pressed the remote and the Audi clicked open. Sliding into the driver's seat, he grabbed the steering wheel and took a deep breath, calming himself. Today was Thursday. This would be the third argument this week. An argument over nothing. Or over something so small that it counted for nothing. Easing the car out of the driveway, he turned left onto the quiet roadway. Ice crackled under his tyres: it would freeze hard later on.

They had been married for eighteen years, and he recognised that an argument never really came from nowhere and it was never – *never* – about the subject under discussion. Today, Kathy was arguing about Christmas cards. Yesterday she'd fought with him because he forgot to bring home some milk, earlier in the week she'd had a go at him because he failed to get home in time to go to a parent-teacher meeting.

He had explained to her – more than once – that this was his busiest period. He simply had not got the time; but she found it difficult to accept that. Plus it was particularly awkward now with Maureen out of the picture. The new receptionist was good, very good indeed, and she came without all the awkward baggage that know-it-all Maureen brought to the job, but he found he had to check and double-check everything and that just increased his work load and his stress levels.

Kathy liked to think that she knew about the business, but in the years since she'd stepped back from being involved in the day-to-day running, things had changed. And not only the business; Kathy had been home for too long and had become isolated from the realities of doing business in the real world. And the real world now included traffic. Incredible traffic. Stand-still traffic. She simply did not understand that it made no sense to leave the office at five thirty and sit in traffic for two hours, when he could just as easily leave at six thirty and sit in moving traffic for forty-five minutes.

Plus, of course, it allowed time for Stephanie to call around.

Robert smiled as he pulled up outside Brendan's school. Both Brendan and Theresa were late home today; they had extra classes. Brendan was slipping behind in just about every subject, whereas Theresa had really come to the fore this year. All her grades were going through the roof. She took after her mother, he thought proudly.

Robert turned off the engine and dropped the window a fraction. Icy wind curled in around the stuffy interior of the car. He pushed the CD button and a Christmas compilation that had been given away free with the *Indo* came on. He found himself humming along with the Bing Crosby, David Bowie version of "The Little Drummer Boy" and he felt a little of the tension ease away.

Maybe after Christmas they would find time to get away together. Have a talk, mend some fences, tell her exactly what was going on with the business. And Stephanie? Would he talk about Stephanie Burroughs? Would he tell her about his mistress, and why he needed to keep her sweet?

"Dad!" Brendan wrenched open the door, with all the force and enthusiasm of a seventeen-year-old, jolting him from his thoughts. "I wasn't expecting to see you here."

"Thought I'd surprise you." Robert reached over and squeezed his son's shoulder. "How was school? And don't say *boring*," he added quickly.

"Almost boring," Brendan grinned. "This maths grind, Dad . . ."

"I know. I know. But you heard what your mother said. She'd like you to continue on in school and get some good grades. And so would I," he added, turning the key in the ignition and easing the car out into traffic.

"But you said I could join you in the company."

"And so you will. But the business is changing. Technology is moving on so quickly. The latest digital video technology is moving ahead in leaps and bounds. Wasn't so long ago video cameras recorded on tape. Now you can record directly onto DVD. There are newer and newer generations of DVD coming on the market all the time." Robert turned down the narrow side road that led to Theresa's school. "I can't keep up with all the new technology – but you can. That's why I really want you to go to college, come out with a degree and take R&K to a new level." He squeezed his son's shoulder again. "You know it makes sense."

"I know," Brendan said unhappily. "But Mam is really on my case about this. I've even got to study over the Christmas holidays, she tells me."

"I'll talk to her."

"Does this mean I won't be able to work in the company at weekends?"

"Of course you can. I'm currently talking to a boy band about shooting their new pop video. I could use you on that."

"That would be so cool. I could be a second-unit director."

"Hey – this is R&K Productions remember, not MGM. We don't have second units. We have one unit – and that's me with a camera on my shoulder. You can be an associate producer maybe."

"OK," Brendan said slowly, "and what's that exactly?"

"Means you make the tea."

"Brilliant," Brendan said glumly. He suddenly leaned forward and pointed. "There's Theresa."

Robert drove back to the house, with the two children chatting happily together in the back of the car, which was now redolent of a combination of Indian and Chinese take-away. There was only two years between them and they got on well together and he was pleased about that. He had no relationship with his three brothers, all of whom were older than he was. His parents had divorced when he was fourteen and although he'd stayed with his mother, his regular weekends with his father and older brothers had been uncomfortable outings. He'd stopped going when he was sixteen. By then all but one of his brothers had emigrated – Australia and the States – and a year later, his eldest brother, Mikey, had gone to Canada. There were still occasional letters, the odd Christmas card, but the last time he'd seen them had been at his father's funeral fifteen years ago. Only Mikey had come home for their mother's funeral nine months later.

"Dad," Theresa chimed up around a mouthful of chips. She was dipping them in curry sauce and Robert felt his stomach grumble. He'd missed lunch – again – and all he'd had to eat since breakfast was a packet of peanut M&M's. "Dad, are we going to have to go down to Julia's for Stephen's Day?"

"Well, you have a choice," he said carefully. "Either we go

down to your Aunt Julia . . . or she will come up to us. Now, if we go down to her," he continued slowly, "we can leave. If she comes up to us, we'll never get rid of her."

"But we go down there every year!" Brendan protested.

"It's a tradition."

"It's time to break the tradition. We're missing some of the best telly."

"I know. I know," Robert sighed. He too hated going down to Kathy's sister for Stephen's Day, but he knew how important it was to her. "Let's do it this year, and we'll see if we can we do something about changing it for next year. So we'll go with the understanding that this is our last year."

"And it would not be a good thing to say this to Mam," Theresa guessed.

"It would not," Robert agreed. He pulled into the driveway and turned off the engine. The bedroom light was on upstairs. As they climbed out of the car, it clicked off. He put his key in the lock and pushed the hall door open, allowing Theresa and Brendan to shove their way into the hallway.

Kathy was halfway down the stairs.

"We got take-away," Brendan called holding up the brown paper bags.

Kathy smiled. "Great. I was going to suggest that anyway."

There was an expression on her face that Robert could not identify, and he wondered if she was ill. "Everything OK?"

"Fine, just fine," she said tightly, then swept past him into the kitchen.

Robert wandered into the dining-room and sank into a chair. He hit the remote to turn on the TV, absently flicking from channel to channel. Soap, soap, soap, marine documentary, cookery programme. All the soaps had a Christmas theme, the marine documentary was set in someplace snowy and the cookery programme was doing a countdown to Christmas. It was probably recorded in June, he thought glumly.

"Are you having yours in here?" Kathy asked, standing in the doorway.

"No, no, I'll come on out to the kitchen." He eased himself out of the chair and went into the kitchen. Theresa and Brendan were sorting through the food, doling it out onto plates, squabbling over the number of chips each had. They put their plates onto trays and carried them into the dining-room to watch TV.

"I got you some Rogan Josh. It's mild," Robert said.

"I'm not really hungry."

"Well, have a few mouthfuls anyway."

"I said I'm not hungry."

Robert concentrated on emptying his own food – plain old Chicken Curry – from the foil containers onto his plate.

"That'll stink up the kitchen," Kathy said, pushing open the windows, "and you'll reek of garlic for the rest of the night."

"Keep the vampires away," he said lightly. He sat and ate, chewing slowly and methodically, determined not to get a stomach ache. He turned on the small TV set high on the wall and found the cookery programme. From the corner of his eye, he watched Kathy open the plastic medicine box and pull out two aspirin. She swallowed them quickly. "Are you all right?" he asked again.

"Just a touch of a headache. I'm off to bed," she said, and hurried from the room, leaving him alone in the kitchen with his take-away meal and the TV for comfort.

Robert watched the cookery programme with the sound off. The two children were a room away and Kathy was upstairs, and he was alone in the kitchen, eating his dinner: just another night in the Walker household. He felt desperately lonely. He couldn't remember the last time the family had sat down to a meal together, nor could he remember the last time Kathy had asked him about work, how things had gone, whether it had been a good day or not.

In fact, he couldn't remember the last time she had shown any interest in anything: in him, in his work, in bed.

CHAPTER 19

"Hi."

The phone popped and crackled, then Stephanie's voice, intimate and clear, whispered down the line. "I was going to phone you later on. I missed you this evening."

Robert crossed the floor of the room he used as a home office and checked to make sure the door was locked. "I know. I'm sorry," he said quietly. "I was working on the DaBoyz proposal. Then I decided to get away before the traffic got too awful."

"How's it coming?"

"Good, I think. I'll make a good presentation."

"You can do it. I know you can."

Robert sank back into his office chair and nodded. "I hope so."

"I've every confidence in you. It'll be a new direction for the company. Do one good pop video and you'll be the next big thing. All the bands will flock to your door."

"You're right. I know you're right." And in that instant he knew he could do it: Stephanie had absolute confidence in him and his abilities. "Thanks again for putting me onto it."

"What's wrong?" Stephanie asked suddenly, surprising him.

"Nothing."

"Yes, there is. I know there is."

"How can you tell?" Robert wondered, genuinely curious now.

"Short sentences. When you're tired or bothered, you reply to me in short sentences."

"You and your college education," Robert grinned.

"Nothing to do with college – besides I'm not sure *"The Interpretation of One's Lover's Moods"* is covered in media studies."

Robert could hear the laughter in her voice and found himself smiling in turn.

"So tell me, what's bothering you?"

"Oh, the usual. But I'm just tired. It was a long day."

"And Kathy?" Stephanie pressed.

Robert shrugged, uncomfortable discussing his wife with his mistress. "She's not in great form," he admitted. "I saw her taking some tablets this evening; I think she may be coming down with something."

There was a silence on the other end of the line.

"You think I'm making excuses for her, don't you?" Robert snapped, filling the silence and immediately regretting it. The last thing he needed was to have an argument with Stephanie. One cold shoulder he could manage: two cold shoulders would leave him none to cry on. "I'm sorry. I shouldn't have said that. I'm tired. Yes," he admitted, "there were a few words this evening. But only to do with Christmas. It's the pressure of the season."

As soon as the words were out of his mouth, Robert squeezed his eyes shut and shook his head from side to side. Christ! But he must be tired. He'd been avoiding bringing up the subject of Christmas with Stephanie!

"Am I going to get to see you over Christmas?" Stephanie asked. He had come to recognise that when she was being serious, the American intonation in her accent became more pronounced. Stephanie Burroughs had gone to college just outside of New York.

"Of course, you will," he said quickly.

"Any idea when?"

"Well, I'll see you on Christmas Eve. Give you your present," he added. "And then probably on Stephen's Day . . . no, not Stephen's Day, the day after."

"What's wrong with Thursday?"

"We go down for dinner with Kathy's sister, Julia, on Stephen's Day. It's a tradition."

There was a pause, then Stephanie said, "I remember you did that last year. I think you said then it was going to be the last one you attended."

"I think I say that every year."

"Do you enjoy it?"

"No," he said simply.

"So, given the choice: dinner with your sister-in-law, or spending time with me. What would it be?"

"No contest. Spending time with you," he said immediately.

"Then do it."

"It's not that easy."

"It is if you want it to be."

"You know I want it to be."

Stephanie sighed. "I know you do. I'm sorry. I shouldn't tease you so. I guess I'm tired too. I'm seeing you tomorrow though?"

"That's what I wanted to talk to you about. I double-booked. I've got Jimmy Moran lined up for dinner tomorrow night. I'm really sorry. Blame it on the situation in the office. I thought Maureen had cancelled him and Illona never thought to check. I'm sorry.

"There's no problem. These things happen. Any sign of Maureen coming back?"

"January. Maybe," he sighed. "She cannot – or will not – give me a straight answer."

"You need to start thinking with your head rather than your heart on this one," Stephanie suggested. "And if you do manage to get the pop-video gig, do you want someone who looks like a glamorous granny managing the front desk?"

"You're right. I know you're right." He sighed. "I'd sort of come to that decision myself. But I don't feel right letting her go before Christmas."

"You're too soft," Stephanie murmured. "Though I usually change that," she added quickly, her voice soft and husky, catching him off guard.

"You're bold!"

"Sometimes. So I won't see you tomorrow at all?"

"I've got the presentation to the band and their manager in the morning, then dinner in the evening."

"Do you want to stay over after dinner?"

"Maybe," he said coyly.

"Maybe," she laughed, the sound high and light. "Just maybe?"

"Would it be worth my while?" he asked.

"Absolutely," she promised.

"I'll see what I can do."

CHAPTER 20

"I was thinking," Kathy said suddenly.

"Always dangerous . . ." he quipped. He hit the switch on the electric toothbrush as his wife began to speak.

"You've been working so hard lately . . ."

She stopped talking and he caught the flash of annoyance on her face in the mirror.

"I can still hear you," he said through a mouthful of toothpaste, but she went back to her magazine. He'd spoken to her a dozen times about the amount of money she spent on women's magazines and novels, but it had no effect and the floor beside her bed was piled high with dog-eared magazines and bundles of half-read paperbacks. Eventually, he'd simply stopped talking about it, because the argument went nowhere, and she retaliated by throwing every expense she could think of in his face. When he'd had his teeth done, she'd given him hell about it for weeks. He turned off the toothbrush and Kathy started immediately.

"I've been thinking, you've been working so hard lately I've barely seen you. I thought we should try and have a night out."

"Good idea," he said automatically. And it was. With Maureen gone and the temp not knowing her way around the office, plus the scramble for new work, combined with the madness of Christmas, he had been working longer and later recently. He hadn't seen a whole lot of his wife and their encounters lately tended to be brief and chilly. After Christmas, when things had settled down, he'd take her out for a nice meal, maybe even talk to her about the situation with the business, try and convince her to cut down a little on her spending . . .

"I was thinking tomorrow night."

"I can't. Not tomorrow night. I'm entertaining a client. Christmas drinks."

"You never said."

"I'm sure I did," he frowned. He had told her, hadn't he? But he'd had so much on his mind recently. Had he told her?

"I'd have remembered."

Robert shrugged and turned to toss the towel back into the en-suite. It missed the rail and slid to the floor.

"Who are you meeting tomorrow?"

"Jimmy Moran," Robert said. "We're having dinner in Shanahan's on the Green." He threw back the covers and slipped into the bed, then jumped with the chill of the sheets. "You didn't turn on the blanket," he said, almost accusingly.

"I didn't think it was that cold." She tossed the magazine onto the floor and slid down in the bed, pulling the covers up to her chin.

Robert glanced sidelong at her. "Are you not going to read?"

"No, my eyes are watering; I think I've got a bit of eye strain." She reached up and turned off the light over her side of the bed.

"Well, I'll read for a bit, if you don't mind." He reached down to the side of the bed and lifted up the book he'd been reading on and off for the past two months, *The Road Less Travelled* by M Scott Peck. Despite Stephanie's recommendation, he simply could not get into it and managed less than a page a night. She was always reading self-help and self-improvement books. He'd enjoyed her last recommendation, the *Chicken Soup for the Soul* series. He loved the little stories that revealed the essential goodness of man. He bought one for Kathy – *Chicken Soup for the Woman's Soul* – thinking she'd enjoy it. It was on the floor, close to the bottom of the pile of paperbacks, unread.

"When do you think we might be able to get a night out? Before Christmas?" Kathy's voice was muffled, coming from beneath the covers.

Next week was Christmas week; the whole idea was too ridiculous for words, but it just went to show how out of touch she was. Robert bit his tongue, taking a moment to work out how to phrase the response properly, determined to go to sleep without a major argument. "We might leave it until after Christmas," he suggested. "It's a nightmare trying to find a place to eat and parking is impossible." He attempted a laugh. "All the restaurants are full of people like me, treating clients like Jimmy to too much wine." He realised he had not read a single word and dropped *The Road Less Travelled* – The Book Never Read in his case – to the floor, and then snapped the light off. "After Christmas, we'll find a little time. Maybe even head off for the weekend. What do you think?"

"That would be nice," Kathy mumbled, but she didn't sound too enthusiastic about it.

Robert lay in the darkness, listening to the house settle and creak around them. A house alarm was wailing in the far distance, the sound like an animal cry, while closer to home, a drunken voice was butchering "White Christmas".

Kathy's breathing settled and shifted into sleep and when he was sure she was fully asleep, he moved closer to her, resting the side of his face against her back.

He couldn't help but compare Kathy's attitude with Stephanie's. Stephanie was encouraging and interested; Kathy was anything but. Kathy simply didn't understand his world and, as far as he could see, had no interest in understanding. Her world had shrunk to the children, the home, her circle of friends, her family and the minutiae of their lives. Because he was running so fast now, running just to stand still, it was a world he had little time for and even less interest in.

And when he came home to a night like tonight, when there was an argument over nothing, then he really appreciated having someone understanding and loving to talk to.

His job required him to be able to compartmentalise and prioritise. The television-production business was essentially one of time and people management and although he could be untogether and disorganised in his personal habits, he was always able to manage his business.

Kathy lived in one compartment; Stephanie in the other. He sometimes liked to imagine the three of them as three circles. His circle intersected with Kathy and Stephanie's; their circles intersected with his. Their circles would never intersect. Kathy was uninterested in him and the business; Stephanie was interested in every aspect of the business – and every aspect of him too, he grinned.

Stephanie had a healthy appetite towards lovemaking, whereas over the years he and Kathy had drifted apart in that department too. He was as much to blame as she was, however; he was often exhausted after too many hours in the office and fell asleep the moment his head hit the pillow. He'd also be the first to admit that they'd become just a little bored with one another sexually. With Stephanie, it was like starting afresh.

Stephanie spoke to him every day, and, more importantly, listened to him. Kathy told him practically nothing. When he asked her how her day had gone, she would say "Fine," and that would be the sum total.

Of the two, Stephanie was the more demanding. She wanted to spend time with him; she loved his company, she said. And he adored spending time with her. She made him feel young, made him feel special again.

Kathy made him feel like an inconvenience.

And yet, and yet, and yet . . . he loved Kathy. Not passionately, not sexually, not extravagantly: he just loved her. She had been with him right from the beginning, had worked with him side by side to build the business, even when she was pregnant, had supported him when he'd left RTE to set up his own company, even though it meant giving up a regular pay cheque and pension. The bond they'd forged together ran deep, and if their relationship had changed . . . well, after eighteen years, that was hardly surprising.

What was surprising was that he had fallen in love with Stephanie too.

That was the problem. He'd never believed it was possible to love two people equally; he'd always imagined that love was some sort of exclusive emotion. He loved the two women, but there was a difference . . . he just wasn't able to differentiate the difference yet.

Robert turned over in the bed and looked at the glowing red digits on the bedside clock: 12:55. He needed to get to sleep: he needed to be refreshed and alert tomorrow morning for the presentation. That meant getting up at six thirty and leaving the house around seven to be in the city at eight. Any later and it would take him an eternity to get across the city and then he'd never get parking around Mount Street.

He loved Stephanie.

Or did he?

The emotion had crept upon him over the past couple of months, surprising and frightening him in equal measure. He'd never really thought about the words, "I love you". Three little words, overused, bandied about with little thought to their real meaning. In the television and advertising business especially, it was a phrase that everyone used. It was a phrase he had used with Kathy every day, last thing at night especially, though he had recently drifted out of the habit of saying it to her. It was a phrase he tucked the children into bed with every night, until they grew too big and he got too busy to be home when they needed tucking in.

And then, about six months ago, he had first used the phrase to Stephanie, and meant it.

It had shocked them both.

Robert first met Stephanie Burroughs almost seven years previously. R&K was struggling, and the position was made all the more difficult because Kathy had stepped back from the business to look after the children. Her mother, Margaret, had been helping out up till then, but she had started to become increasing bitter and gloomy and both Robert and Kathy became genuinely concerned for the children's welfare around her. Also, Brendan and Theresa simply did not want to spend any more time with Granny Childs.

Stephanie joined the company as a researcher. She'd been a freelancer working around the city for a number of years and they'd bumped into one another on the circuit. R&K had landed a small, but lucrative project: *One Hundred Years Ago On This Day* – little two-minute inserts which told, in news-report form, the events of one hundred years previously. The pieces needed to be intensively researched and sharply written. Stephanie ended up doing all the work on the pieces herself: researching, writing, finding the pictures and archive footage where needed, and also the costumes and jewellery for the dramatic reconstructions.

They worked very closely together on the *One Hundred Years* project, which had, by necessity, taken them all across Ireland, keeping them away from home for days at a time. He had to admit that he'd found himself attracted to her. But that's all it had been: an attraction and he'd never done anything about it, never tried to take it any further. She was a bright, vivacious, lively, fun-loving young woman. Neither Stephanie nor he had said or done anything to move it onto another level. It was only later, much later, that he realised that all he had been waiting for was a hint from Stephanie that she was interested. If he'd got that he might have been tempted . . .

Close to the end of the *One Hundred Years* project, when everything had been shot and they were in the final stages of editing, Kathy had come out and accused him of having an affair with Stephanie. He'd felt sick to the pit of his stomach as he stood in the back garden, with hamburgers and sausages burning on the barbeque, listening to Kathy's wild allegations. He'd denied them, of course, because they were not true, but deep in his heart and soul he felt guilty, because he realised how close he'd come. He'd never told Stephanie, of course, but he'd immediately terminated her contract early with a little cash bonus as a thank-you. She'd moved on to another research role. They'd kept in touch intermittently, and then she'd left the country and the next he heard she was working on breakfast-time television in Britain.

Two years ago, Stephanie returned to the Celtic Tiger Dublin, as the accounts manager of an international advertising agency. They'd bumped into one another at a product launch and rekindled their previous friendship.

Kathy turned over in bed, breathing in short sighing breaths. Robert turned to look at her. In sleep her features changed, the lines on her forehead and around her mouth disappeared altogether and her mouth drooped open, elongating her face. In sleep, Stephanie's face remained unchanged.

The comparison came unbidden and he turned away from his wife, glancing at the clock again: 1:20.

He remembered the first time he'd slept with Stephanie. Ironically, it was on a Midsummer's Eve, the anniversary of the day five years previously his wife had accused him of having an affair with the woman. He and Stephanie had been drifting towards the event for weeks, he realised. Their casual lunches had turned into regular events, their occasional dinners in the evenings were becoming habit and their conversations were becoming more and more suggestive. Stephanie had got R&K a lucrative little contract to shoot an ad for bottled water. She gave Robert a list of locations and told him to scout the best one. He'd recommended Glendalough and she suggested they both visit it, check out the light in the evening and again in the morning.

They both knew it was completely unnecessary, but they both knew where the evening was leading.

There had been absolutely no doubts in his mind as they drove down to Wicklow in his car, that they were going to end up in bed together. But that was it: he wasn't thinking beyond that. They would have an enjoyable meal, and then . . . well, then the old adage beloved of television and film crews everywhere would apply: what goes on on the road, stays on the road.

Robert could remember every detail of that night. All his senses were heightened. He could remember the meal, the intense flavours of the meat, the sharp bitterness of the wine, the hint of Stephanie's perfume, the peaty odour from the fire. She was wearing a white silk blouse over stonewashed jeans, a thin gold chain around her neck, gold-ball studs in her ears, no rings. Her nails were short and blunt and coated with an iridescent clear lacquer and she'd allowed her hair to tumble onto her shoulders.

They'd taken adjoining rooms in the little hotel.

When the meal was finished, they'd retired upstairs. They stopped outside Stephanie's room and Robert had dipped his head to kiss her goodnight. She turned her head at the last moment and instead of brushing her cheek, he'd kissed her lips. And she had returned the kiss.

They made love for hours that first night. Robert had been shocked by Stephanie's enthusiasm, inventiveness and obvious enjoyment. He always had the impression that Kathy treated lovemaking as a duty, something to get finished as quickly as possible. Stephanie obviously relished it.

And later, much later, as the first rays of the Wicklow sun were touching the window, and he was lying naked in bed, with Stephanie wrapped into his body, he realised that he felt alive. He felt energised, creative and excited.

And not the slightest bit guilty.

CHAPTER 21

Friday 20th December

Eyes gritty, head thumping, Robert Walker pushed open the door of R&K Productions with his foot. He was carrying a large cup of steaming coffee in one hand and was juggling his laptop, briefcase and keys in the other. The alarm started to blip warningly. He placed the coffee on Illona's desk, and returned to the box behind the door to punch in the alarm code #32. He kept promising to change it. Maybe if he really did pluck up the courage and let Maureen go, that would give him the impetus to change the code and locks.

There were two calls flashing on the answering machine. Robert hit the play button and left the door to his office open so that he could listen to them as he carried his coffee and briefcase inside.

The mechanical female voice announced: *"You have two new messages. New message left Thursday, December 19th at six fifty-nine pm."*

"Bob, this is Jimmy. It's about seven o'clock, Thursday evening, at the moment. I'm just phoning to confirm that dinner is still on tomorrow night. Really looking forward to it. If it gets too late, or there's a little too much of the red stuff consumed, you can always stay over in my place. You know I've still got that apartment in Temple Bar. My God, but it was the best investment I ever made. Talk to you tomorrow."

"New message left today, Friday, December 20th at seven fifty-five am."

"Good morning, Robert, Eddie Carson, DaBoyz Management here, I understand from Stephanie that you start early. Will you give me a call as soon as you get in? I'll need to rearrange our appointment."

"End of new messages."

Robert glanced at the clock. Ten past eight. The message had come in fifteen minutes ago. Most of the DaBoyz presentation was spread out on the conference table and he had the latest updates on his laptop. The band and their manager were due to come in at ten thirty, but it would only take him half an hour to get his act together, so he could see them at nine if they needed to pull the appointment forward.

Before he phoned DaBoyz however, he had one other call to make. It had become a habit: the first call of the day, and the last call at night. He hit the speed dial on his mobile. "Hi, it's your Phone-A-Friend."

"My God, what time is it?" Stephanie's voice was muffled and woolly with sleep.

"Ten past eight, nearly a quarter past. Wake up, sleepyhead. I thought you'd be on the way into the office."

"I'm going in later. I'd a late call with LA last night; the eight-hour time difference is a killer."

Robert moved around the office, opening the blinds. "Speaking of calls, there was a message from Carson on my answer machine this morning; wants to rearrange the appointment. Shouldn't be a problem."

There was a rustle of bedclothes, and when Stephanie spoke again, her voice was awake and more alert. "Tell me what he said, exactly what he said."

"Well, he just said . . . actually, hang on a second and I'll play you the call." He carried his mobile phone to the outer office and hit the Play button.

"You have no new messages. You have two old messages".

Robert fast forwarded through the first message, then he hit play again and held his phone to the speaker.

"*Good morning, Robert. Eddie Carson, DaBoyz Management here, I understand from Stephanie that you start early. Will you give me a call as soon as you get in? I'll need to re-arrange our appointment.*"

"That's it," he said brightly. "It's not a problem. I'll clear my diary to see them, you know that."

"It *is* a problem," Stephanie snapped. "This is just bullshit. I told Carson that we were very lucky to get you. You phone him back and do not – do you hear me – do *not* allow him to rearrange the appointment. You've got to show this little bastard who's boss, otherwise he'll walk all over you."

"It really isn't a problem –" Robert began.

"Just do as I say. Be tough with him. Tell him you must meet this morning or not at all, then shut up and say nothing. Wait for his response."

"OK," Robert said dubiously.

"Trust me on this," Stephanie said in a slightly gentler tone. "Right, go and do it now, and then phone me back."

"Yes, ma'am!" Robert mimed a salute as he hung up. He went over to the conference table and rooted through the pages until he got Carson's business card. Left to his own devices he would phone Carson and arrange to see the band at their convenience. But he had to accept that Stephanie was very good at what she did, and she handled some of the biggest accounts in the show-business world.

"Eddie Carson." The call was answered on the first ring.

"Morning, Eddie, Robert Walker, R&K Productions. I just missed you."

"Yeah, Bob, thanks for calling back. Listen I need to rearrange DaBoyz meeting for tomorrow or maybe Sunday. What's good for you?"

Robert opened his briefcase and took out his laptop, settling it onto his desk. "None of those work for me, Eddie. Today works for me. I made time for you today."

There was a long pause. Robert could hear traffic hissing by and guessed that Eddie was still a little way out of Dublin. Nothing whizzed once it hit the capital's outskirts. He fired up the laptop and rattled in his password. The screen cleared and opened to an almost empty desktop, with just a few icons lining the left-hand side of the screen. He clicked into *My Documents*, then *My Pictures*. He highlighted one picture and hit *Enter*. It opened immediately: he had taken the picture the previous Christmas. It showed Stephanie wearing only tinsel and Christmas balls, sitting beside a tiny Christmas tree in her apartment. There was a sign on the carpet by her feet: *Robert's Christmas Present. Can be opened anytime.* He zoomed in on her face. She was smiling impishly. She was always in control, always knew just what to do. He just hoped that she knew what she was doing now.

"That's really not possible. DaBoyz are in great demand –"

"So am I, Mr Carson," Robert said coldly. "It's this morning or not at all."

There was a long pause. Robert opened his mouth several times to break the silence, but, mindful of Stephanie's advice, closed it again.

"I might be able to fit you in later today," Carson said smoothly, and in that moment, Robert knew he had won.

"I have you down for ten o'clock. Will you be here or not?"

There was another silence. "I'll juggle some stuff. We'll be there." Then he hung up.

Robert's fingers were trembling as he hit the speed dial. The call was picked up on the first ring. "You were right. What would I do without you?"

"Let's hope you never have to find out."

"I owe you one."

"Oh, and I'll make sure I collect," Stephanie promised.

CHAPTER 22

"I told you." Stephanie strode around the office. She was dressed in a pinstriped power suit whose severe lines were only softened by the cream silk blouse she wore beneath the jacket. She wore her hair pulled back off her face, looped and held in a short tight pony-tail with an ornate butterfly clasp, which had been a gift from Robert.

Robert was sitting behind his desk, staring intently at his computer monitor. He was putting the finishing touches to the latest version of the DaBoyz presentation, which incorporated the changes he had agreed with Carson and the band members earlier that morning. "Your advice was absolutely spot on," he said without looking up from the screen. "They turned up at ten on the spot. The boys were as good as gold, a little overawed by everything, I thought, and very much under Carson's thumb. He made all the creative decisions."

Stephanie stopped at the conference table and spread out the drawings. "These look very good, very exciting. Different.

"Carson was complimentary." Robert came out from behind the desk and joined Stephanie by the table. He arranged the images into a sequence, laying out the pop video. "You'd think I'd been doing this all my life," he muttered. "Carson wanted some changes here, here and here."

"Of course, he did. It's a power thing with him, like trying to change the time of the appointment this morning. I've seen him do that so often. He thinks he's managing U2, not just another cloned boy band."

Robert was abruptly conscious of Stephanie's perfume, something sharp and citrus, and the heat from her body as she bent over the table alongside him. A stray curl of hair brushed his face; it felt like an electric shock.

"And if you hadn't called him on it, then he would have given you the run-around for the next couple of weeks. Even if you had got the gig, he would have interfered every step of the way . . ." Stephanie's voice trailed away to a husky whisper. She turned to look at Robert. Her face was inches away from his. He could smell the coffee on her breath. As he watched, her pupils dilated and she brushed the tip of her tongue across her lips. She smiled and raised her eyebrows a fraction, then glanced towards the open door.

Robert took a deep breath to settle his fluttering heartbeat and stepped away from Stephanie. Glancing at the clock, he strode out into the outer office to where Illona, the secretary, was systematically working her way through an office-supplies catalogue. "Are you busy, Illona?"

The slim Eastern European girl looked up, eyes huge and dark in her pale face. She spoke English with an American twang that was now showing traces of a Dublin accent, which Robert found incredibly disconcerting. "Not especially. Phones are quiet."

"Look, it's just after four. Why don't you head on? Maybe get some shopping done?"

"Well, if you are sure you don't need me . . .?"

"Stephanie and I have a few bits to sort out on the DaBoyz contract. We'll be a while, and there are no other appointments this afternoon, are there?"

"None."

"OK. Switch the phones over to the answering machine, but leave your computer on; I'll shut down the system before I leave."

Illona gathered up her coat and bag, and headed for the door. She stopped and glanced back over her shoulder, looking past Robert to where Stephanie was standing at the conference table, seemingly absorbed in the designs. She raised her voice slightly. "Goodnight, Miss Burroughs."

"Goodnight, Illona," Stephanie called, without looking up.

She looked back at Robert. "Goodnight. Try not to work too late."

Robert just nodded. Was there something in Illona's expression, something knowing, a smirk almost. Did she suspect? He knew for a certainty that Maureen suspected – she revealed her dislike of Stephanie in a score of ways. It was one of the reasons he was seriously thinking about letting her go. But even that was no longer a clean decision: if he let Maureen go, then she might take her suspicions to Kathy.

Who would have thought that a simple affair would have had such complications? There was not a single aspect of his life left untouched and unaltered by the relationship.

He'd tried very carefully to keep his relationship with Stephanie a closely guarded secret. When he'd finally become aware that what had started out as a fling was turning into something more serious, he'd consciously tried to ensure that they never ate in the same restaurant more than once and, when they stayed away overnight, it was always outside of Dublin where they stood less chance of being recognised. It was really no-one's business but his and Stephanie's, but Dublin was a small town, and people talked and the last thing he wanted was for the news to get back to Kathy. If anyone was going to tell her, then he would.

When the time was right.

And the time was most certainly not right, not now.

Robert followed Illona to the door and held it open for her. "See you on Monday, Illona."

"Good night, Robert." Illona wrapped her coat tighter around her shoulders and disappeared into the night.

Robert waited until she had rounded the corner onto Mount Street, then closed the door and shot the bolts. "I think she suspects –" he began, walking back into the office.

"Who cares?" Stephanie snapped. "She's a secretary." Then she caught Robert by his lapels and pulled him towards her, tilting her head and pressing her lips against his.

Her passion took him by surprise. His own response – immediate and hungry – shocked him. Every time with Stephanie was like the first time: exhilarating and exhausting. He backed her up against the conference table and pushed her back onto it, scattering pages in every direction. His fingers fumbled at the buttons of her blouse.

Before he met Stephanie, the only place Robert had ever made love was in bed. In the early years of their marriage, he and Kathy sometimes made love in the daylight, but as the years went by, that changed too, and they'd fallen into the routine of many married couples: Saturday or Sunday morning when the house was still quiet and the children were either in bed or downstairs watching TV.

Stephanie sat up on the table and pushed him away from her. She shrugged out of her jacket and tossed it on a chair, then pulled off her blouse. Robert tugged off his shirt, hearing a button pop and dance across the room.

More often that not, Stephanie was the one who instigated their lovemaking. Robert could never remember Kathy initiating lovemaking; he always had to make the first move. Before he made love to Stephanie that first time, he had not made love with Kathy for over four months. Since he began his relationship with Stephanie, he had not made love to his wife once. Nor had he tried; it didn't seem right somehow.

And suddenly, Stephanie was naked on the conference table and he was pulling off his socks. "Now, where were we?" she asked, opening her arms, lifting her legs, inviting him, welcoming him, into her body.

Stephanie stepped out of the tiny shower and accepted the towel Robert wrapped around her. The shower cubicle in R&K was too small to take two people, so they had to wash in turn. This was not the first time they had made love in the office. There was always something especially exciting about it, Robert thought. Only earlier that day, as he'd sat at the table with the boy band, he'd had a sudden flash of a naked Stephanie spread-eagled on the table. It was very difficult to hold a sensible conversation after that.

He stepped into the shower and adjusted the heat, pushing it up to its highest level. Even at full power, the water pressure was little more than a trickle. Through the frosted glass, he could see Stephanie drying herself unselfconsciously. He watched the sway of her hips as she stepped out of the bathroom and began to gather her clothes off the chairs where she had tossed them. His clothing was tossed around the room. The neat drawings and printouts he had prepared for the DaBoyz presentation were scattered across the floor, many of them crumpled and crushed. He didn't care. When he made love to Stephanie, nothing else mattered. He gave himself fully and wholeheartedly to the act. So did she. Whenever Kathy made love to him, he was always aware that she was distracted, distant even, almost as if she was going through the motions. After eighteen years, he wondered, was that so unusual?

Robert turned off the shower and stepped out into the bathroom. Stephanie's towel was still damp, but he used it, unwilling to use a second towel. If Illona was suspicious then he didn't want to leave her clues that anything was going on.

"Will I see you tonight?" Stephanie stood in the doorway, wearing only her white lace-trimmed bra.

"I'm not sure. Do me a favour," he added. "Get dressed, please."

"Why?" she said archly.

"Because, if you don't, I'll just have to have you again."

"Promises, promises," she smiled, but stepped away from the door and started to dress. "What about tonight?" she asked again.

"Tonight is all screwed up." He tossed the towel on the rail and padded naked out into the office and started to dress. "You know Jimmy and I were supposed to have dinner in Shanahan's? Well, I got Illona to phone to confirm the reservation. And it turns out there was none."

"What happened?" Stephanie tugged on her trousers, but her blouse was still undone and Robert reached out and stroked the swell of her breast with the back of his hand. The movement was unconscious, tender. Stephanie caught his hand and pressed it against her skin. Then she brought his fingertips to her lips and kissed them.

And it was these movements, the small tender intimate movements which meant so much to Robert. These were what he missed with Kathy: the tiny intimacies, the touches, the casualness, the comfortableness with one another. For a long time, he'd felt like a stranger with her.

"I'm not sure whose problem it is, Illona's or Maureen's. Maureen's, I think. But that's not the point. I've got a good client meeting me here in just over an hour, and I've no place to take him to dinner."

"It'll be difficult finding a place to eat this close to Christmas."

"I know. And Jimmy won't want to go out of the city: he was talking about spending the night in his apartment in Temple Bar."

Stephanie finished dressing. She grabbed her tiny handbag and went back into the bathroom to repair her make-up.

"Be upfront with him," Stephanie advised. "You never know, maybe all he wants are drinks. If you get out relatively early, you might check out the Market Bar off George's Street. You'll get drinks and nibbles there."

"Great idea."

"But that doesn't answer the question I asked earlier: are you going to spend the night with me? Should I wait up?"

Robert grinned. "If I do spend the night, I'll be sleeping. You exhaust me."

"Well, look, I've an early start in the morning. If you can get to me before one in the morning, then come on over, but if you are going to be any later, forget about it. Send me a text when you've got an idea what's happening."

"Good plan."

Stephanie appeared out of the bathroom, looking immaculate and composed.

"There is no way to tell that less than half an hour ago you were lying on this table making passionate love."

Stephanie blinked at him in surprise. "I've no idea what you are talking about, Mr Walker. I was closing a very important business deal." She leaned over and kissed him, a gossamer brushing of her lips against his. "And I do like the way you close a deal."

Chapter 23

When Stephanie left, Robert tried to put some order on his office. It looked as if a bomb had gone off in it. Papers were scattered all over the floor, some of them clearly bearing the imprint of damp bare feet, others crushed beyond all recognition. Making love with Stephanie could not be done in halves. At the point of orgasm she cried aloud, a sound between a grunt and a shout of pain. It wasn't so bad in the office, but he was sure that the neighbours in the apartments adjoining hers could clearly hear what was going on. In the beginning it had embarrassed him; now he had no such reservations. It was another of Stephanie's gifts: she had taught him to be free.

Clearing up the papers, he turned his attention to the table. It was covered with sweaty palm-prints and there was the clear imprint of a bottom on the polished wood. He found some paper roll and furniture polish under the sink in the tiny kitchen and set to work on it.

It was just after six when he finished. He sprayed some air freshener around the room to disguise the scent of sex, then stood back to examine his handiwork. The office looked pristine, the table was gleaming, papers piled neatly, pens arranged alongside.

Hard to image that two naked people had recently cavorted on the table.

Before he left the office, he hit the speed dial on his desk phone to call home.

"Hello?"

For an instant he thought he had phoned the wrong number. It sounded like Kathy's voice, but altered somewhat.

"Hello?"

Then he recognised his sister-in-law Julia's waspish tone. He forced a pleasant tone into his voice. "Julia, it's Robert."

"I thought it was."

"I take it if you're there, then Kathy is not."

"She had a few things to do; I said I'd keep an eye on the children, though, to be perfectly honest," she added quickly, "they're old enough to look after themselves."

"I agree with you, but at least if you're there, they will study rather than just watch TV," he said, unconsciously mirroring the same words his wife had used a little earlier that day. "Can I speak to Brendan – is he anywhere about?"

Robert had no time for Julia. There was simply too much bad blood between them, going back over too many years; she considered him beneath Kathy and had made no secret of her feelings for him. He thought she was a stuck-up cow. He had some sympathies for Ben, her long-suffering husband.

"Dad?"

"Bren. Where's your mum?"

"Gone into town."

"At this time of day!"

"And she's left Aunt Julia in charge of us," Brendan added, lowering his voice to a whisper. "I'm seventeen, Dad. I don't need a baby-sitter."

"I know. How long has your mother been gone?"

"About twenty minutes, half an hour. Can we get takeaway tonight?"

"You had takeaway last night,"

"But Mam's not left anything prepared."

Robert frowned. That was totally unlike Kathy. She was a wonderful mother and the children wanted for nothing. "Any idea where she's gone?"

"No idea. She just announced it out of the blue."

"And that's all she said? She didn't say anything else?"

"She wondered what you had given her for a Christmas present last year. Maybe she's gone into town looking for your present."

"Maybe." He experienced a twinge of guilt. He still hadn't got Kathy her present and he swore, after last year's debacle, when he'd ended up grabbing a few things in the Stephen's Green Centre, that he would get her something nice this year. "I'll give her a ring on the mobile. Be good for Julia. I'll be late tonight."

"Later, Dad." Brendan hung up.

Robert sat at his desk and tried to make sense out of what he had just heard. Kathy did and didn't do many things, but she never did anything without a good reason. And why was she coming into the city, for Christ's sake? He hit another speed dial and transferred the call to the speaker. It rang six times before it connected.

"Hello?"

"Kathy, where are you?"

"In the car."

Robert took a deep breath. He knew she was in the car. He was phoning her in the car. Telling him that she was in the car was telling him nothing. But, if nothing else, it revealed that she was still pissed off at him. He wasn't quite sure what it was about this time, but lately there didn't need to be a reason. He tried a different tack. "I've just phoned home; the kids tell me you're heading into the city to go shopping." Even as he was saying it, he was aware of just how ludicrous it sounded.

"Yes," Kathy said, her voice neutral and flat.

Robert put elbows on his desk and cradled his head in his hands. "I really don't think this is a good idea. This is the last Friday before Christmas. Traffic is shite, and the weather is closing in. Forecasters are promising snow and maybe black ice this evening."

"I need to get a few things. I thought I'd head into Stephen's Green," she pressed on, ignoring him. "If there's a problem with the weather, I might drop down to Shanahan's, meet you there. We can drive home in your car and I'll come in with you in the morning to pick up my car."

Somewhere at the back of his mind a warning bell – a tiny bitter sound – went off. Something was amiss here. Why was she coming into town in the first place – it was completely out of character – and why was she talking about popping into Shanahan's? It was almost as if she was checking up on him. "Have I lost you?" he asked, when he realised that there had been a long moment of silence.

"I'm still here," she said shortly. "Where are you?"

"Still at the office. Jimmy's coming here around seven or so." There was a hiss of static. "I really don't think it's a good idea to head into the city tonight. And if I have a few drinks with Jimmy I might have to leave the car myself. That'll be two cars in town. I was half-thinking I might even stay overnight in the city. He says I can kip down in his apartment; he's got a place in Temple Bar."

There was another long pause.

"Kathy . . .?" he asked eventually.

"I'm at the back of the airport. Signal is patchy."

"Can you not get what you're looking for in the Pavilions in Swords?"

"No," she said shortly. "I'll see you in Shanahan's later . . ."

"No, not Shanahan's . . ."

"I thought you said last night you were going to Shanahan's . . ."

There it was: the note of suspicion in her voice. He'd lived with her long enough to recognise it. And he'd heard it before, on that terrible occasion when she'd accused him of having an affair. But she didn't know, couldn't know about Stephanie. He'd been so careful. "I know, but there was a cock-up. I phoned earlier to confirm and they'd no record of the booking."

"So where are you going to go?"

"Don't know yet."

"Well look, ring me when you find a place, and I'll drop by."

Robert nodded. That was the third time in the same conversation she'd made a definite reference to dropping by and seeing him. He could not remember the last time – certainly not in the last year, maybe even the last two years – that she'd made such a suggestion. She was definitely suspicious. He frowned; had he said or done something to alert her, had someone said something, had she discovered something?

"I haven't seen Jimmy for ages. How is Angela?"

"Ah, best not to mention Angela. They've separated. He wants a divorce. She says no."

"I've got to go. I think I can see a police checkpoint ahead."

The call finished and the phone started blipping. Robert took off the speed dial and the office descended into silence. Did she suspect or was this just his paranoia?

He had never set out to have an affair with Stephanie, but once it happened it was the most exciting thing in his life. But he was also determined that he would do nothing in the world to upset Kathy. He'd spent eighteen years of his married life protecting and looking after her; he would continue to do that. He wasn't one of those men who went to bed with a woman and were then forced by a guilty conscience to confess all. But there would come a time when she would find out, he knew that. And the longer it went on, the likelihood became greater. How long could he keep it from his wife? And what would happen when she found out?

He never imagined that the affair would continue on this long.

At first he thought he and Stephanie would drift apart after a couple of weeks or maybe months. Instead the affair had deepened, intensified.

And then it had become complicated.

He had actually been on the verge of breaking up with her six months ago. He'd gone through an intensely busy patch looking for work, and they hadn't seen each other for the best part of a month. In that time, he had made the decision to break it off; he was becoming fearful of the feelings he was having for the woman. This was no longer sex, or affection or some combination of the two: this was love.

He decided he would speak to her on a Friday night. He would invite her around to the office and break the news gently to her over a nice bottle of wine. They would remain friends, but he could not be her lover. That was the plan: on the Wednesday, she'd come to him with a proposal. She knew R&K were in trouble and she suddenly found herself in a position to put a little business his way, good business, lucrative business. Was he interested?

R&K were not just in trouble, the company was on the verge of going under: of course, he was interested. Stephanie had only one condition: no-one in her office must know that she was involved with him. She could lose her job if people knew she was directing contracts towards her lover's company. There was nothing illegal in what she was doing, but there was certainly a conflict of interest. Also, she did not push him for the lowest possible price and she was not quite as tough on him as she was with some of her other accounts.

That single job kept the company afloat.

Suddenly he could not let her go: he could not afford to. The jobs, large and small, that she put his way saved R&K from going bankrupt.

But if they got the DaBoyz contract things would be different. He would not need to rely so heavily on Stephanie for work.

Also, because of some of the work she got him, small jobs had started to trickle his way again. It was mainly advertising work, shooting TV commercials for toothpaste and bread, which he hated, but it paid the bills. He also knew R&K were in the running to shoot the new Renault ad, and he'd pitched what he thought was a very good idea for the forthcoming Guinness campaign.

After Christmas, he promised himself. He would do something about his relationship with Stephanie after Christmas; he would break up with her. She would understand; he was sure she would. She'd see the sense in it. He couldn't carry on this way, splitting himself in two.

Christmas really highlighted the problems of trying to juggle a marriage and mistress.

He desperately wanted to spend time with Stephanie – it would be fun and sexy, and they would laugh and eat and make love. Kathy, on the other hand, might condescend to speak to him and then again, she might not. There would certainly be an argument over something – there almost always was. So really there was no argument about whom he wanted to spend Christmas with . . . except . . . there were the children to consider.

Robert got up and began to move around the office, shutting off lights and locking up for the night. Where was Jimmy?

Robert was extremely proud of Brendan and Theresa. He could truthfully say that they had brought nothing but joy into his and Kathy's lives. And he would never hurt them. He loved the way they looked up to him, the way they came to him for advice, the way they shared their triumphs and disasters with him. They loved him, of that he had absolutely no doubts: he could not afford to lose that love. That would destroy him. His own father, Robert Senior, had been a cold, distant, aloof man. Never once did he remember his father saying, "I love you," to him. His own children would not be able to say that: he told them he loved them every day. If it ever came to a toss-up between the children and Stephanie, then Stephanie would lose.

It was a cliché to say that he was staying with Kathy for the sake of the children, but it was very close to the truth. There were so many great things in his life – including Kathy, when she was in good humour – and he knew that his affair with Stephanie was casting a shadow over all of them. One slip, one stupid mistake and he stood to lose everything: wife, children, home and house. The few friends he and Kathy had were joint friends – he would probably find himself ostracised from them. At least he'd be able to hang onto the business . . . except, he realised with a sinking feeling, Kathy owned half of it. What would happen if they split up? He veered away from that thought: it was not going to happen.

There was a tapping on the glass and he could see Jimmy's round face peering in.

But when Stephanie touched him, pressed herself against him, breathed in his ear, he could feel his resolve failing.

Jimmy tapped on the glass again.

Robert shook his head fiercely. He wasn't going to lose anything. He was too careful. Much too careful.

CHAPTER 24

"I'm really sorry about Shanahan's," Robert said again, as they walked past the front door of the restaurant, facing out onto Stephen's Green.

"There's no problem," Jimmy said again. "Really. None at all." He reached out and squeezed Robert's arm. "Forget about it."

In his youth, Jimmy Moran had been one of the handsomest men in Dublin. Tall, elegant and fine-featured, the director and producer had been a regular in the social pages and had been involved in bringing some of the huge movie productions to Ireland in the Seventies and early Eighties. It was confidently expected that he was going to be Ireland's answer to Francis Ford Coppola. He had never quite lived up to those expectations; two hugely expensive productions foundered with enormous debts and had tainted him with the whiff of scandal when it was discovered that he'd made sure to pay himself before anyone else, including the internationally famous stars. Time moved on, and a lifetime of excess had blurred his fine features, bloating his nose and dappling his cheeks with broken veins. He was fifty-two, and looked it, though his hair was still jet-black and he swore he didn't dye it.

When Robert had first joined RTE, he'd worked with Jimmy on a series of live dramatised plays. That had been at the height of Jimmy's drinking and often weeks went by when Robert never saw Jimmy sober, though it never seemed to affect his work. But his temper was legendary. When other young directors refused to work with Jimmy Moran, Robert stepped in; he recognised early on that Jimmy knew more about the business than the rest of the other so-called directors put together. Also, his contacts in the movie business were very attractive to the younger Robert who had pretensions then of being The Great Irish director. By the time he realised that Jimmy had burned far too many bridges at home and abroad to ever again be a force in the Irish movie business, it didn't matter: the two men had become friends.

Jimmy left RTE years before Robert. He set up in a dilapidated office off Leeson Street as an independent production company, one of the first in the country. He called in every favour he could find and managed to get a quiz show on the air. The show was simple, no frills, no expensive special effects, no set-up, just two teams, a live audience and a quizmaster. It had run on RTE for years and when it was cancelled in favour of glitzier quiz shows, it successfully transferred to radio, where it was still regularly revived. The show spun off a series of live pub-quiz type events, a number of best-selling quiz books and a cheap and cheerful board game – and all of this was years before the phenomenon that was *Millionaire*. Jimmy owned the format; it was one of the very few that he had actually bother to register and keep. The show re-established his fortunes and also proved to Robert, who had become increasingly unhappy in RTE with its lack of promotion opportunities, that he could make a go of it as an independent producer.

The two men kept in touch over the years, often collaborating on projects, sharing resources and pooling their talents to pitch ideas into the various commission rounds when RTE looked for new programme ideas.

"So, where are we going?" Jimmy asked again.

"Wherever we can get in," Robert grinned. "I'll buy you a drink or two, even if we can't have dinner."

There were carol singers at the top of Grafton Street, gathered around the huge Christmas tree. Wearing white coats with tinsel-trimmed Christmas hats, they were singing "Silent Night" with more enthusiasm than skill. A girl whose cheeks matched the colour of her red hair shook a plastic bucket under their noses. "Help the homeless!"

Jimmy laughed as he dropped a handful of coins into the bucket. "That's me," he said brightly.

"What?" Robert asked, unsure if he was joking or not.

"Technically, I'm homeless at the moment," Jimmy said ruefully. "Angela is going to take the house from me." They turned left off Grafton Street, heading towards the Gaiety, and suddenly further speech was impossible. "Fill you in later," Jimmy shouted. The noise in the narrow street was incredible. A brass band just beyond the Gaiety entrance was playing something vaguely Christmassy, while the enormous queue of chattering, laughing and singing punters stretched the length of the street waiting to get in for the early evening panto. Further down the street, a fire-eater was juggling flaming torches to roars of applause. The two men pushed their way through the crowd and turned to the right, past the old Mercer's hospital.

"What about Break for the Border?"

"Even we're too old for that noise," Jimmy grinned.

"We could try some of the Indian or Chinese restaurants down here," Robert suggested.

"Can't, I'm afraid," Jimmy said, patting his stomach. "The MSG kills me."

"I thought you said it was an ulcer."

"It was. Until I had the docs look at it." Jimmy glanced sidelong at his friend. "Don't look so alarmed. It's nothing major. I'm just getting old. There are certain foods I can no longer eat, and I'm afraid anything with MSG in it is out for me."

"That's a shame." Robert shook his head. He had a lot of happy memories of the pair of them on location, always looking for the Chinese or the Indian with the hottest curry on the menu. A little place in a Glasgow back street still held the record.

"I'm finally paying for my lifetime of sins," Jimmy said, then added, "but they were great sins, and I enjoyed every one of them."

They turned left into Fade Street and into the Market Bar. The old sausage factory which was part of George's Arcade had been converted into one of Dublin's trendiest bars, a huge open space dotted with tables. It was busy, but not outrageously full. Robert stepped into the bar and turned to look at the mezzanine over his head. "There're tables upstairs. You go and grab one. I'll get us a drink and something to eat. What are you having?"

"No spirits. House red is good for me."

Robert blinked in surprise. "Cutting down?"

"Cutting out. Doctor's orders."

When Robert returned a few moments later with the drinks, he found Jimmy at a small round table positioned alongside the railing, staring out over the room below. "I've not been here before."

"I only discovered it recently." Robert put the glass of red wine down in front of Jimmy, and a matching glass for himself. "I got us glasses rather than a bottle."

"Good thinking; I'd never be able to finish a bottle," Jimmy shrugged ruefully.

"And I'm driving," Robert added. "I haven't seen you in an age. We've a lot of catching up to do."

"I know." Jimmy raised his glass, and Robert raised his. Glasses pinged together. "What'll we drink to?"

"That next year is better?"

Jimmy grinned ruefully. "That might be too much to ask for and is probably tempting fate. Let's drink to health and happiness. If we have one, the other will follow."

164

"Health and happiness," Robert agreed. He sipped the wine. It was bitter and sharp and as he swallowed, he realised he could still taste Stephanie's flesh on his tongue. "You don't sound too sure about next year?"

"I'm not." Jimmy glanced sidelong at him. "This has been a pisser of a year. An absolute pisser. I'll be glad to see the back of it."

In the dim light of the bar, Robert saw that Jimmy looked old – more than old, he looked weary, beaten. There were bags under his eyes and his normally spotless suit was shabby, with the evidence of an old stain on the lapel. The collar was dappled with dandruff.

"Do you want to tell me?" he asked gently.

"What's to tell?" Jimmy sighed. "Remember I told you that Angela would not give me a divorce; well, she's changed her mind, or rather her very expensive lawyer has changed her mind for her. But she wants the house as part of the deal."

"But the house is fabulous!"

Jimmy and Angela owned a spectacular house in Wicklow, two miles beyond the town. It had been a ruined Church of Ireland rectory when he bought it. Over the years, he had restored it with an extraordinary amount of love and too much money.

"Well, to be honest, I don't get down there much any more, so I'm resigned to letting it go."

"You spent the last twenty years fixing it up."

"I know. But if it's the cost of getting out a loveless marriage, then that's the price I'm prepared to pay."

"That's what you meant when you said you were homeless earlier?"

Jimmy nodded.

"But you have the place in Temple Bar."

"For the moment, yes. Angela wants a bite of that too. I may end up paying her half its value."

"But it must be worth what: half a million?"

Jimmy smiled, showing startlingly white teeth. "Double that. Angela's lawyers had it valued recently: two estate agents estimated it at just under one million euro. So, I'll either have to pay Angela half a mill – which I can't afford – or put it on the market and give her half of whatever I get."

"Jesus, Jimmy, what a mess."

Jimmy Moran finished the last of the drink in one quick swallow, then grimaced as it hit his stomach. "Of my own making, remember. I've always told you: everything has a cost; you just have to be prepared to pay the cost. Angela just got fed up with me screwing around and my drinking. You can't blame her."

Robert couldn't. Angela had put up with a lot. Events had come to a head three years ago when Jimmy's long-running relationship with Frances, an actress many years his junior, had hit the headlines. The girl had been desperate for a part in an upcoming movie and had sold the story to the newspapers, hoping that the resultant publicity would help her get the job. It hadn't, and Frances hadn't worked since. Surprisingly, Jimmy had continued the relationship with the actress and eighteen months ago she'd borne him a child.

Remarkably, the press had not yet got wind of the fact that Frances had borne Jimmy a son. Following her disastrous publicity stunt, she had disappeared completely from the public eye. Robert was one of the few people who knew that Jimmy had set her up in a small bookshop in the west of Ireland. "Someone told Angela. I expect to see a piece about it in the Sundays any day soon. Anyway, Angela contacted me through her solicitor, said that if she'd known I had fathered a child she would have given me the divorce I wanted ages ago. No child deserved to be without a father, she said." He shook his head at what was obviously a painful memory. "She's bitter, very bitter indeed. She'll take me for everything she can."

"What are you going to do?" Robert asked.

Before Jimmy could answer, their food arrived, plates of

appetisers, pâté, mushrooms, chicken wings, bowls of olives and baskets of different types of bread. The waitress took their order for two more glasses of wine.

Jimmy shrugged. "I'll divorce Angela – it'll probably bankrupt me, and I'll marry Frances, which will probably kill me. I'm fifty-two; I'm too told to be a first-time father. I'd be a lousy father."

"Jesus, Jimmy, I'm not sure if I'm supposed to say sorry, or congratulations."

"Neither am I, to be truthful."

The two men nibbled at the food without speaking. The noise level from the floor below had increased appreciably.

"How are things with you?" Jimmy asked, arranging the stones from the olives he'd eaten in a neat circle on the tabletop.

"They're OK. Struggling a bit; there's not a lot of work out there. But I've been lucky recently."

"And Kathy, how is she?"

"Good. She's good. She's busy with the Christmas preparations. I was talking to her earlier; she said she might drop in to see us in Shanahan's." He fished out his mobile phone. "In fact, I really should let her know where we are. She might call around if she's close by." Also, it actually suited him to have her call around now; at least then she'd get to see that he was genuinely out with a client. His screen said *Network Search*. "I've no signal. What about you?"

Jimmy pulled out an overlarge mobile phone that was at least five years out of date. He tilted it to the light and squinted at the small green screen. "No. No signal. Must be the thickness of the walls."

"You need to upgrade that," Robert smiled. "Noah probably used that model to talk to God about the Flood."

"It works for me. It's retro chic. I'm not one of these early adapters." He reached out for Robert's phone. "Very fancy. I presume it does everything except make tea."

"I think it might even do that."

"And tell me," Jimmy continued smoothly, "what about the delectable Stephanie? How is she?"

Robert paused for a beat before responding. "Oh she's good, she's good. She got us a little business earlier this year, and is trying to push a little more our way."

Jimmy stared down onto the floor below. Without looking at Robert, he said, "I heard that you and she might be . . . together."

"What?" For a single instant, Robert wasn't sure if he had heard right. He felt his stomach cramp. "Who said that?"

"This is a small city. Small minds and big mouths. People talk and make assumptions. Some people saw you together, and made the connection."

"People should mind their own fucking business!" Robert snapped, surprising himself with his vehemence.

"So it's true then?"

Robert opened his mouth to bark a response, then he abruptly nodded. "I'll not lie to you. It's true." Even as he was saying the words, he felt an extraordinary rush of emotion: it took him a moment to recognise it as relief. Jimmy was the first person – the only person – he'd told about his affair with Stephanie.

Jimmy leaned across the table, and caught both of Robert's hands in his. "Is she worth it?"

Startled, Robert drew back. "What?" This was not the reaction he'd expected. Jimmy's affairs and one-night stands were legendary.

"Is she worth it?"

Their second round of drinks arrived and the two men drew apart. Robert immediately ordered another round, knowing it would take the waitress at least fifteen minutes to battle her way through the crowd back to them. He also needed some time to gather his thoughts. Jimmy knew about his affair. Other people knew about the relationship. The question was: who else knew, and for how long? Even though the Market Bar was now hot and noisy, he felt surrounded by a bubble of chilly silence.

"Is she worth it?" Jimmy asked again.

"Yes. Yes. I think so. Who told you?"

"I was at a directors' seminar recently. I was in a group, and someone was talking about Stephanie's company. He mentioned that they had given you three major contracts over the past year and wondered how that had come about when you hadn't exactly got a track record in shooting advertisements. Simon Farmer –"

"Little bastard," Robert interjected immediately.

"Exactly. Little bastard said it was because you were knocking off their accounts manager. He said it like it was common knowledge."

The wine curdled and soured in Robert's stomach and he felt as if he was about to throw up. His fingers were trembling slightly as he lifted the wineglass and drained it in one long swallow. It seared its way down his throat. He should have been feeling a little buzz from the wine on an empty stomach, but right now he was stone cold sober and he imagined that no matter how much he drank tonight, he would not be able to get drunk.

Jimmy sipped his wine, then pulled Robert's glass over and emptied half of his into it. "It took me a moment to realise that it was Stephanie he was talking about."

"Oh shit. And is it . . . common knowledge, I mean?"

"I'd not heard it before," Jimmy admitted. "I've suspected about the pair of you for a while however. I will confess whenever I saw the two of you together there was a comfortableness between you that made me uneasy."

"Uneasy? How?"

"Because I recognised myself and Frances in the way the two of you stood, the way you casually looked at one another, the innocent and apparently accidental touching of hands. The casual chat that was anything but."

"And you never said anything to me about it?"

"None of my business, was it? Besides, with my reputation, I'm not the one to be telling you how to live your life."

"I need to talk to Stephanie. I need to let her know. She might lose her job over this."

"I doubt it. She wouldn't be the first woman to do favours for her lover, and besides, I'm sure the work you did for her company was top-notch. As long as you weren't overpaid and didn't under-deliver, you'll be OK."

"She said she might lose her job if anyone found out."

Jimmy shrugged. "If she worked for me, I'd be asking hard questions," he admitted, "but if she'd done nothing illegal, I would have no cause to sack her. She's a tough cookie; she'll have protected herself somehow."

Robert put his elbows on the table and cupped his head in his hands. "I didn't think anyone knew. I've been so careful."

"Robert, even if there was nothing between you and Stephanie, if people saw you together, of course they are going to talk. In this day and age, a man and a woman simply cannot be seen together without tongues wagging. But put two people of the same sex together and there is no suggestion that they are conducting a homosexual relationship! It's just the way of the world."

"You been in this position before," Robert said desperately. "What should I do?"

"You're really asking me two questions: what should you do, and what should you do if anyone asks?"

Robert thought about it for a moment and then nodded in agreement. There were two questions. He opted for the easier one. "What do I say if anyone asks?"

"You have two choices: deny or accept. If you accept it, you have to be prepared for the fallout, which will affect home, family, friends and work. My advice is to deny it. Deny it and stick to your guns. Make sure Stephanie denies it. But make sure that Kathy knows about the rumours before anyone tells her. Tell her you've heard that this story is going around and you're bringing it to her attention first. You have to make her believe it's not true.

If Kathy suspects that nothing is going on, then you're OK; however, if she has any suspicions then you will only be confirming them.

Robert opened his mouth to say something, but Jimmy held up a hand.

"And don't tell me you don't want to lie to her. You've already done that. This is just an extension of the lie."

Robert slumped back in the chair as the next round of drinks arrived. "Can I have the bill, please?" He looked at Jimmy. "I'm really sorry. I need to get out, get a breath of air, clear my head."

"I understand."

Robert laughed, a short bark. "You know what's so ironic here? I had decided just a couple of hours ago that I'd suggest to Stephanie that we really should consider stepping back from one another in the New Year."

Jimmy's face remained a blank mask.

"Maybe this will precipitate that," Robert continued.

"Robert, try not to overreact. I'm telling you what I heard. Hearsay. Repeated by a bitter little man, jealous because he did not get the contracts. And because he wasn't sleeping with Stephanie Burroughs," Jimmy added with a cheeky grin.

Robert smiled wanly. "Well, that is true."

Jimmy's smile faded. "However, let me give you a piece of advice if I may?"

"Please."

"Well, let me ask you a question first. Do you love her? Do you love Stephanie?"

It took Robert a long moment before he nodded yes.

"And Kathy? Do you love her?"

He nodded more quickly this time. Yes.

"And Stephanie? Does she love you?"

"I believe she does."

Jimmy squirmed uncomfortably. "Then you do have a problem. It's always so much easier if it's just sex."

"I know that. What's the advice?"

"Never tell a woman that you're dumping her – no matter how nicely you phrase it. That road leads to disaster."

"Shit! I should never have got into this situation. But at the time . . ."

"I know. It was easy. Easier to get into than to get out of. Remember what I said about everything having a price. Well, payment is a bitch."

CHAPTER 25

"I never did ask you what I should do."

The two men shivered as they came out of the Market Bar. The temperature had plummeted, though that seemed to have no effect on the line of people queuing to get in, or the milling crowd of smokers gathered on the street, or sat and stood by the big barrels that served as tables in the arched entrance foyer.

"That's not a question you should be asking me," the older man said.

They turned to the right, heading for George's Street. Robert had offered to walk Jimmy back to his apartment in Temple Bar, but, in light of the new information, had refused his offer of staying over. They turned right at the corner of Fade Street and walked down George's Street, towards Dame Street.

Robert dug his hands into the pockets of his long black overcoat. "I just don't know what to do. I've never been in this situation before and you . . ."

"And I have, you mean." Jimmy smiled, but there was nothing humorous in the twisting of his lips. "Oh, I have. But you know something? All of the affairs I had – and I'll not deny that there were many – none of them tempted me to leave Angela. Except Frances. And, I'll admit this to you and to no-one else, if she hadn't got pregnant, I'd not be in the mess I'm in now. Angela and I never had children. We tried; we wanted them. We got medical advice, but there was nothing wrong: we just never conceived. We talked about adopting, but my life was too erratic, I was all over the place, the money was too irregular. Even if we had managed to adopt, it would have meant Angela would have been left to raise the child herself. We kept putting it off, and suddenly that option was closed off to us. But when Angela learned that Frances had given birth, that was the last straw in our relationship. She had forgiven me so much over the years: but I think she saw that as the ultimate betrayal."

"You're saying not to leave Kathy."

"I didn't say that."

"I love them both!" Robert said, shocked by the sound of desperation in his own voice. Pedestrians waiting at the traffic lights to cross Dame Street looked at him in bemusement.

Jimmy gripped his arm and hurried him across the road, weaving through traffic which was at a standstill. "So what? Love is not some exclusive emotion that you give to one person. We love lots of people, our parents, wives, children. We love them unconditionally. I'm not talking about love. I'm talking about commitment. Which one of the women are you committed to?"

They turned left into Crow Street, heading down towards Temple Bar. The narrow cobbled street was jammed with smokers spilling out from the pubs and restaurants, some sitting on the icy kerb. A hen party in matching Santa outfits that ended high on their thighs, one of them wearing a big L sign, were click-clacking their way across the cobbles. Their bare flesh looked blue and alabaster with the cold.

Jimmy paused at the bottom of the street. "Here's where I leave you. Are you sure you won't come in for a nightcap?"

"I'd better not. I'm driving."

"Think about what I've said. This is no longer about love – since you love them both – this is about commitment. Commitment in the past, commitment now and commitment in the future. You wouldn't be where you are today if Kathy hadn't been there to support you."

"I know that. But the business would not have survived without Stephanie's commitment."

"Yes, it would, Robert. It would just have survived differently. Which is more important to you: your marriage and your family, or your mistress and your business?" Jimmy suddenly reached forward and embraced Robert, hugging him closely. "This time next year, Robert, where do you want to be? Who do you want to be with?" He broke away and took half a dozen steps, before glancing over his shoulder. "Oh, and Happy Christmas." Then he turned and was swallowed up by the milling crowd.

Robert waited until he was out of Temple Bar before reaching for his phone. He was about to call Stephanie, then he stopped. What was he going to say to her? His head was spinning. Events were slipping out of control; there was just too much to deal with at the moment.

He darted across the road, car horns blaring, an angry shout fading behind him, and walked towards Trinity College, washed gold and black with its uplit illumination. Couples walked towards him, arm-in-arm, happy, laughing, smiling and he found himself wondering how many of them were having affairs, how many of them were in genuine relationships. But was that to suggest that an affair was not a genuine relationship? It was. He found himself nodding. His relationship with Stephanie was genuine. But was it fair?

No.

The answer was stark and simple. It wasn't fair on anyone. He fished his phone out of his pocket and hit the speed dial for Stephanie. It was answered almost immediately.

"I wasn't expecting to hear from you for ages," she began.

"Where are you?"

"In the car, heading home. I met Sally for a drink in the Shelbourne. Is everything all right?"

"I'm not sure. I'll meet you at home. I'm just heading down Nassau Street; I left the car outside the office. It'll take me forty-five minutes to get to you."

"Robert –" Stephanie began, but he snapped off the phone. He didn't want to talk to her just now; he needed a little time to think.

This was not how he had planned to end his day, walking cold and heartsick through the streets of Dublin. This should have been a good day: it looked as if he had tied up the DaBoyz contract, had made love to a beautiful woman and then had dinner with an old friend.

Until Jimmy had told him about the rumours. And then everything changed. Was he overreacting? Jimmy said that Simon Farmer told the group that Robert was having an affair with Stephanie. He knew Farmer, an obnoxious little no-talent shit, but who was incredibly well-connected. His company managed, year-after-year-after-year, to get some plum contracts. Farmer was a loud-mouthed drunk and he and Robert had bumped heads on a couple of occasions. They sat on a couple of committees together some years ago and had simply not got along. Thinking back to those committee days, one of the things Robert particularly disliked about Farmer was that he was a gossip, delighting in telling tales and spreading bad news. How many people had he told?

Robert turned right, cutting up Kildare Street, heading for the Green. He had to accept that if Farmer knew about his relationship with Stephanie and had noticed that she was directing business towards Robert's company, then Farmer would complain. His stomach lurched: maybe he already had!

Robert pulled out his XDA and stepped into a doorway to look at the screen. He scrolled down through the names in his address book until he eventually found Jimmy's. The call was answered on the first ring.

"Jimmy Moran."

"It's Robert."

"Changed your mind? Come on over." Robert distinctly heard a pop and then a clink as Jimmy opened a bottle and poured liquid into a glass.

"No, I can't. I'm going to see Stephanie. We need to talk."

"Good idea."

"I just want to ask you one question. How long ago were you talking to Farmer? You said you'd been at a directors' conference recently. How recently?"

"It was the last weekend in November. I can get you the exact dates if you like."

"No, that's great. I just was trying to work out how long Farmer had known."

"Robert," Jimmy said seriously, "when he announced the news, no-one reacted like it was a big surprise. A couple of heads nodded, as if they already knew. I think you have to accept that people know and have known for a while . . . and you know something: most people simply don't care, which is as it should be. Now go and talk to Stephanie. And you know you can call me anytime. Anytime," he emphasised.

"I know that. Thank you, Jimmy, you're a good friend." He hung up, pushed his phone back into his pocket and hurried up the street. He needed to get back to the car, needed to get to Stephanie, desperately needed to talk to her.

But if people knew, then why had no-one said anything to him? He'd been at a BBC Northern Ireland meet-and-greet in Belfast recently. The Beeb were introducing their new commissioning editors and discussing their documentary and drama requirements and just about every independent production company in the North and the Republic were represented. No-one had said anything to him about Stephanie. Not even Farmer.

They'd exchanged a few civil words. He frowned, trying to re-run the event in his head. Was there something he missed, some subtle hints, some knowing looks? When he had been sitting in the middle of the conference room in the Europa Hotel had people been looking at him, whispering behind his back, talking about him?

He laughed, a sudden barking sound that made the young couple walking towards him veer away suddenly. He was being stupid. Of course no-one was talking about him; Jimmy was right. No-one cared.

But this was no way to live his life, wondering if people were talking about him, concerned about what they thought of him, terrified in case his wife got to hear about it. He had to sort this out.

Now.

Tonight.

CHAPTER 26

Robert used his swipe card to open the gates that led into the small apartment and townhouse complex where Stephanie lived off the Grand Canal. The complex was in almost total darkness, just a few of the duplexes lit up. It was mainly populated by singles or young professional couples, though there were also one or two retired couples in the larger townhouses. Most of the occupants of the complex were probably out on the town tonight; Christmas party season was in full swing. He pulled the Audi into the empty space before Number 28, alongside Stephanie's silver BMW. Although he had a key to Stephanie's apartment, he rarely used it, and he hit the bell, two short distinct rings.

There was movement behind the bubbled glass, and then Stephanie appeared, wearing a peach-coloured silk dressing-gown, her hair wrapped in a towel. Her body, still damp from the recent shower, was clearly outlined against the thin fabric, nipples hard and pointed against the cloth. She smiled archly. "I really wasn't expecting you."

"There was a change of plan." He kissed her quickly and brushed past her into the apartment.

Stephanie's apartment was in stark contrast to his home. He

always felt slightly claustrophobic in the small rooms. Stephanie preferred comfort over form and the sitting-room was cluttered with heavy overstuffed furniture covered in corded material, a hideous dark-wood display cabinet filled with scores of little hand-painted houses, while dozens of pictures in just about every medium – oils and watercolours predominating – crowded each wall. Tall banks of dried flowers in fluted glasses dominated either side of the coal-effect gas fire. A flat panel TV was discreetly tucked into the sparsely populated bookshelves and below it, a micro-CD player was running, filling the air with the ambient new age music which Robert hated and Stephanie adored.

"You look like you need a drink." Without waiting for a response, she turned away into the small kitchen.

"Coffee, no alcohol," Robert called after her. He shrugged off his coat and tossed it onto a chair, then followed her out to the kitchen to lean against the doorway. The kitchen was tiny and pristine, and it was obvious that she rarely used it. The gas cooker looked unused, but the worktop was strewn with kitchen devices: kettle, toaster, microwave and water filter and a state-of-the-art black and silver coffee machine.

She bent over to open the fridge. "I've got a nice white wine chilling . . ."

"I'd better not. I'm driving."

Stephanie straightened and a frown flickered across her face. "You're not staying?"

"No, not tonight. I can't."

"That wasn't the initial plan," she smiled.

"The plan changed."

Stephanie tugged her dressing-gown across her body. "I'll make some coffee."

Robert watched her in silence while she poured ground coffee into the filter. What was it about this woman that he loved; how had she captivated him so? She was pretty, but not spectacular. Her breasts were full, but not overlarge, she was slender, but not to the point of emaciation. She was ordinary. Very ordinary. In fact, he suddenly realised, with what felt like a growing sense of panic: she looked a little . . . she looked a lot like Kathy, a slimmer, younger Kathy. Robert stared intently at the woman, shocked, horrified and fascinated by what he had just discovered. How had he never seen it before? Because, he realised, he'd never asked himself what had attracted him to her in the first place.

He watched her move, aware – all too aware – that she was naked beneath the dressing-gown. She poured water into the coffee-maker and her dressing-gown gaped open, allowing him a glimpse of her breast. She flicked him a quick sidelong glance and he realised he'd been caught.

"You've seen them before."

"The day I get tired of looking at them is the day I'm dead."

But there were differences, huge differences between the two women. Kathy would never make coffee in the kitchen wearing nothing more than a flimsy dressing-gown. Kathy didn't make him laugh any more, didn't arouse him any more either. Stephanie did all of that, and more.

But somewhere at the back of his mind, he realised that he was not being entirely fair to Kathy: he worked harder with Stephanie, worked to make her laugh, to make her happy, bringing her little presents, small treats, occasional bunches of flowers. He couldn't remember the last time he'd brought Kathy a small present or a bunch of flowers.

"Tell me what happened?" she said. "I presume it's something to do with Jimmy, since you were fine – more than fine – when I left you a couple of hours ago? He's OK, is he?"

"He's OK. His life's a mess, as usual."

"I think he thrives on it," Stephanie remarked.

"He's not getting any younger. And this time the mess is bigger than usual. His wife is finally giving him the divorce he's wanted."

"Well, that's good news . . ."

"And taking half of everything he owns into the bargain."

Stephanie looked at him sharply. "Good for her. That is her right."

"I know that. He's going to marry Frances so they can raise the child together."

"So he should."

Robert shrugged noncommittally. He found he was vaguely uncomfortable with Stephanie's reaction; she wasn't exactly sympathetic towards Jimmy's plight.

"You don't look so sure," Stephanie observed, watching him closely.

"I just remember that Frances was the woman who sold her story to the press. She used him to get free publicity, hoping she'd get that movie part."

The coffee started to percolate and the rich aroma of Kenyan filled the small kitchen.

"That revelation was really the beginning of the end for him and Angela."

"But he's still with Frances though," Stephanie said, pulling open cupboard doors and lifting out two tiny coffee cups. "He went back to her, got her pregnant."

"Put it in a mug, would you? Something a bit more substantial than those thumbnails."

Stephanie reached into the cupboard and brought out a mug emblazoned with a yellow smiley face.

"I gave you that."

"I know."

"Frances ruined his reputation in return for a few column inches."

Stephanie laughed, the sound high and bright. "She did not. He had no reputation to ruin. You know he was notorious around Dublin. One of the reasons he could never get female researchers to work with him on projects was because he always came on to them – and expected them to reciprocate." She poured coffee, thick and black, into the mug, and then filled her own tiny cup. "Everyone knew about him."

Robert accepted the mug from her hand. He sipped it, grimacing and yet relishing the harsh bitter taste. "People know about us, Stephanie," he said quietly. "Jimmy told me tonight."

She paused, holding the cup and saucer in both hands. Then she nodded and walked past Robert into the sitting-room. In one deft movement, she curled up on the sofa, tucking her bare legs beneath her.

Robert followed her into the room. "Did you hear what I said?" He sat down in the easy chair facing Stephanie. "People know about us."

The room was still, silent save for the ghostly wind chimes coming from the CD player. Something about Stephanie's stony demeanour and her reaction finally clicked: she hadn't been surprised by the news. He had been stunned when Jimmy told him; her reaction should have been similar, unless . . .

"You knew." He was shocked and felt curiously betrayed. "You knew and you never told me."

"Yes, I knew."

Robert licked dry lips and drank deeply from the coffee. "How long . . . I mean why didn't you . . . what about your office?"

"There have been rumours floating about us for the last couple of months," Stephanie said evenly. "I ignored them. This business of ours thrives on rumour and gossip. And when two people are regularly seen together tongues will wag, even if there is no truth to the rumours. About a month ago, I was called into head office. Charles Flintoff himself asked me outright if you and I were an item."

"You said no," Robert said immediately.

"I said yes."

Robert looked at her blankly.

"Having a relationship with you is one thing – he doesn't give a damn about that. Putting business your way is another. But so long as it's above board, well, that's still marginally OK. However, lying to him was out of the question. The very fact that he was asking me a question suggested that he already knew the answer. I told him the truth."

Robert was speechless. There were questions he wanted, needed, to ask, but he could not formulate the words.

"And it was the right thing to do. He had contracts for the jobs I'd given you, plus the costings. He'd done some comparisons with the other bidders and had an independent assessment of the final result." She shrugged. "He could find no fault with it."

Robert finally managed to find his voice. "So how many people know?"

Stephanie frowned. "Why? What's the problem?"

"Because if people know, then it's only a matter of time before Kathy gets to hear."

Stephanie's face became an expressionless mask. She concentrated on her coffee.

"I wanted to be in a position to tell her myself. When the time was right."

"And when would the time be right, Robert?"

"When it's right. When I get myself sorted out," he muttered.

"And when would that be? And what constitutes 'sorting out'?"

Robert concentrated on his coffee. This was not going the way he planned. On the drive over, he had rehearsed versions of the conversation he intended having with Stephanie. He was going to explain to her that people in the business suspected that they were having a relationship and that, for the sake of her job, it might be best if they were to cool it for a while. They'd let things cool down, not see one another for a few weeks or a couple of months maybe, and then pretty soon people would forget. Stephanie's revelation – that her boss knew and that she had admitted to him that the stories were true – changed all that.

"We've been lovers now for eighteen months, Robert. Where do we go from here? What's the future?"

He had asked himself the same questions.

"You told me how unhappy you are at home. You suggested to me – no, more than suggested, you told me, that you would leave Kathy . . ."

"I'm sure I never said that."

"Maybe not in those words, but that was my clear understanding. I would never have got involved with you otherwise. You told me you would leave her when the time was right."

He heard the bitterness, the anger clearly in her voice.

He nodded briefly. He had said that. He remembered saying it. They'd spent the day in bed, here in this very apartment. He was exhausted, a little drunk. He'd said a lot of things.

"Well, when is the right time? This month? No, it cannot be this month because it's Christmas, and you don't want to ruin Christmas for the family. But you've no problem ruining my Christmas. OK then, next month, but that's the start of the New Year and you probably don't want to ruin that for them either. Maybe February, but that's Theresa's birthday and that's not a nice birthday present to give her. March? But you know something, there's bound to be a problem with that too." Stephanie stopped suddenly. Then she sighed. "Look, I'm tired. I don't want to be having this conversation with you now."

Robert nodded. He didn't want to have it either. He had been shocked by the vehemence in her voice.

"I had a drink with Sally earlier . . ."

"Does she know?"

"Of course, she knows. She knew from the very beginning."

Robert squeezed his eyes shut. Who didn't know?

"She warned me, right from the git-go not to get involved with a married man. She explained to me exactly what would happen, and you know what: so far, she's been right. Just spot on."

"Stephanie," Robert began. He was alarmed to see tears in her eyes. "Maybe this isn't a good time. We're both tired. Let's get some sleep."

185

"I think that's a really good idea." She stood up smoothly, picked up Robert's coat and handed it to him.

"I'll see you tomorrow. We'll talk."

She nodded as she walked him to the door, then she laid a hand on his arm. "I don't want to think that you've been making a fool of me. I don't want to think that you've been using me." Then she leaned up and kissed him gently, brushing her lips against his. "Tomorrow. Tell me the truth. Don't disappoint me."

"We'll talk tomorrow," Robert said, tasting her lipstick on his lips, surprised by how husky his voice sounded. He walked out to the car, hit the remote, opened the doors and climbed in without looking back. Sitting in the driver's seat, he was facing the hall door. Stephanie had already closed it and he could see the peach colour of her dressing gown as she retreated down the hallway. Usually, she waited in the doorway until he reached the gates. Seconds later the light in the sitting-room went off. Then the kitchen light clicked off. He turned the key in the engine and backed out. The bedroom light came on, warm and yellow against the drapes and he saw her shadow move behind them. He knew what that bedroom looked like, knew what the bed felt like beneath his naked flesh. He waited a moment, wondering if she would look out. She didn't and the light flicked off.

Robert put the car in gear and drove away.

CHAPTER 27

"I wasn't sure if you were coming home tonight."

The voice whispered out of the darkness, startling him. "I didn't mean to wake you."

"You didn't wake me."

Kathy was awake. He could tell her now. He could sit on the edge of the bed and tell her, whispering his secrets into the darkness.

And tell her what?

Once he started to tell this story, he had to go right through to the conclusion. And he wasn't sure what the conclusion was. Which version of the truth did he want to tell – that he was involved with Stephanie, or that he'd heard a rumour from Jimmy that he was involved with Stephanie, and that it was untrue. What did he want to do: it was the question that had gnawed at him on the drive home. Did he want to stay with Kathy, or did he want to go with Stephanie?

He tugged at the knot in his tie, pulled it open, the raw silk hissing like a zipper and threw it onto the chair by the dressing-table. It whispered onto the floor.

Of course, it wasn't quite that simple. If he told Kathy that he'd been having an affair, would she still want him? He remembered how she had reacted when she suspected six years previously. Maybe if he admitted it to her now, she would tell him to get out, and the decision would be made. Is that what he'd wanted all along? For Kathy to find out, for Kathy to make the decision? Robert squeezed his eyes shut, disgusted with himself.

"I only had a couple of drinks and the roads weren't too bad." He pulled off his suit jacket, folded it over the chair and began to unbutton his shirt.

"I phoned earlier." Her voice was crisp and clear; she didn't sound as if she had awakened from sleep.

"I didn't get a call," he said.

"It went straight to your machine."

"We went to the Market Bar off George's Street; the stone walls probably killed the signal."

Driving home, he'd thought about telling Kathy. About waking her up, taking her hands in his and confessing. But, Stephanie was right, it was too close to Christmas. *Happy Christmas, I'm having an affair.*

That was the emotional response. Then the rational part of his mind kicked in, asking him why he should tell Kathy anything. Simple. He wanted to get to her before anyone else spoke to her, so he could tell her the story in his way, put his spin on it. Then he recalled that Kathy was no longer really involved in the business. He couldn't remember the last time she dropped into the office, even when she was in town. And now that Maureen was out of the picture, that closed off that avenue of communication. So maybe there was no need to jump the gun. Maybe all he needed to do was to talk to Stephanie tomorrow, so they could sort it out between themselves, before he had to tackle Kathy.

The only problem was that he didn't know what Stephanie wanted. He hadn't like the way the conversation had drifted this evening. Previously, it had been light-hearted and fun: they dined well, made love when it suited them, enjoyed one another's company. He'd always been vaguely aware that Stephanie expected more, and was aware too that he'd promised more, but that was always going to happen at some future date, some indefinable time when "things would be different".

Whatever that meant.

Whenever that was.

"How is Jimmy?"

"Jimmy is fine. He sends his love."

"I'm surprised he remembered me."

"Of course, he remembered you."

"So you didn't get into Shanahan's?"

And there it was again, the probing suspicion. This was not paranoia brought on by the events of the day; this was something more, something definite. "I'm going to phone and complain in the morning. I'm sure Maureen booked, but they said they'd no record of the booking." He abruptly realised that this was probably the longest conversation they'd had in a long time.

"What does Maureen say?"

"Maureen's out sick at the moment."

"You never said."

He could hear the accusation in her voice. "Oh, I'm sure I did."

"You did not!" she snapped. "I most certainly would have remembered. I worked with Maureen, remember. How long has she been out sick?"

"Three weeks . . . four," Robert mumbled. Shit, shit, shit. Why had he opened his mouth and mentioned Maureen's name. Now there was every possibility that Kathy would want to talk to her. And that was the last thing he wanted at this moment. He'd decided on that way home that he really needed to get to see Maureen before Christmas, bring her a little present, tell her about the new business which Stephanie had brought the company.

"And you never told me. . ." Her voice rose and she lowered it again. "You never told me. I would have called her, visited her."

189

Christ, couldn't she understand that he'd a lot on his mind at the moment? Maybe, if she'd shown more interest in the company, she'd have known about Maureen. Maybe if she'd shown more interest in him, he would not have had an affair. "I've been busy. I must have forgotten."

"What's wrong with her?"

"Chest infection or something. Doctor's note says she won't be back till next year. And it's the busiest time too."

"You make it sound as if she went sick deliberately. I can't remember the last time she was ill. Can you?"

Robert didn't answer. He stepped into the en suite, pulled the door closed, clicked on the light, and picked up his electric toothbrush. So what if she wanted to visit Maureen? He suspected that Maureen knew about his affair – shit, it sounded as if the entire TV industry knew about it. Even if Kathy got to her before him, Maureen was no fool. She knew the state the company was in, knew too that it was only the business Stephanie put their way so far that kept them afloat and paid her salary. She'd say nothing. Still, it would be better if he could get to her quickly. Maybe tomorrow. No, Sunday maybe, or Monday. Maybe he'd phone her. It wouldn't do any harm to remind her – subtly – who paid her salary and, at her age she wasn't going to get another job as cushy as this, so easily. She liked to think that her contacts in the business were second-to-none. But time was passing her by, and slowly, one-by-one, her contacts were becoming useless as her old friends were replaced by new people.

He'd phone her in the morning because women, in Robert's limited experience, stuck together. Like Stephanie's friend Sally warning her off him in the first place: why didn't she just mind her own business? If Kathy went to Maureen voicing some vague suspicion, God only knows what Maureen would say. Actually, it might be better if he called around in the morning, maybe bring a bunch of flowers and a Christmas bonus. That would keep her sweet.

"Who's on reception now?" Kathy asked, when he came out of the en-suite. White light flooded the bedroom and he watched her raise her hand to shield her eyes. He quickly closed the door again.

"A temp. Illona. Russian, I think. I got her from an agency. She's very good."

"Perhaps Illona made the reservation?" she suggested.

Robert pulled out a fresh pair of pyjamas and tugged on the top. "Maybe. But it was about four weeks ago; I'm sure Maureen was still around then. I'll still complain to the restaurant in the morning, if I get a minute."

"Do you want me to do it for you?"

Something in her voice, some eagerness, some expectation alerted him. He'd heard that tone before, and he knew then, knew for a certainty that Kathy was suspicious of him. Again. Only this time there was a reason. He was aware that his heart was thumping solidly against his chest. He could actually feel the skin vibrate. He took a deep breath and forced his voice to remain calm, and then he smiled in the darkness. "If you get a chance – yes, that would be great. Table for two, Friday night, 7:30, in either my name or Jimmy Moran's. I used his name too just in case he arrived first." Let her check up; she'd find nothing and it might allay some of her suspicions.

Robert got into bed. The sheets were icy, but maybe that was because he felt as if he was burning up. He leaned across and kissed his wife quickly on the cheek.

"Night." She muttered the single word as she rolled over, turning away from him. As usual. She didn't ask him how his day had gone, didn't ask him what he'd done, barely asked him about his evening. He found himself getting angry. Why did he put up with this? Was this his future? Was he destined to spend years going though this loveless routine, gradually becoming more and more distant from Kathy until there was nothing left between them but bitterness?

But there was an alternative.

There was Stephanie.

She loved him and he loved her. She loved being with him. There was an opportunity for a future for both of them. A happy future. But she wouldn't wait forever. From what she had said earlier, she was not prepared to wait much longer.

But the children? What about the children?

He fell asleep, then tossed and turned in dreams where he chased Brendan and Theresa through the tables in the Market Bar. They were always just out of reach, and Kathy and Stephanie occupied every table.

CHAPTER 28

Saturday 21st December

"I told you we should have got the smaller tree."

"Dad! You know we always get the biggest tree we can find," Theresa said.

"And then we always spend ages cutting the end off," Brendan reminded his sister.

"Who's this 'we?'" Robert asked. "Looks like I'm the only one sawing at the moment."

"We're holding it steady," Brendan reminded him.

Robert, along with Brendan and Theresa, had gone into Swords to buy a Christmas tree. It had become a tradition over the years to buy their tree as close to Christmas as possible, a tradition it was becoming increasingly difficult to keep as trees began appearing in neighbours' windows earlier and earlier in December and surviving long into January. The other part of the tradition, of course, was that Kathy would complain about the tree – it was too big, too bushy, too thin, too lopsided.

But at least they were spared that this morning and for that small mercy, Robert was grateful. Although Kathy had been in bed when the trio had set out to buy the tree, she'd left the house by the time they returned less than an hour later. A scribbled note on the kitchen table said: *"Gone Shopping."*

It suited Robert perfectly. Once he got the tree into the house, and dug the decorations out of the garage, he needed to see Stephanie. He glanced at his watch; he wanted to be gone before Kathy came back and maybe started an argument.

But the tree was too tall; it would not go into the house.

He spent a frustrating half hour sawing off the base of the tree, getting covered in sticky sap and pricked by scores of needles. And every moment he expected to see Kathy's car turn down the road. Finally, he managed to chop and saw eighteen inches off the end of the tree and, with Theresa holding the top, Brendan in the middle and he taking up the rear, they backed the tree through the kitchen door and into the house.

"We could set it up in the hall," Robert said, voice muffled behind branches which kept swatting him across the face.

"Dad!" Theresa squealed in disgust. He made the same suggestion every year, and every year they placed the tree in the dining-room.

With the tree finally set up in a corner, standing in a bucket filled with stones, and more or less straight, Robert turned to Brendan.

"I know, I know," the young man said. "Hoover up the needles. I'll get on it."

"Right, I'll get out the decorations, then I need to wash up and head into the office for an hour or so."

"Dad! Do you have to?"

"This is to do with DaBoyz!" He leaned over and patted Theresa's cheek. "Just think, if I get this gig, you can come on set as I shoot their pop video."

Theresa looked distinctly unimpressed, with that look which only teenage girls perfect. "I don't think so!"

"I thought they were good," he said surprised. "Up-and-coming. They were on *Top of the Pops*."

"And they were rubbish," she said. "Their last single didn't even chart. And Ben, the lead singer –"

"Which one is he?"

"Shaved head, little pointy beard."

Robert nodded, vaguely remembering the young man. He'd thought all five band members looked alike.

"Ben is in a gay relationship with Viv, the drummer," she said seriously.

Robert nodded seriously and bit the inside of his cheek to prevent himself from smiling. He hoped his baby girl did not know what "gay relationship" meant, but was afraid to ask, just in case she did.

"It was on MTV recently that they're about to break up," she added. She saw the look on her father's face and grinned. "Are you sure you want to shoot their video?"

Robert licked dry lips, tasting pine and bile in equal measure. "I'm not sure."

"Might be a mistake, Dad," Brendan said, coming back into the dining-room, lugging the upright Hoover. "If they are about to go bust, these bands usually blame everyone but themselves. Blaming the pop video is high on their list."

"Wish I'd spoken to you two sooner," he muttered, leaving the room.

"Anytime, Dad," Brendan called after him. "Say, do we get a consultancy fee for this?"

Robert stepped into his home office, shut the door, then, as an afterthought, turned the key in the lock. Folding his arms across his chest, he stared out across the bare winter garden, not quite sure what to think. The big gig, the great opportunity, might just turn out to be not so big, not so great as he had imagined. He'd talk to Stephanie about it; she'd know what to do.

He sat in his chair and reached for his mobile. He never phoned Stephanie on the home phone; he didn't want the itemised billing showing up numerous calls to a single number. He hit the speed dial and while he waited for the call to connect, he riffled through the correspondence in his basket. He'd been so busy in work, he hadn't had a chance to attend to it. He'd stuffed it all in his briefcase on Monday last, intending to take care of it during the week, but so far, he hadn't even had a chance to glance through it.

The call connected.

"How . . . how are you feeling?" he asked immediately.

"I'm tired, Robert."

"Do you want to see me?"

"I always want to see you." He could almost hear the smile in her voice.

"I was going to call over. I don't know how long it will take me; traffic is sure to be appalling."

"I'm actually heading into the city; there is an open-air carol service being held in Stephen's Green."

"What time?"

"Starts about two."

"Why don't I meet you there? We can listen to some carols, then go and get something to eat."

"OK," she said shortly. "Give me a call when you're in the city." The phone went dead.

Robert sat looking at the handset for a long moment. That had been very short and not so very sweet. He put the phone down and quickly sorted through the basket.

And for a moment thought he was having a heart attack.

His MBNA Visa bill was in the pile. What was that doing here? He must have bundled it up with the post he'd brought home from the office. He'd taken up the offer of the credit card shortly after he started his relationship with Stephanie, thinking that it might be a useful way of allowing him to spend money unbeknownst to Kathy. Kathy did the household accounts and paid all the bills and the last thing he needed was for her to start questioning some of his expenditure. He still put his legitimate business expenses on the BOI card, but expenses which were specifically to do with Stephanie went on the new card. Statements were sent to the office, and he wrote them a cheque every month. He filled in the cheque stub with fictitious business meetings, usually lunches.

Robert turned the statement over and over in his fingers. Had Kathy seen this? Unlikely. She rarely came into his room, and she would have no reason to go rooting through his post.

Unless she was suspicious.

The thought crept slowly and insidiously into his consciousness.

And he knew she was.

He looked through the bill. It wasn't as bad as he thought: most of the items on it he could claim as legitimate business expenses, even the books and CD's, which he'd given as gifts to Stephanie, he could claim as research material for a documentary. Documentary research covered a multitude of sins. He turned the page. "Shit!" There were three items on the second page which might be more difficult to explain. He had satellite TV piped into the office and often watched QVC, the shopping channel, when he was working, particularly when they were selling movie memorabilia, which he collected. However, he'd bought a bracelet for Stephanie – part of her birthday present – with the card and he'd also ordered a bouquet of flowers online to be sent to her. He'd taken Stephanie to the White Orchid Restaurant in Dublin city, and he'd used the card to pay for that.

OK. What was the worst-case scenario? Kathy had seen this page. If she had, then she was bound to raise the issue of the card. He could explain that away. The books, the CD's, he could explain away also. These three items however . . .

Well, the statement only showed the amount; it did not show the item.

The QVC bill could have been something for his computer.

He had a couple of items in the office – wireless mice, memory sticks – which he could show her if necessary; she'd never know how much they cost.

The flowers. A birthday present, a thank-you gift. Maybe a get-well bouquet for Maureen. He must remember to really send her a bouquet, just in case Kathy asked about the flowers.

The dinner. Well, that could have been just any business dinner.

Sorted.

He sat back in the creaking chair, and then stopped, suddenly realising what he was doing. He was creating a worst-case scenario – just in case Kathy tackled him. But only last night he'd been on the verge of confessing to her. So just what the fuck did he want: to stay with Kathy or go with Stephanie?

Both, the little perverse thought at the back of his head whispered. Both.

CHAPTER 29

"Oh shit. Oh shit. Oh shit. She didn't waste any time."

Robert slowed as he turned off the Finglas Road. Kathy's car was parked outside Maureen's house. He remembered the house well; when R&K had pitched a DIY programme to RTE, they'd used Maureen's home for the pilot. She'd got a very nice conservatory out of it. He hoped that she and Kathy were now sitting out in that conservatory at the back of the house, rather than watching him drive by. He glanced at the bouquet of flowers on the seat beside him. Looked like Maureen would not be getting her flowers today; he had planned to drop in on her unannounced, just to "see how she was" and give her a Christmas bonus, a cheque for one thousand euro which was in the card with the flowers. He was going to be very careful to explain that one of the reasons he could pay the bonus was because of the work that Stephanie had brought them in. Well, she wouldn't be getting that today either. He accelerated past the house, desperately resisting the temptation to look in.

It took him another hour to get from Finglas into the city, and he eventually abandoned the car in Christchurch carpark which, even though the big parking signs dotted over the city were showing was full, still had plenty of spaces on the top floor.

199

Pulling on his heavy tweed overcoat and wrapping a silk scarf around his neck, he hurried across the city. The temperature was hovering around zero, but Dublin looked glorious in crisp December light. It was one of those rare winter days when the sky was cloudless and the low sunlight painted the streets in gold and shadow. St Patrick's Cathedral directly in front of him was etched against the blue sky, each brick, each slate picked out in incredible detail. All across the city, bells were tolling as the bell-ringers put in some practice for Christmas Eve, and, with his breath pluming on the air before him, he felt the first touch of Christmas spirit.

This had never been his favourite time of year. There were too many bitter memories from his youth; his parents' constant arguing, and his mother's drinking – exacerbated by his father's icy temper – made holidays, or indeed any time they were forced to spend together as a family unit, difficult and uncomfortable. When his parents had finally seperated, he ended up spending Christmas Day with his mother, listening to her bitch about his father, and then Stephen's Day with his father, listening to him rant about his mother.

He did not want that to happen to his children, to make them choose between one parent or another. He didn't want to place them in that position . . . and yet, his actions had certainly made that a very real possibility. When he'd first taken Stephanie to bed, he'd never imagined the potential consequences. It was just a bit of fun, two adults, doing what adults did, not harming anyone . . .

Except that it had. Even if Kathy and the children never got to hear about his affair, it had damaged his marriage. He shook his head quickly: no, the affair hadn't damaged his marriage. He had.

The long drive into the city had, however, allowed him to come to one decision. He was determined to get through Christmas without an argument if that was possible. He knew, deep in his heart and soul, that what he really meant was that he hoped to get through Christmas without having to make a decision. If he boxed clever, he thought he might just be able to do that. He just needed a little more time to think things through. A couple of days, a week, maybe a month to make a decision.

Coward, something that might have been his conscience hissed. And he had to agree.

He cut through the mall that ran alongside the Westbury Hotel and headed out into Grafton Street. It was virtually at a standstill and he battled his way through hordes of shoppers: teenagers wrapped around one another, mothers pushing prams, fathers carrying children in their arms or dragging older children along behind them. Who in their right mind brought children into the city a couple of days before Christmas? But when he looked at the children and parents again, none of them seemed to be upset. They were smiling, happy, and he remembered that when Brendan and Theresa were young, he and Kathy had taken them into the city to see the lights strung across the streets, look into the shop windows and enjoy the festive atmosphere. They had been happy then, just the four of them; they'd laughed a lot, as a couple and as a family. He tried to remember when they'd stopped doing that. There was no one moment. It had just happened; things changed. The children had grown up, he'd started working harder and harder to support a particular lifestyle, and he and Kathy had just drifted apart.

He ducked into the entrance to the Stephen's Green shopping centre, pulled out his phone and hit the speed dial for Stephanie. The call went for ten rings before it was finally answered.

"Where are you?" she asked, without preamble.

"In the door to the shopping centre."

"Stay there. Don't move. I'll find you. It's chaos here."

Robert turned off the phone and stood nervously in the circular foyer. This was probably one of the most visible spots in Dublin with crowds of people milling around, meeting and greeting in the entrance to the shopping centre or streaming in and out. He'd already caught glimpses of a couple of neighbours.

And then suddenly Stephanie was standing in front of him. She was bundled against the chill air in a bright red skiing jacket, black skiing pants tucked into woolly-topped boots and wearing a bright red woollen skiing cap on her head. With the bulky clothing disguising her body and only a tiny section of her face visible – eyes, nose and mouth – the similarity to his wife was startling.

He leaned forward to kiss her, a quick peck on the cheek, and then caught her arm, easing her away from the doorway. "Where did you leave your toboggan?"

"Parked it upstairs alongside the sleigh."

Robert hurried her across the road, back towards the high arched entrance to the Green. From within the park came the sound of "Away in a Manger" clearly audible above the noise of the traffic, the pinging of the Luas trams and the drone of the massed people. "Do you want to go back in?"

She shook her head. "The choir are loud, but not good and the park is jammed. Let's walk around and look at the art."

A huge open-air art exhibition was taking place on the railings surrounding the Green. Dozens of artists were exhibiting their works, the younger artists standing nervously alongside their paintings, talking to everyone who stopped to look, the older, more experienced exhibitors sitting on chairs and standing beside their open cars, allowing their art to speak for them.

"Left or right?" Stephanie asked brightly.

"Right," Robert said, linking her arm and leading her to the right, towards the Luas stop, but, more importantly, away from the crowds. If they had gone to the left, it would have taken them past Dawson Street and the Shelbourne.

"I'm sorry about last night," he began.

"So am I," she said immediately. "I should have told you that our relationship had been discovered. But I knew you were under so much pressure, I simply didn't want to add to it."

"It might have been better if you had. When Jimmy dropped it on me last night, I thought I was going to have a stroke."

Stephanie glanced at him curiously. She stopped to look at a spectacularly abstract oil, vivid in green and gold, slashed across with daubs of red and violet. She leaned forward, into the painting. "Tell me," she murmured, so softly that Robert had to lean close to hear her, "do you love me?"

His instinct was to snap a quick 'yes,' but something about the apparent casualness of the question stopped him.

When he didn't answer immediately, she turned her head to look at him. "No answer?"

"I suppose I was just startled that you had to ask me."

"Because I want to know." She moved away from the painting and he followed her. "I want to know how much."

"I've told you often enough."

"I know that. But have you shown me?"

"I've given you presents . . ."

A flash of annoyance in her dark eyes shut him up. "What is love, Robert?"

"Love is. . ." he floundered, ". . . well, love."

"Typical man!" she snapped. "Think about it: what is love? You tell me you love me. What does that mean?"

"It means . . . it means I want to be with you. That I love being with you."

"Would you be talking about commitment now?"

He suddenly saw where the conversation was going, but had no way to change it. "Yes. Commitment," he agreed.

Stephanie stopped to peer at another painting, a tiny delicate watercolour of a single daffodil. "And are you committed to me?" she continued.

"Yes."

Stephanie straightened. "Committed? How do you show that commitment?"

Robert was about to answer, but the over-eager artist, a young woman with huge glasses and too much hair, came forward. "We're not interested," Robert said, before she could utter a word.

203

He caught Stephanie by the arm and led her into the Green through a small side gate opposite the College of Surgeons. "If we're going to talk, then let's talk. Let's leave the art for another day. What do you want from me?"

"The truth," Stephanie said. "I told you that last night. Just tell me the truth."

"I've told you I love you. That's the truth."

"And I believe you."

Her response stopped him. She walked on a couple of paces, before turning to look back at him. The path was busy and for a moment he lost her in the crowd and there was the temptation simply to turn his back and walk away. When the path cleared, she was standing in the same position, waiting for him.

"If you have something to ask me, then ask me out straight," he said.

Stephanie dug her hands into the pockets of her jacket. Her eyes were glittering and her cheeks were red, but he wasn't sure if it was from the cold or emotion.

"You tell me you love me. You tell me you want to be with me. You seem to enjoy my company. You certainly enjoy my body." She stopped and took a deep breath. "I need to know if there is more. If there is going to be more."

"More?"

"More of us. Together. Not snatched half-hour lunches or one-hour dinners, not fumbles in your office or dirty weekends away. I need to know if we're going to be together. As a couple. Openly." She looked away from him, across the park, which was bright with people. "That's all."

And in the end, this was what it came down to, Robert decided. The answer he gave now was going to determine the rest of his life. All the thoughts of the previous night, his rambling thought processes of the day had revealed nothing, had not prepared him for this moment. He could try and be cold and calculating, try and choose between the two women, choose the security that Kathy represented, the uncertain future which Stephanie promised. He could refuse to make the decision and lose Stephanie, but in doing so, that might force her to go to Kathy and then he would lose her too. Jimmy Moran was right: everything had a price.

"I've had relationships before, Robert. You know that. I've never felt about anyone the way I feel about you. I love you. I need to know if you love me. I need to know if you love me enough to do something about it."

They walked out of the Green together and crossed the street, heading up Harcourt Street. Two Luas trams passed by, bells jingling brightly; neither Robert nor Stephanie turned to look at them.

Robert was watching Stephanie out of the corner of his eye. When they were first falling in love, but before they had made love for the first time, they walked. They spent weekends together, striding through the streets of Dublin, of Galway, of Cork and Kilkenny, walking side-by-side, not touching, not holding hands. She was fitter than he was; there were times when he struggled to keep up. Later, he recognised what had been happening. They were both so full of energy – nervous energy, sexual energy – this was how they had channelled it. Once they started making love regularly, they stopped walking.

Now they were walking again, but with a different energy, a different motive. Their steps were slow, grudging.

"You want me to commit to you."

"I don't want to be your bit on the side any more. That was fine for a while, because I wasn't sure if you were the one."

"The one?"

"The one I loved. And I allowed myself to fall in love with you – even though you were a married man, because I believed that there might be a chance for us." Stephanie took a deep breath, and Robert realised that his heart was hammering. "Then it came home to me. My girlfriends have gone away for Christmas, but I was going to be spending Christmas alone, because I wanted to be close to my lover. But my lover was spending time with his family. It was that way last year too; I don't want it to be that way next year."

"Stephanie, I –" he said quickly.

"If there is no future for us, then just say so. I'm not going to be stupid about it. I'm a big girl. I won't make a scene. I won't tell Kathy, if that's what you're worried about."

So there it was. Robert took a deep breath. In a single sentence, Stephanie had removed one of his huge fears. He could tell Stephanie now that there was no future for them, at least not for a few years until the children had grown up. He could go back to Kathy, and she would never know anything about his affair. Stephanie would drift away. And things would continue on with Kathy until . . . well, until they drifted completely apart. The children would have their own lives, their own families. He would be left with nothing.

Except now he had an opportunity.

An opportunity to make a selfish decision: to do something for himself for once in his life. From the moment he married, he'd ended up in a trap, running faster and faster to stand still, scrambling for work to keep everyone satisfied, to keep a roof over their heads. He'd sacrificed friendships and holidays, weekends and late nights in the desperate search for work in a business which was, ultimately, worthless. What had happened to his dreams of being a great director, of producing documentaries of worth, of making people think, of making a difference? He'd sacrificed that too.

He was in a loveless marriage to a woman who had no interest in him other than the pay cheque he deposited in the bank every week. The children loved him, he was sure, and he would always make sure they were taken care of. He would never become his father, telling a child how bad his mother was. And he'd see them regularly, probably even more regularly that he did now. He'd make time for them, dedicate time to them, with no interruptions, no phone calls, no meetings.

Could he throw it all away? Wife and family, home and friends? He was too old to start again.

Or had he thrown it away a long time ago? Was this the opportunity to start again, with a woman who loved him, and whom he would work with to make sure they stayed in love?

His head was spinning and he physically swayed. Stephanie reached out and caught his arm. Even through the layers of cloth, her touch was electric.

The decision, when it came, was almost a shock to him. He felt as if pieces were sliding and slipping into place. He moved around to stand in front of Stephanie, catching both of her shoulders, looking down into her dark eyes, magnified now by unshed tears. His breath was coming in quick gasps as if he had been running.

"I love you. I want to be with you. To marry you. Will you marry me?"

And then the tears came. Stephanie wrapped her arms around his shoulders and pulled his face down and kissed him. He could feel her tears running down his collar and was sure there were tears on his own face. He heard her voice buzzing in his head, whispering, breathing, saying, "Yes, yes, yes."

CHAPTER 30

Saturday 21st/Sunday 22nd December

Robert stayed up late, watching *Run, Lola, Run* on Sky Movies. It was a movie he loved, a German movie with three different endings, so you got to see how things might have been if only things had been done a little differently.

The remainder of Saturday had passed in a blur. Since making the commitment to Stephanie, he felt as if a huge weight had been lifted off his shoulders. Bizarrely, he wanted to phone people and tell them his good news, his great news: he was in love with a woman who loved him.

No decisions had been made, Stephanie had been satisfied that he'd made the commitment. She'd been laughing, crying, and when they'd walked back to her apartment complex on the canal, they'd strode along with their old energy. She'd invited him in, but he resisted the temptation: once they were inside, he knew they would end up in bed together and for some indefinable reason, he felt that would be unfair on her. Standing by the gate she kissed him, lovingly, passionately, and thanked him.

"For what?" he asked.

"For making me happy."

It was half past midnight when the movie finished. The house was silent. Kathy had gone to bed early, claiming another of her interminable headaches. The children had drifted off to bed much later. Robert moved around the house, checking the doors, pulling out plugs, turning off lights. Who would do this when he was gone? He was startled to find himself thinking this already. He climbed the stairs and turned off the landing light, then stepped into the bedroom, closing the door gently behind him. He undressed in the dark, tossing his clothes onto the back of the chair and slid into bed, sighing as his head hit the pillow. This was a day he was not going to forget.

"I went to see Maureen today."

Kathy's voice startled him; he thought she was long asleep.

He doubted there was any possibility of sleep tonight – he was too wired with thoughts and emotions – but the last thing he wanted to do was to chat about Maureen. Besides, once the news broke, Maureen would have no hold – real or imagined – over him. He could let her go without a second thought. It would be a chance to make a clean sweep and start afresh in the office too. Maybe Stephanie could join him in the business. That was an exciting thought. He shifted in the bed to look at Kathy. He could see her wide-open eyes sparkling in the dim reflected streetlight. "How is she?"

"Getting better. But she won't be back till the New Year."

"Didn't think so," he mumbled.

"She's not as young as she pretends to be."

"I know that." Maureen sometimes thought – and dressed – as if she was in her twenties. He shifted again, rolling onto his back. "This new girl, the Russian . . ."

"Illona?"

"Yes, Illona." He was vaguely surprised that Kathy still remembered the girl's name. "She's very good. Does what she's told, gives no cheek, is in on time, takes exactly an hour for lunch. Maureen does it her way, treats me like a boy and has no concept of a one-hour lunch."

"You're not thinking about sacking her, are you?"

"I've been thinking about it," he admitted.

"I'll not have it," Kathy snapped. "I forbid it."

"Forbid it?" He was genuinely shocked. He bit back the crack of anger in his voice. "You *forbid* it?"

"I still own half the company, remember? Maybe it's time I reminded you of that. Maybe it's time I started to take a more active interest in it." She sat up in bed and snapped on the light.

Robert groaned and shielded his eyes. "It's after one, for Christ's sake! Can we talk about this in the morning?"

Although the company was in both their names, he ran it, he did all the work; he'd always thought of it as his business. Kathy had a perfect right – a legal right – to query any decisions and even veto ones she didn't approve of. So, what happened now . . . but in truth, he knew what happened now. Exactly what had happened to Jimmy. Kathy would want half of it. Maybe he could do a deal with the house. . .

"Now that the children are older," said Kathy, "I'm thinking in the New Year I might start coming in with you three or four times a week. Even when Maureen comes back she's not going to be able to work full time. I can go back to doing what I used to do: help you run the company. Put the K back into R&K Productions."

This was getting worse! Much worse. He rubbed dry lips with an equally dry tongue. "Where are you going to find the time?"

"I'll make the time. I'll concentrate on getting new business; you concentrate on making the material."

"Yea, that would be great, I'm sure. Let's talk about it in the morning." He didn't want this conversation to proceed. He needed time to think through the ramifications of what he was hearing.

"Maureen suggested that things were not going too well for the company."

Robert shuffled up in the bed. "Can we talk about it in the morning?"

"We rarely get a chance to talk any more, Robert, have you realised that? We're running in opposite directions."

That was hardly some newsflash! "It's only temporarily, and it's Christmas," he said. "That always brings its own madness." He closed his eyes, trying to end the conversation, but Kathy pressed on.

"No, it's not temporarily and it's not just Christmas. We've been doing it for months, maybe longer. I rarely see you any more. You're home late four nights out of five, you go in at the weekends, and when you are home, you're locked in your room, working."

So she had noticed. Where was this coming from, what had brought it on? He shrugged. "It's been busy. I'll admit that."

"Put my mind at ease: tell me the business is going well."

This had to have something to do with Maureen. What had that bitch told her? First thing in the morning, he was going to tear up the Christmas bonus cheque. "We've gone through a rough patch, but I've landed a few new accounts. We're OK again. Next year will be good."

"Does that mean you'll end up working all the hours God sends next year too?"

Next year would definitely be different, he promised himself, but not in ways she would expect. "While the work is there, I'll do it. I don't have an option. It's one of the joys of being self-employed. You know that."

"Then I'm even more determined to help you. Starting in the New Year, you've got a new employee: me. You can give your Russian girl notice."

Fuck that! Robert made a face and shook his head. She'd been out of the business this long: she could now stay out of it. What he believed he was hearing was some sort of guilty conscience talking.

"What's wrong?" she asked.

"Nothing is wrong." He was getting annoyed with this nonsense. "Here's what will happen. You'll come to work with me for a week, maybe two, then you'll have to take time off to be home here for

211

some reason. Then you'll take more and more time off, and soon enough, you'll be back to the way we are now. Except I'll have to go looking for a secretary again."

"You sound as if you don't want me to work with you."

"I didn't say that. I'd love you to be more interested in the business," he lied. But her offer was coming at least two years, or three years or even five years too late. He lifted the clock off the bedside locker and held it up before her face. "Look at the time. Can we please continue this in the morning?"

"OK," she agreed, turning off her light and sliding down beneath the covers. "But we will continue it."

He heard what sounded like a threat in her voice.

"Absolutely," he said.

That settled it: there would definitely be no sleep for him that night. The rational part of his mind knew that he should not be getting upset with Kathy because she was offering to help him. On any other day of the year, he might have been delighted that she'd finally decided to become his partner again. Obviously something Maureen had told her had twinged her conscience: maybe she had revealed just how rocky things were, just how hard he worked to keep the business afloat. However, right now he was more concerned with her reminders that she was half of R&K. He was going to need legal advice on this one. He didn't want to end up in a stupid and expensive litigious process; he was rather hoping they would be able to decide things amicably.

That same voice, the little conscience voice deep in his skull, started to laugh hysterically. He was about to separate from his wife of eighteen years and he hoped they would do it amicably? She'd take him for everything he had.

And he couldn't really blame her.

It was dawn when he finally rolled out of bed, jittery and exhausted, eyes gritty with sleep, not-quite-a-headache occupying the back of his skull. Gathering up some clothes, he bundled them into the en-suite and dressed there, unwilling to wake Kathy. He simply did not want to talk to her; he did not know what to say. He dashed off a quick note and left it on the pillow.

"*Gone into the office to finish off some work. Will be home later. Love R.*"

Writing "Love R" was a habit, and this time he hesitated before scribbling it. It wasn't that he did not love Kathy, he decided, he just didn't love her enough. Not as much as he loved Stephanie.

CHAPTER 31

Monday 23rd December

Robert had been on the treadmill for fifteen minutes and had worked up a sweat when Stephanie came out of the changing rooms and joined him on the machine next to his. She gripped the handles and hit the button to turn the machine on. The narrow pad beneath her feet started to move and she fell into an easy pace on it.

"Sorry I'm late. The office is closing today and there were drinks in the boardroom."

"No problem. I got your message. Any issues in work about . . ."

"About us? Nothing. No mentions. And I did hear on the grapevine that it looks as if you got the DaBoyz gig."

"That's great, I think! I was meaning to ask you about that. Theresa said that two of the lads are gay."

Stephanie shook her head. "I've not heard. Wouldn't surprise me. Is that a problem?"

"Not at all. But she also said she heard on MTV that they are thinking of breaking up."

"They were. That's why this single is so important. There's been a lot of investment in this group, and the investors are unwilling to cut loose their investment without one last shot. That's you by the way. Do the pop video right and you will have saved a lot of people a lot of money. Screw it up however and you'll never work in this town again," she laughed.

"I'm not sure whether you're joking or serious."

"A bit of both, I think. You'll do a great job. Remember, I've staked my career on it."

"So, no pressure there then," he murmured.

"And I'm sorry about yesterday. I really wanted to see you, but I'd already agreed to go shopping with Sally before . . ."

Robert glanced sidelong at her and smiled. "Before?"

"Before us." She was wearing a simple black leotard under a black jogging pants. He loved the way it showed off her flawless skin.

"It was probably just as well. It gave me a chance to get a lot done in the office. If you and I had got together, we would have . . ."

Now it was her turn to look sidelong. "What would we have done?"

"Talked. Planned."

"I know. You've made me so happy. Even Sally is pleased."

Robert bit the inside of his cheek to prevent a comment he knew would only cause an argument. "One of these days I'd like to meet this mysterious Sally."

"She's looking forward to meeting you too. I've told her a lot about you."

Robert had never met Stephanie's friend and confidante, Sally. All he knew was that Sally had not approved of him and had done her best to separate them. "I supposed she was surprised by the news."

"Surprised. She was stunned. I said we'd get together after Christmas and celebrate. She's paying."

"Good idea." Robert eased up the controls on the side of his treadmill, increasing the speed. "Why is she paying?"

"Because she once bet me the best meal money could buy that you would never leave your wife for me."

"Well, let's make sure that's an expensive bet. I'll book Shanahan's on the Green myself for this one."

"Have you given any further thought to Christmas?" Stephanie asked.

Robert frowned, wondering where this was leading. "I've thought about nothing else," he said truthfully.

"Will you spend Christmas Day with me?"

Robert increased the speed of the machine again. The humming whine would make conversation difficult. "Ah, no." He caught the flicker of disappointment on her face. "Be reasonable." Realising that some of the other patrons of the gym were looking in their direction, he discovered that he'd raised his voice. He leaned across to Stephanie. "Be reasonable. I can hardly go to Kathy and the kids tonight or tomorrow and say, 'Guess what? I'm leaving. Happy Christmas.' Can I?"

Stephanie nodded. "No, of course not."

"But I will see you tomorrow. And I'll get down on Christmas Day," he added, though he was not exactly sure what excuse he'd use to get out of the house. Maybe say the office alarm had gone off, something like that.

Stephanie patted at her forehead with the towel draped around her neck. "And when do you intend telling her?"

"I was thinking the twenty-seventh, which is Friday."

"Why not Thursday?"

"Well, we're committed to going down to her sister's for dinner. All the arrangements have been made."

"So what do I do for Christmas Day; hang around until you appear?"

Robert ignored the question. "I will tell her on Friday and I will spend New Year's Eve with you. We will see in the New Year together. It will be the start of a new year for us too. Come on – meet me halfway on this. This is a big decision, a huge move for me to make. You've only got yourself to think of; I've got Kathy and the kids to consider."

Stephanie nodded. "You're right, of course. Absolutely right. Another couple of days is not going to make that much difference to us, is it? And Christmas Day is just another Wednesday."

They moved off the treadmills and onto the bikes. Stephanie set a high gear and began to pedal, the muscles in her legs pushing hard as the covered wheel whirred around. Robert pedalled at an easier pace.

"I need a little advice however."

Stephanie looked at him. "What sort of advice?"

"It's about the company. R&K Productions. You know the K stands for Kathy and that she has a fifty-per cent share in it."

"I know that."

"I was wondering if you would like to join with me in the company, take over Kathy's share. We could call it R&S Productions. That is, if I can buy Kathy out, of course."

He thought Stephanie was looking at him in surprise and she took a long moment before she replied. "I'm not sure I'd want to give up my present position. I would think going to work in your company might be seen as a retrograde step, career-wise."

For a moment, Robert thought she was joking. He even started to laugh, until he realised that she was deadly serious.

"The other thing we'll have to bear in mind is that I will not be able to put any more business your way. It would not look good for me to be seen to be pushing business to my partner's company."

He was shocked. "No more business . . ."

"Not from me. But I'll keep my ear to the ground. I'll keep you well up to speed with what happening; there'll be no problems."

Robert felt his head spin. Yesterday, sitting in the cold office, trying to get through to Stephanie, and only getting her machine, he'd doodled new R&S logos on the computer, interlocking R's and S's, symbolically entwined. And with the relationship between himself and Stephanie out in the open, he imagined there would be no problem with her sending him clients. Which was a good thing, because he reckoned he was going to need the extra money to pay off Kathy.

"Anyway," Stephanie continued, "I was thinking you might close R&K."

"What?"

"Get a job with one of the big companies."

Robert concentrated on the pedalling. He'd spent most of his adult life building up R&K, and now she was suggesting closing it down!

"It would be easier on you mentally and physically," she continued. "There would be a regular pay cheque, and you could walk out at five thirty or six and not have to think about it again until the following morning. Your weekends would be yours again."

"I'd be working for someone. I've been my own boss for a long time."

"At the moment you're working for Kathy and the children and the bank. They're your boss. This way you end up with more free time; time to spend with me. Time to spend with your children," she added.

And Robert admitted it was a persuasive argument. Ironically, he'd even broached something similar with Kathy a year previously. Then it was her reminding him of the huge investment in time and money he had put into the firm over the years. He started laughing, a dry rasp, which turned into a cough.

Stephanie climbed off the bike and thumped his back. "Are you all right?"

"I'm fine. I was just thinking . . ."

"Thinking what?"

"Thinking that you're some sort of catalyst. Change happens around you."

Stephanie leaned into him, pushing her breasts against his chest. "We make our own changes, but sometimes you just need someone or something to do a little nudging. Now, I'm going to get changed."

Robert watched her move across the floor, hips swaying. One or two of the other men in the huge gym also turned to follow her progress. He was surprised to discover that he did not feel jealous of their interest in her. They knew she was with him, which meant that they were jealous of him.

He climbed stiffly off the bike and rotated his back. Christ: but when changes came, they were like buses – all together. Here he was, forty-two years of age and already thinking of a new woman, a new home and a new job. All he needed was a child to complete the set.

"Well, I'd like children," Stephanie said as they came through the door of the gym and out into the bitter night air. Robert had mentioned his realisation as they walked across the foyer towards the entrance. He expected her to laugh; instead she took him seriously.

"When would you like to have them?" he wondered. He felt her hand slip into his and he opened his fingers, entwining them.

"Not immediately, of course. Well, it's a bit of a Catch-22. I'm thirty-five now. I can't wait too long and yet, I need another two years at least before I'm promoted. Then we could start trying for the year after that."

The little perverse imp that seemed to be his constant companion these days reminded him that he and Kathy had tried for children immediately after they'd married, and she had cut back on her hours in the office the moment she learned she'd become pregnant.

The cars were parked alongside one another in the darkened corner of the carpark. They hit the alarm toggles together and both sets of lights blinked simultaneously.

Robert opened the door of Stephanie's silver BMW for her. The roof light popped on, flooding the interior in soft pearl light, washing over the leather seats. Stephanie threw her gym bag onto the passenger seat, then turned to Robert. She wrapped her arms around his neck, pressed the palm of her right hand against the back of his skull to bring his head down to a level with hers. "Think of all the fun we'll have practising to conceive children," she whispered. Then she kissed him. Robert responded by dropping his gym bag to the ground and pulling her close. He loved the feel of this woman in his arms, the heat of her, the strength of her. He adored the pressure of his lips on hers. He loved her passion.

Finally they broke apart and Stephanie climbed into the car. She waved once and drove away. Robert picked up his bag and moved around the front of the car. His phone rang. He fished it out of his jacket pocket and answered without looking at the screen.

"Hi, it's me," Kathy's voice crackled across a surprisingly clear connection. He thought she sounded in good humour for a change. "I'm just wondering what time you'll be home?"

Robert checked his watch. "I'm just leaving the office. I should be there in about forty minutes."

When he hung up, he suddenly found himself wondering why he had told the stupid lie. She knew he went to the gym, it was no secret. But he just supposed he'd got into the habit of lying to Kathy. It was time to start telling the truth.

But not tonight.

Not tonight.

BOOK 3

The Mistress's Story

Of course I knew he was married. I knew he was lying to his wife about us, and I knew, in my heart and soul, that he was also lying to me.

But I loved him.

Or I thought I loved him.

CHAPTER 32

Thursday 19th December

Stephanie Burroughs ran the back of her hand down the length of the raw silk tie. It hissed against her skin. She glanced up at the young woman standing behind the counter. The girl was staring at her blankly, a professional smile fixed on her lips, but with that empty expressionless face of someone who is desperately tired.

"Long day?" Stephanie asked sympathetically, folding the tie back into its box.

"Long week," the girl murmured, glancing around quickly to make sure her supervisor was nowhere near. "And no end in sight."

Stephanie put the two boxes side by side on the counter and compared the ties – one a deep powerful crimson, the other a rich gold – and tried to choose between them.

"You're not off for the weekend?"

"I wish!" the girl said, obviously grateful for someone to talk to. "But with Christmas not falling until Wednesday, we're working right through until Christmas Eve."

"What time will you finish then?"

"Probably five thirty. Christmas Eve is always incredibly busy as people rush in for last-minute presents."

"When are you back?"

"We're open again on Friday. But I've got the following Monday off," the girl added with a smile, "and Wednesday, New Year's Day, of course. Then we're back to normal. December is the longest month."

Stephanie smiled understandingly and handed over the two ties. "I'll take both," she said. She felt suddenly sorry for the shop assistant forced to spend long hours on a shop floor for a mediocre wage. She'd never really thought about working in a retail environment where you started at nine and finished at five thirty or six, with a late night on Thursday and open at the weekend. She thought it must be like prison. When she'd come out of college, she'd drifted into the world of television research, which more or less allowed her to set her own pace. Now, as Senior Accounts Manager for one of the largest advertising agencies in the world, she was moving steadily along a career path that often demanded long hours, but equally allowed a lot of free time, and when the work came up, she could do it in her own time. And it paid very well. December for her was turning out to be a remarkably short month. There were only a few bits and pieces of work to complete, then the office closed on Monday and would not reopen until the second of January

"Cash or charge?"

"Charge." Stephanie handed over her American Express card.

The shop assistant made the sale and slipped the two long rectangular tie boxes into a black bag. "A Christmas present?" she asked.

Stephanie nodded. "For someone special," she smiled. "Happy Christmas."

"I'm sure he'll love them. Happy Christmas."

Stephanie Burroughs wandered out into Grafton Street and allowed herself to be carried along by the crowd. She had a few small items to get and wanted to pop into BT's. She knew Robert would like the ties; she'd seen him wearing the ones she'd bought him over the past few months. They matched the Pinks shirts he'd initially been so sceptical about. She still hadn't picked him up his "big" present and, as time went by, she was finding him more and more difficult to buy for. He had the unfortunate habit of buying himself whatever he wanted. She'd had her eye on a new personal digital assistant for him, one of the ultra-slim Palm Tungsten's PDA's, but then he'd gone and bought himself the XDA combination phone and PDA. He had the latest in cameras – he'd got a new one the previous Christmas. She was now thinking about the Apple iPod, the tiny box no bigger than a cigarette package which held thousands of songs and hours of music. The only problem was, he simply did not listen much to music. She found that absolutely astonishing. For her, music was one of the great joys of life. It went everywhere with her, it played through each room in her home, even the loo, on her computer, her laptop, in the car, in the office. She owned thousands of CD's; she thought he might own ten. For an otherwise remarkable and creative man, she found it a curious lack in his character.

Stephanie pushed her way into BT's. She loved the new look of the shop, she thought it was much more open and welcoming and no matter how busy the shop was, there always seemed to be space to move around. She headed up the stairs towards the men's department.

The other problem was that she loved to buy him presents. She didn't need an excuse or an event, and over the course of their eighteen-month relationship, she hadn't let a month go by without buying him something.

And he had done the same for her.

But this would be their second Christmas together and she was determined to outdo herself. So far she'd got him some shirts in a nice Oxford weave, and now she had these ties to match. She'd picked up a stunning book of aerial photographs of the world, which she thought he'd like, and a little book of *Celtic Wisdom for Business*, which was full of inspirational quotes and sayings, which she thought might make a nice stocking-filler, but she needed just one more present, something special . . .

Of course, she could always do as she'd done last year: wrap herself up in tinsel and bows and present herself as his Christmas present. They'd both enjoyed unwrapping that present.

She touched the Louis Vuitton handbag he'd given her. It was incredibly impractical and the butter-soft black leather attracted scratches and nicks like a magnet, but she adored the weight and feel of it . . . and the envious looks of the other girls in the office, or women walking down the street who recognised it for what it was.

Stephanie dipped into her handbag and pulled out a tiny Siemens phone. Robert was the first number on her list. She tried his direct line in the office, bypassing Illona on the reception desk, but the phone rang out. She glanced at the clock: three thirty. A little early to have closed the office. She cancelled the call and tried his mobile.

It rang for twelve rings and she rang off before it transferred to his answering machine. She'd catch him later.

Stephanie wandered through the men's department in BT's. What exactly did you get the man who had everything he wanted and wanted nothing? Clothes certainly, but they weren't exactly the most exciting of presents, and he didn't play golf. He had no real hobbies as far as she could determine: his entire life revolved around his work.

Finding nothing in BT's, she left the shop, and manoeuvred her way across the street towards Weir's the jeweller's. Maybe a watch. A watch wasn't really jewellery. Watches tended to fall into two types, very thin or very chunky and she wondered which one he would prefer. Maybe something in silver, with lots of dials and buttons – he was just like a big kid that way. She nodded, seeing her reflection in the shop-window mirror the movement. A watch, a diver's watch, with three dials and a rotating bezel, silver with a black face . . .

Then came the little practical thought, the one which now

accompanied, touched and tainted everything she bought him: would he be able to wear it without his wife noticing, and asking questions about where he got it?

She sighed, her breath misting the glass before her face. Who would have thought that buying a present would be so complicated, and would have so many conditions attached?

Robert said that his wife had no interest in him – and Stephanie believed him. She saw absolutely no signs that Kathy showed any interest in his work or whereabouts, but that didn't mean that the woman wouldn't notice if he turned up wearing a nice chunky watch. She supposed he could always say it was a gift from a client. But she didn't want that: she wanted him to be able to wear it and say: 'My girlfriend gave me this.'

Girlfriend sounded better than mistress, she thought.

Maybe not a watch then. She pushed away from Weir's window, crossed Grafton Street again and stepped into the Grafton Arcade, which she used as a short cut, via Hodges Figgis bookshop, to make her way out into Dawson Street. The bookshop was absolutely jammed with people, and she thought it was such a shame he read so little that books were a limited option. He claimed he simply had no time. She'd bought him some books on CD for the car stereo for his birthday earlier in the year, but she'd noted the last time she sat in his car that they were still in their plastic wrappers, unopened.

OK then, what about a print, or a nice original painting? But, although they shared an interest in so many things, they were diametrically opposed in others, especially art. She preferred modern art: bright primary daubs of colours. She loved the energy and emotion they conveyed. He preferred – if he had any real preference that is – photo-realism.

Besides, if she got him a picture or a print, where would he hang it? It came back to the same question, one she was beginning to tire of asking: what would his wife say? He could hardly bring it home and hang it on the wall, could he?

She turned to the right as she came out of the bookshop and headed up Dawson Street, glancing cursorily in the windows of the shops as she hurried past. An overcoat was an option – something in mohair perhaps, or a nice briefcase, a wallet, pens . . .

She stopped and grinned. She was getting desperate and stupid. She could hardly give her lover a fancy biro, could she? Besides, last year he had given her a magnificent antique gold pendant inset with a chip of opal as big as her thumbnail. And for her birthday recently, he'd given her a fabulous modern silver bracelet. He took time to look for and choose her presents. The final option would be a voucher, but she hated giving vouchers for presents, because they were so impersonal.

His wife had given him a voucher last year; that's what he told her.

Stephanie felt her cheery mood slip a little. Some days she felt as if she was living with Kathy Walker! Glancing up and down the street, she darted across the road almost directly across from the Mansion House. A Salvation Army band was gathered around the huge Christmas tree set up outside and the rich sounds of trumpets and cymbals were just audible over the noise of the traffic.

Lately, she'd discovered that Robert's wife was never too far from her thoughts. At times like these, when she was buying Robert a present, she'd find herself wondering what Kathy was going to get him for Christmas, or what she'd got him for his birthday. Sometimes she even found herself wondering what Robert was giving his wife.

When she'd first begun her relationship with Robert, it hadn't been a problem. She knew he was married; but she also knew that he was emotionally separated from a woman who seemed to have stopped caring for him. He was attracted to her and she to him, and they were two adults, and so long as they were hurting no-one . . .

Stephanie turned left at the top of Dawson Street, heading for the Shelbourne.

Also, when she'd started the relationship, she never expected it to last. She gave it three months, maybe six at the outside. She'd never thought about his wife or children, of that other life he had with them, a life apart from her. As time went by, and she had slowly, inexorably, almost unconsciously fallen in love with him, she did what every woman in love with a man did: she wanted to know everything about him. His likes and dislikes, his dreams, his plans, his past . . . and that's where it became complicated, because Robert's past was still very much with him, wrapped around a wife and two children, a home on the other side of the city and a job that he obsessed about.

Shit! Why did she have to go and fall in love with him?

Because you're a fool.

You don't fall in love with a married man.

She'd given the same answer to girlfriends who had ended up in similar situations, and she'd always sworn she was not going to make the same mistake.

You don't fall in love with a married man.

But she had.

The fading notes of the Sally Army trumpets sounded like mocking laughter following her down the street.

CHAPTER 33

The apartment was still and silent as she pushed open the door, then picked up her shopping off the step and carried it into the hall. Old Mrs Moore, Stephanie's neighbour, was watching from her sitting-room window directly across the courtyard and for a single instant she had the mad temptation to wave at her. But the woman was better than a burglar alarm; she phoned the police at the slightest intimation that something was amiss. Three weeks ago, catching sight of two young men skulking along the canal, she'd called the local station and a roaming Garda car had stopped the two men for questioning. They were found to be carrying gloves, screwdrivers, and masking tape in their bag. They claimed they were apprentice carpenters. They found it slightly more difficult to explain the dozen twists of silver paper containing heroin and an assortment of credit cards in different names in the same bag. The local sergeant had called to personally thank Mrs Moore for her assistance. Since then Mrs Moore had assumed the role of security guard for the small apartment and townhouse complex. Stephanie made a note to get her a nice Christmas present.

She hit the button on the answering machine and listened to

the messages as she unpacked the few groceries she'd picked up on her way home. Robert always teased her because she had so little food in the house, but she rarely ate there – snacked, breakfasted, had tea and supper certainly, but she'd never cooked a full meal in the oven. That's why God invented the microwave.

"Stef . . . this is your mother. Are you there? Why aren't you there?"

Stephanie pulled open the fridge and added the half litre of low-fat milk to the tray in the door, alongside the half-empty carton of pure orange juice and the unopened bottle of champagne. She hated when people called her Stef.

"You're probably out enjoying yourself . . ."

Stephanie shook her head in resignation. No matter how many occasions she'd explained to her mother about the time difference between Dublin and New York, Toni Burroughs never quite got it. Sometimes she was sure her mother thought she was living in Australia.

"I was just checking to make sure that you were not going to come home for Christmas . . ."

Stephanie added yoghurts to the fridge. She had told her mother at least a dozen times that she would be staying in Ireland for Christmas. One year – just one – she had made the mistake of returning to the family home on Long Island for the holiday and every year thereafter her mother had phoned and put pressure – subtle and none too subtle – on her to come again.

"All your brothers and sisters will be here. Your cousins too."

Stephanie Burroughs had grown up on Long Island, the daughter of a college professor and a high school teacher. The family were staunchly Catholic and the seven children, four boys and three girls, had grown up in a four-bedroom house, in a Catholic neighbourhood living a quiet, respectable version of the American dream. There was only a twelve-year age difference between the oldest, Bill, and the youngest, Joan. Stephanie fell more or less in the middle of the group and had somehow managed to avoid the cliques, pairings and groups that form in any large family. That had left her feeling slightly distant from the rest of her extended family who seemed to spend an inordinate amount of time living in one another's pockets. She had always felt like the outsider, which had actually made it easier, much easier, to leave home and move away, first to New York, then Chicago. She was also the first member of the family to leave the country and was now, at the ripe old age of thirty-five, the last one left unmarried. Billy was on his third wife, much to their mother's disgust.

"Your father went online last night and discovered some late availability of tickets. If there's a problem with money, you know he will send it on to you . . ."

Stephanie poured herself a glass of water from the filter jug and shook her head. Including salary, bonuses and expenses, she drew down about one hundred and fifty thousand euro a year. She – and the bank – were buying this townhouse, she owned her own car, went on frequent holidays, ate out regularly, went to the theatre, cinema and the gym whenever she wished. She flew business or first class, and was probably the most successful and financially secure of all of the Burroughs children and yet somehow Toni still thought of her daughter as a secretary or a lowly researcher earning a pittance. Also, because she was not married with at least one child, Stephanie knew her mother was seriously worried about her. The last time she'd been home – for Thanksgiving the previous year – Toni had arranged for a string of young and eligible and not-so-young and even less eligible men to troop through the house in a very unsubtle attempt at matchmaking.

"It would be lovely to see you. Maybe if you ask nicely, your bosses would give you a little extra time off. Tell them you'll make it up to them in the New Year."

She still had ten days' holidays left to take out of this year's allocation. She was going to try and carry them forward into the

New Year. If she could persuade Robert to take a few days off, she might take him to NY and they could travel out to Long Island to meet her parents. She stopped, suddenly struck by the thought. Meeting the parents: that was a very formal thing to do. She knew they would both adore him – a successful Irish businessman, a few years older than her. But you only introduced your young man to your parents if you were serious about him. And then she smiled, and her face lit up. She guessed she was serious about him – then the smile faded slightly – and becoming increasingly serious as time went by.

"*Well, ring me if you get a chance, but I guess you're worked off your feet over there. You might ring on Christmas Eve. All the family will be here, your brothers and sisters and their wives and children. We'll have a full house here . . .*"

Here it comes, Stephanie thought, and mouthed the words along with her mother.

" *. . . all except you, of course.*"

Stephanie lay back in the thick foaming bubble bath and pressed her mobile phone to her ear. "So then she said, '*We'll have a full house here, all except you, of course.*' Talk about emotional blackmail!"

Sally Wilson, Stephanie's oldest friend, laughed delightedly. "My mother is exactly the same. Mothers the world over are the same. I'm sure they take lessons."

Stephanie lifted her leg out of the water and allowed the bubbles to run down her smooth skin. Putting the bath into the townhouse had been outrageously expensive, but money very well spent. After a long day on your feet, nothing beat a bath. "But you know, for half a moment there, I was actually tempted. It would be fun to go home, be with all the family one more time. I'm really conscious that both Mom and Dad are getting older."

"Well, why don't you?" Sally asked, seriously. There was a

sharp intake of breath and Stephanie clearly heard the crackle of cigarette paper burning. She could just visualise Sally standing outside a pub or bar somewhere, drink in one hand, cigarette in the other.

"Why don't I what?"

"Why don't you get on a plane Christmas Eve, go over and surprise everyone? Don't tell anyone you're coming. Just turn up."

"Oh, but I couldn't!"

"Why not? What's stopping you?" Sally asked sharply. "I bet your mother would be thrilled to see you."

"Absolutely. I'm sure she would."

"And you said yourself, as times go by, one of these Christmases will be their last."

"I know."

"But . . .?" Sally prompted.

"But what about Robert?" Stephanie squeezed her eyes shut as soon as she mentioned her lover's name. She knew what was coming.

"Oh yes, Robert," Sally said coldly and Stephanie could just visualise her sucking hard on the cigarette. "Let's see: I wonder where Robert will be. Oh, I know: Robert will be at home with his wife and children. As he was last year and the year before that, as he will be next year and the year after that."

Stephanie sat up and reached for the glass of mineral water perched on the edge of the bath. "You really don't like him, do you?" she said brightly, trying to avoid another argument with Sally over Robert.

"Not much. No."

"He's a really nice man. One of these days I'm going to get you together."

"I'm sure he's a wonderful man, pats dogs, gives money to the Church, kisses his children and loves his wife too. While he's lying to her, of course."

Stephanie sighed.

"I'm sorry," Sally said immediately. "I don't want to have a fight with you. I just don't want to see you sitting home on Christmas Eve hoping for an hour with Robert, and then waiting in all day Christmas Day for a visit that will not happen. That's all."

"I know," Stephanie sighed. And she did know. It had been slipping in and out of her thoughts as Christmas approached: what was she going to do on Christmas Day? She remembered last Christmas; she had never felt so lonely, so lost, so alone in all her life. "I know you're right. I've been meaning to have a chat with him about it."

"Better do it soon, sweetie – less than a week to go to the big day," Sally advised.

"Tomorrow night. We're having dinner. I'll talk about it to him over dinner."

"OK then. What are your plans for tonight?"

"Absolutely none. I took a half-day, then walked the feet off myself, looking for a present for Robert, but with no success. What are you getting Dave?"

"I've got him a nice leather jacket, plus the *Star Wars* DVD boxed set. He has them on video, but I know he'll watch them on DVD and enjoy them all over again. He's nothing but a big kid."

"You're lucky; at least your Dave watches movies and reads. My Robert does neither."

"Your Robert is a peculiar fish," Sally agreed. Stephanie braced herself for another diatribe, but then Sally said, "Gotta go. Dave is here. Talk to you tomorrow."

She rang off and Stephanie switched off her own phone. She was sure there was a distinct tone of sarcasm in Sally's voice when she used the phrase "*your Robert*". Because, of course, he was not "*her*" Robert, he was someone else's Robert.

Sally and Robert had never met; Stephanie deliberately kept them apart. Sally made no secret of her dislike for Robert: he was a married man playing around with a single woman. She'd been tough on Stephanie too, reminding her how stupid she was taking up with someone like him. The two women fought and Stephanie's relationship with Robert almost cost them their friendship. Finally, she came to her senses and realised that Sally was only looking out for her, was only trying to save her friend from what she saw as inevitable pain and heartache.

And she had been stupid, she knew that. She'd broken one of her own long-standing rules: don't get between another woman and her man. There were plenty more men out there. But not like Robert; Robert was different.

Stephanie sat forward and reached down to add more hot water to the bath. She tossed in bath salts and the slightly spicy odour of green tea permeated the damp air. She stretched out in the bath, resting her head back on the foam pillow. Over her right shoulder a short fat candle guttered out. The original layout of the townhouse came with a power shower but no bath. Before she'd moved in, Stephanie had brought in a team of interior designers to reconfigure part of the second bedroom and incorporate it into the bathroom, effectively taking a corner off the unused bedroom and creating a larger bathroom. She'd gone for a country estate look for the room: an antique-style free-standing bath, treated to look like copper, standing in the centre of the terracotta floor, while hand-painted tiles covered three of the walls, and the fourth was covered with a mural which gave the impression of a door opening out onto a Tuscan landscape. When she'd had a particularly stressful day, she'd fill the bath almost to the brim, add green tea or Dead Sea Salts, light some candles and just lie back and stare at the mural. Within moments, she could feel the stupid tensions and anxieties of the day drifting away.

The irony was, of course, when she'd first met Robert six years previously, she hadn't really liked him. He wasn't especially handsome, he was certainly arrogant and brusque to the point of rudeness and he seemed very much under the thumb of his wife and Maureen, the old dragon of a secretary who effectively ran the company.

She'd been aware even then that relations had been strained between himself and his wife. He was very careful not to say anything directly about it, but she picked up enough by what he said, and how he said it. She learned more by simply listening to Kathy and Maureen talk about him: it was obvious that neither woman respected him and she did feel sorry for him.

Stephanie had been brought in to do the research for what seemed like a simple premise for a TV show – *One Hundred Years Ago On This Day*: events from the last century presented as if they were contemporary news pieces, but with a strong Irish bias. It should have been a straightforward gig, but the pieces had to be intensively researched and every fact had to be spot on inasmuch as R&K Productions were hoping to sell on the series to the Discovery Channel, and there was talk of a video and a companion book. None of which had ever transpired. The real problem was the number of programmes: they had secured a twelve-week run, five days a week, which came to sixty programmes. The more she researched, the more she found it was difficult to find interesting news for every day one hundred years ago. The past could be boring too and some days nothing happened, which made filling the two-minute slot difficult. The other problem was that Robert could not afford to get in another researcher, so she was absolutely swamped. That was when they first started working together, travelling all across Ireland, trying to shoot the Irish segments on site. She started to get to know him on those trips and was surprised to discover that beneath the bluster and the arrogance was a clever and sensitive man, who had traded dreams of producing important and worthy documentaries in return for putting bread on the table.

Eventually, she ended up practically producing the series herself: researching and writing the scripts, then finding the pictures and archive footage to match the words, even going out to the costume houses to find the costumes and jewellery needed for the dramatic reconstructions. Robert was so impressed that he gave her on-screen credit as writer and producer and took the executive producer role for himself. That screen credit had, in so many ways, kicked off her own career and she would be forever grateful for that.

She hadn't the slightest romantic or sexual interest in Robert then. She'd just been coming out of a relationship with a footballer, who was as poor as a church mouse when he was with her and allowed her to pay for everything, but as soon as he left, signed a multi-million pound sterling contract with an English club. Nowadays she saw him on the back and front pages of the tabloids practically every second week having committed another gaffe either on or off the field, and considered that she'd had a very lucky escape.

The gig had ended suddenly too, she remembered that. With still three weeks to run on her contract, he called her into the office on Monday morning . . . no, Tuesday, it was just after the Bank Holiday weekend. He gave her three weeks' money, plus a bonus of an extra two weeks' pay, and told her she was to finish up that day. He never gave any explanation, and it wasn't until years later, when she and Robert had become an item, that she discovered Kathy had accused her husband of having an affair with her. Talk about the shape of things to come!

With the two weeks' unexpected bonus, she'd taken a holiday in Spain, where she met a young woman who worked as a researcher on breakfast-time TV in Britain. They exchanged addresses, and six weeks later Stephanie was working on *Good Morning*, first as a researcher, then, when it was discovered that she had producer credits for *One Hundred Years*, as Associate Producer. She stuck at that for a year before joining one of the largest advertising agencies in the world. Again, it was through a fortuitous meeting: Charles Flintoff, the MD of the agency, was a guest of the show, and had been impressed by her. He offered her a job on the spot and she accepted.

Life was full of small instances, little moments where a simple decision had extraordinary consequences years down the road. If she had not taken the job as researcher with R&K, she would not have gone to Spain, would not have got the job on breakfast-time television, would not have met Charles and got her present position, which brought her back to Dublin, and back into Robert's world.

Two years ago, she returned to Dublin as the accounts manager for the agency. She'd been in the city less than a week when she bumped into Robert. They'd chatted about old times, then gone for a drink, in Dobbins of all places: not exactly the most romantic pub in Dublin. But that drink had led to dinner a few nights later. She wondered if that was when the affair really began, with that single drink in Dobbins.

CHAPTER 34

Stephanie stood in the kitchen, wrapped in her heavy quilted dressing-gown, waiting for the microwave to ping. A low-calorie, low-sodium, low-taste can-be-used-as-part-of-a-calorie-controlled-diet excuse for a meal spun slowly behind the glass. *"Instant Meal"* it said on the package: that meant it took fifteen minutes to cook, including standing time, which she now knew really translated as the time you spent standing in front of the microwave.

Her mobile rang and she automatically opened the microwave door before she realised what she was doing. She'd left her phone on top of the counter. Grinning, she snatched it up and glanced at the screen, seeing the three XXX's she used instead of his name, and felt her insides physically shift. Jesus: but she had it bad, she realised.

"Hi."

There was a crackle of static and she moved away from the microwave. "I was going to phone you later on. I missed you this evening."

She heard movement on the other end of the line, the signal dipping in and out. She wondered where he was now, what he looked like, what he was wearing.

"I know. I'm sorry," Robert said quietly.

She could tell immediately by the tone of his voice that he was at home. He always spoke to her in softer tones there, as if he was afraid of being overhead.

"I was working on the DaBoyz proposal. Then I decided to get away before traffic got too awful."

"How's it coming?" The DaBoyz contract was the biggest job she had so far managed to put his way and the one she had the most doubts about. He'd never shot a pop video before, and although she was sure he could, she was beginning to regret having done it. She left the kitchen and wandered into the sitting-room, curling up on the sofa.

"Good, I think. I'll make a good presentation."

"You can do it. I know you can."

"I hope so."

She heard it then, the self-doubt in his voice. "I've every confidence in you. It'll be a new direction for the company. Do one good pop video and you'll be the next big thing. All the bands will flock to your door." She wondered who she was trying to convince. This was DaBoyz' last chance. They were on the verge of splitting up and their manager, Eddie Carson, looked as if he was going to take one of the boys under his wing and manage him as a solo artist, and dump the rest.

"You're right. I know you're right. Thanks again for putting me onto it."

He sounded flat, beaten. She'd come to recognise the signs: he'd fought with Kathy. There was a time when she thought he was simply a coward, unwilling or unable to stand up to his wife. More recently, she'd understood that he didn't fight with her because he hated upsetting her. It had been a shocking revelation, because it begged the question: did he still have feelings for Kathy? He said he didn't, but . . .

"What's wrong?" she asked gently.

"Nothing."

"Yes, there is. I know there is."

"How can you tell?"

"Short sentences. When you're tired or bothered, you reply to me in short sentences."

"You and your college education," Robert said quickly, but she could hear the lift in his tone and she knew he was smiling.

"Nothing to do with college – besides I'm not sure *"The Interpretation of One's Lover's Moods"* is covered in media studies." She forced herself to keep her tone light and bantering. She needed him positive and focussed on the meeting in the morning. "So tell me, what's bothering you?"

"Oh, the usual. And I'm just tired. It's been a long day."

"And Kathy?" she pressed.

There was a long moment of silence, then he said, "She's not in great form. I saw her taking some tablets this evening; I think she may be coming down with something."

Stephanie opened her mouth to respond, but closed it tightly without saying a word. He knew there was a problem in their marriage, but simply refused to face it, and, more importantly, deal with it. He always made excuses for her: Kathy fought with him because she was tired, because she was ill, because she was upset. When was he going to realise that maybe she fought with him because it was the only form of communication open to her?

"You think I'm making excuses for her, don't you?" he snapped, his quick touch of temper surprising her. "I'm sorry. I shouldn't have said that," he added immediately in a much more conciliatory tone. "I'm tired. Yes, there were a few words this evening. But only to do with Christmas. It's the pressure of the season."

It was the opening she was looking for. "Am I going to get to see you over Christmas?" she asked. If he said no, then she might very well book that flight back home and surprise the family. It might be nice to have a family Christmas, especially when considering the lonely alternative. And at least if she went back to Long Island, it would most certainly not be lonely or quiet. It would be loud and joyous, with lots of shouting, arguments, and food. Lots and lots of food. Her mother would bring out the old photo albums, her father would set up the cine projector. She found herself nodding: it was beginning to look very attractive.

"Of course, you will," he said quickly.

"Any idea when?"

"Well, I'll see you on Christmas Eve. Give you your present. And then probably on Stephen's Day . . . no, not Stephen's Day, the day after."

"What's wrong with Thursday?" So, she wouldn't see him Wednesday or Thursday; maybe if she went online now she'd be able to book a ticket. Dublin-JFK direct would be good, but she could head home via London. There was bound to be a Heathrow-JFK flight. The microwave pinged and she uncurled from the sofa to return to the kitchen.

"We go down for dinner with Kathy's sister, Julia, on Stephen's Day. It's a tradition."

Spending Christmas with loved ones was also a tradition, she thought, but resisted the temptation to say it aloud. "I remember you did that last year. I think you said then it was going to be the last one you attended." She juggled the hot container out onto a plate and jabbed the top with a fork to allow steam to escape. The faint aroma of Indian spices filled the kitchen.

"I think I say that every year."

"Do you enjoy it?"

"No."

"So, given the choice: dinner with your sister-in-law, or spending time with me – what would it be?"

"No contest. Spending time with you," he said immediately.

"Then do it." But even as she was saying it, she knew that he was going to find a problem with the suggestion.

"It's not that easy."

"It is if you want it to be."

"You know I want it to be."

245

And suddenly she was tired of the sparring. She had to accept that she was not going to see him on those two days; this was part of the price of a relationship with a married man.

"I know you do. I'm sorry. I shouldn't tease you so. I guess I'm tired too. I'm seeing you tomorrow though?"

"That's what I wanted to talk to you about. I double-booked. I've got Jimmy Moran lined up for dinner tomorrow night. I'm really sorry. Blame it on the situation in the office. I thought Maureen had cancelled him and Illona never thought to check. I'm sorry."

"There's no problem." She was pleased she managed to keep her voice even and disguise her disappointment. "These things happen. Any sign of Maureen coming back?"

"January. Maybe. She cannot – or will not – give me a straight answer."

"You need to start thinking with your head rather than your heart on this one," Stephanie suggested. "And if you do manage to get the pop video gig, do you want someone who looks like a glamorous granny managing the front desk?"

"You're right. I know you're right." He sighed. "I'd sort of come to that decision myself. But I don't feel right letting her go before Christmas."

"You're too soft," Stephanie murmured. "Though I usually change that," she added quickly, her voice soft and husky, catching him off guard.

"You're bold!"

"Sometimes. So I won't see you tomorrow at all?"

"I've got the presentation to the band and their manager in the morning, then dinner in the evening."

"Do you want to stay over after dinner?"

"Maybe," he said coyly.

"Maybe," she laughed, the sound high and light. "Just maybe?"

"Would it be worth my while?" he asked.

"Absolutely," she promised.

"I'll see what I can do."

Stephanie carried her simple dinner back into the sitting-room. She hit the remote control on the arm of the chair and the CD clicked on. Medwyn Goodall's appropriately named "Timeless" filled the air. She loved the simple, ethereal music. She concentrated on the gently lilting guitars, and mechanically ate the meal, not tasting it, trying unsuccessfully not to rerun the conversation she'd just had.

Sally was right. Sally was always right when it came to men. Her friend had one rule: no married men. Sally had had scores of boyfriends, mostly casual acquaintances, and three very serious relationships in the fifteen years Stephanie had known her, but none of them with a married man. She even tried to keep her casual friendships with married or attached men to an absolute minimum. When Stephanie teased that platonic relationships were possible, Sally laughed at her, claiming that sooner or later platonic eventually drifted into sexual, and once sex entered a friendship, then everything changed.

It had certainly changed for her when she and Robert went to bed together. The sexual tension had been building for a while. She recognised what was happening a long time before he did. In those early days together, they would visit sites across Ireland, "scouting locations" they called it, and walk and talk together. She'd learned a lot about him on those walks, about the young man he'd been, full of dreams and plans and hopes for the future and she'd learned even more about the man he'd become, with no real plan and a lot of broken dreams, trapped in a loveless marriage, and a job that was slowly spiralling into the ground.

The first time they made love had been . . . extraordinary. He had been passionate and gentle, fearful of hurting her, terrified of letting go, and afterwards he had wept. She was never entirely sure why; he told her it was because he was happy and hadn't, until that moment, known he was unhappy. But she wasn't entirely sure if she believed him.

She never had any sense that she was taking him away from a loving wife. He was always incredibly loyal to Kathy, and never said anything against her, but from the little bits and pieces she had picked up on their walks and talks, she'd come to understand that a great gulf had opened up between them. If there had been no children, they might have split up and gone their separate ways, but their relationship – both Robert's and Kathy's – was wrapped around house and home, children and the business. It was complicated. He acted like a single man and Stephanie treated him like one. They made love because they wanted to; she didn't feel guilty, and neither did he. He was an old-fashioned and unimaginative lover, but he was considerate and she enjoyed the physical aspect of their relationship. She especially loved waking in his arms, feeling the warmth and comfort of them around her.

Stephanie pushed away the plate; she hadn't tasted a single mouthful. She climbed slowly to her feet and carried the plate out to the kitchen where she dropped it into the sink. She knew she should wash it now, but a growing numbing exhaustion had crept over her and all she wanted to do was to climb into bed and sleep. The CD had finished and the house was still and silent. She moved through the rooms, checking that the doors were locked and the lights were off. She recognised what was happening. It had taken her a long time to put a name to the emotion she was now feeling, and when she had, it had surprised and frightened her. She felt lonely.

This was Stephanie Burroughs who, from the age of seventeen, when she had first left home, was resilient, confident and self-sufficient. She was always in control, needing no-one, wanting no-one, in her life.

But no more.

Now she was lonely.

These moments, she called them blue notes, had happened

occasionally in the past when she wanted to have Robert around and, for various reasons, he couldn't be there. She was experiencing the blue notes much more frequently of late. The problem was she'd got used to having Robert around, of having him in her life. It had been easier, so much easier, when she'd been alone.

But she hadn't known what she was missing from her life. And she wasn't just talking about a man – she despised that nonsense that a woman needed a man to make her complete. She was talking about a partner, a companion, a lover, a friend. In the beginning it had been nothing but sex. They were like teenagers again, enjoying one another's bodies, making out in the car, in the back of the cinema, spending an entire day in bed, coming home from the office, making love, going out for dinner, then coming back and making love again. It had been a game.

But the game turned serious when she fell in love with him.

If only she could be sure that he loved her. He said he did.

Did she believe him?

CHAPTER 35

Friday 20th December

The buzzing of the bedside phone woke her out of a deep and dreamless sleep. She scrabbled blindly for it, almost knocking it off the table.

"Hi, it's your Phone-A-Friend."

Recognising Robert's voice, she pushed herself into an upright position and discovered that the bedclothes were in a knotted heap on the floor. When she slept alone she tossed and turned, but when Robert was in bed with her, she slept still and unmoving. She squinted at the clock, trying to make sense of the digits. "My God, what time is it?"

"Ten past eight, nearly a quarter past. Wake up, sleepyhead! I thought you'd be on the way into the office."

"I'm going in later. I'd a late call with LA last night; the eight-hour time difference is a killer."

The call had come in around midnight, shocking her from a deep sleep. It was Billy, her brother, wanting to know if she was coming over to the States for Christmas. She knew immediately that their mother, in her deeply unsubtle way, had set this up and encouraged her eldest brother to phone her. They chatted for ten minutes, slight inconsequential chit-chat before he rang off, but she'd not been able to get back to sleep until the early hours of the morning. She wished, desperately wished, that Robert was there with her; not to make love, just to hold her.

She was aware that Robert was speaking to her, and abruptly his half-heard words leapt out at her. "Speaking of calls, there was a message from Carson on my answer machine this morning; wants to rearrange the appointment. Shouldn't be a problem."

She sat bolt upright in the bed, rubbing the heels of her hands into her eyes. Her intuition and business acumen was telling her that something was wrong. "Tell me what he said, exactly what he said."

"Well, he just said . . . actually, hang on a second and I'll play you the call." She heard him walking across the room, then a click as he hit the play button on his answer machine.

You have no new messages. You have two old messages.

She heard the high-pitched squeal of a voice as Robert fast-forwarded through another message, then suddenly Eddie Carson's smug voice came clearly down the line.

"Good morning, Robert. Eddie Carson, DaBoyz Management here. I understand from Stephanie that you start early. Will you give me a call as soon as you get in? I'll need to re-arrange our appointment."

Stephanie shook her head in astonishment. Eddie tried the same trick with just about everyone he worked with.

"That's it," Robert said cheerfully. "It's not a problem. I'll clear my diary to see them, you know that."

"It *is* a problem," she snapped. "This is just bullshit. I told Carson that we were very lucky to get you. You phone him back and do not – do you hear me – do *not* allow him to rearrange the appointment. You've got to show this little bastard who's boss, otherwise he'll walk all over you."

"It really isn't a problem –" Robert began.

"Just do as I say," she snapped. "Be tough with him. Tell him you must meet this morning or not at all, then shut up and say nothing. Wait for his response." She hopped out of bed and went to stand by the window, looking down over the courtyard. Mrs Moore was out sweeping dead leaves away from the front of her house. She was getting sick and tired of Eddie Carson and his second-rate band. If they were not already on the way out, she'd be recommending that the agency drop them.

"OK," Robert said, but she could hear the doubt and indecision in his voice. Why the fuck couldn't he trust her? Because she was a woman and he was a man, and men always knew what they were doing in business? Well, not this time.

"Trust me on this. Right, go and do it now, and then phone me back."

"Yes, ma'am!"

She hung up. Carrying the phone in her hand, she headed into the bathroom and turned on the shower. It would be interesting now to see how Robert handled this: if he gave in to Carson, then the video would be a disaster, because Carson would effectively take charge. If he kept control of the DaBoyz manager, then there was some hope for him.

But Stephanie also knew that Robert was so desperate for business that he might very well give in to Carson. He'd be even more desperate if he discovered that this was the last job he was getting from her agency. She was already compromised. She wasn't sure how badly.

The recent conversation she'd had with her boss, Charles Flintoff, had been very strained. This was the man who'd found her on breakfast-time TV and offered her a job on the basis of a half-hour meeting. He'd mentored her and she'd proven to be an excellent student. She got the feeling that he regarded her almost like a daughter – he had three of his own, none of whom was following him into the business – and she, in turn, was incredibly fond of him. He'd heard a whisper in the trade about her involvement with Robert, and called her in immediately to ask her out straight for an answer. For a single instant, she'd been tempted to lie to him and deny the rumour, but instead had opted for the truth. It had probably saved her job, she realised later. Charles once told her that he only ever asked questions he knew the answer to. The other thing in her favour was that the few small jobs she'd put Robert's way had been competitively priced and he'd delivered the goods. Charles made no comment about the fact that Robert was married, but he had advised Stephanie that she had compromised the agency by becoming involved with a client. She admitted that when she was giving him the work, she'd never thought about that. "Love can be blind," Charles said, "but infatuation can be stupid." If she wanted to remain with the business, she had a choice: she could either break up with Robert, or refrain from giving him any more business. She had to do one or the other and although he didn't say it, she got the distinct impression that he would prefer if she did both. She gave Charles Flintoff an assurance that she would not allow R&K to pitch for any further business or if they did pitch she would not consider them. "Then, we can consider the matter closed," Flintoff said, in his avuncular, cut-glass accent. "There's no need to revisit it." Stephanie knew he would never mention it again, but she could see the disappointment in his face and knew also that her credibility with the man had been damaged and she was going to have to work hard to restore it.

Stephanie wondered how Robert was going to react when he realised that he was not going to get any more business out of her agency? She knew he was counting on her putting more business his way in the coming year. He'd even, rather cheekily, she thought, created a budget based upon that premise. She decided she would break the news to him some time in January. Let him enjoy his Christmas.

Stephanie stared at herself in the mirror. Her hair was wild and her eyes were bloodshot after her disturbed night. The flesh on her face was sagging and creased with pillow-marks. She stepped back and looked at herself critically: her body was in relatively good condition, her breasts were still more or less firm, stomach reasonably flat, but she was losing the battle with cellulite on her thighs. She was no beauty; she was ordinary. What exactly did Robert see in her, she wondered? What had attracted him to her?

A line in the budget, she wondered, business for the company? The thought was nasty and spiteful, but not the first time it had occurred to her.

Her phone rang.

"You were right. What would I do without you?"

"Let's hope you never have to find out."

CHAPTER 36

"Well, I like him," Eddie Carson said, voice crackling and distorted as it came through her hands-free phone system in the BMW.

Stephanie was tracking a pedestrian walking down Mount Street with car keys jangling in his hand. Was he walking to his car, or away from it? "I knew you'd like him, Eddie," she said brightly. "Plus he's a new face, with new ideas, so you can be sure you'll get something different, a new look, for the band."

"Yeah, yeah, he had some good stuff, some nice ideas." Carson sounded bored.

"You didn't try to change the time of the appointment this morning, Eddie, did you?"

"Would I do that, Miss Burroughs?" Eddie Carson asked innocently.

"Absolutely."

The pedestrian stopped beside a five-year-old Peugeot estate and climbed in. Stephanie pulled right up beside the car, indicator ticking. The trick now was to make sure that no-one stole her space.

"Well, it's a game, Stef. You just got to play the game. But this new boy, this Roger . . ."

"Robert," she corrected him.

"Robert. Yeah, he seems to know the rules. I understand you know this boy too." The leer in his voice was clearly audible.

The Peugeot driver showed no sign of moving. Stephanie ground her teeth. "What are the chances of DaBoyz breaking up?" she asked, not answering his question, keeping him off balance. If he wanted to play games, she could play just as well – better! – than he ever could.

"None. I'm drip-feeding the press the story myself. The single is not going to make number one for Christmas, which is a shame, but if Roger . . ."

"Robert."

"Robert can shoot a good vid, we'll have a reasonable chance at the charts with the next single in the early spring."

Stephanie knew he was lying through his teeth. The new video would be released probably a week before the band announced they were going their separate ways for "creative reasons". The creative reasons being that only one of them could sing. The sympathy vote from the dwindling numbers of fans might push the single into the top five.

The Peugeot finally pulled out and Stephanie nipped the BMW into the space. "Sounds good. You have a great Christmas, Eddie. I'll talk to you in the New Year."

"Same to you, Stef."

"And Eddie . . . don't let me read in the papers that the band has broken up. Let's get the video out first."

"Keen to show off your boyfriend's handiwork, eh?" Carson said and rang off before she could respond.

Stephanie nodded. He'd won that round.

"I told you." Stephanie strode around the office, having related an edited version of the conversation she'd just had with Eddie.

Robert was sitting behind his desk, staring intently at his

computer monitor. "Your advice was absolutely spot on," he said without looking up. "They turned up at ten on the dot. The boys were as good as gold, a little overawed by everything, I thought, and very much under Carson's thumb. He made all the creative decisions."

Stephanie fanned out the drawings across the conference table. This was the first time she'd seen the finished presentation and it looked great. Robert had chosen to shoot the band's new single, "Heart of Stone" in the middle of the Burren landscape in Co Clare. He was going to shoot in colour, but treat the image, making it look black and white, giving the video a stark minimalist look. The latter sequence of the video, which incorporated elements from Celtic mythology, was charged with a primitive eroticism. She was reminded, looking at the neat precise drawings he'd made of each frame, just how good he was when he was given the opportunity. "These look very good, very exciting. Different."

"Carson was complimentary." Robert came to stand beside her and started shuffling the pages into order. "You'd think I'd been doing this all my life," he said. "Carson wanted some changes here, here and here."

"Of course, he did. It's a power thing with him, like trying to change the time of the appointment this morning. I've seen him do that so often. He thinks he's managing U2, not just another cloned boy band. And if you hadn't called him on it, then he would have given you the run around for the next couple of weeks. Even if you had got the gig, he would have interfered every step of the way. . ."

Her voice trailed away. She was abruptly, erotically conscious that Robert was standing close – much too close – to her. She could feel the heat radiating from his body and in that instant she wanted him, with a hungry animal passion. She had to have him, in her arms, in her body. Watching his eyes, she saw the lust bloom in them and knew that he wanted her too.

She smiled and raised her eyebrows a fraction, then glanced

towards the open door to where the secretary was pretending to be busy with a catalogue, but was obviously listening in. Robert nodded imperceptibly and stepped into the outer office.

Stephanie fanned out the images again, vaguely aware that he was sending the Russian girl home. There was a great power to the images, a strong primal energy, and the irony of it was that this would probably be the best pop video the band ever had. And it was going to be released a week before they broke up. With any luck someone would see it and commission Robert to do another one for another band. She was relieved too; Charles Flintoff could not help but be impressed.

"Goodnight, Miss Burroughs," the Russian girl's voice disturbed her thoughts.

"Goodnight, Illona," Stephanie called, without looking up. She didn't particularly like the Russian girl, didn't like the way she looked knowingly at her every time she came in. And there was also the doubt, just the tiniest insidious doubt that what had happened between her and Robert could just as easily happen between the blonde Russian and Robert. It wasn't the first time the thought had struck her. Since Robert had betrayed his wife, Stephanie had lived with the awareness that he could just as easily betray her too, which really begged the question: did she trust him?

And it bothered her – bothered her tremendously – that she could not answer yes to that question.

"I think she suspects –" Robert began, walking back into the office.

"Who cares?" Stephanie snapped. "She's a secretary." Then she caught Robert by his lapels and pulled him towards her, tilting her head and pressing her lips against his. The need for him was a physical thing, a hunger, shocking and surprising in its intensity.

She pulled him back against the conference table, kissing him deeply as his fingers fumbled at the buttons of her blouse. She lifted herself up onto the table and pushed him away from her, giving her time to shrug out of her jacket and toss it on a chair. She undid the buttons on her blouse as Robert pulled urgently at his shirt. A button broke away, pinged off the table and skipped across the room.

She was the one who usually initiated their lovemaking. The first time they had made love, she had been forced to make the initial move, letting him know that she was available. She remember feeling a sick queasiness in the pit of her stomach that first time she stood naked before him, waiting for him to take her or reject her, wondering why he hadn't come on to her sooner.

Later, much later in their relationship, she'd come to realise that he'd simply fallen out of the habit of initiating lovemaking. Later still he'd admitted to her that he and Kathy had not made love for a very long time. On the several occasions when he tried to initiate lovemaking with his wife, she was always too tired and he felt she was rejecting him: that formed the habit of not trying, because the rejection hurt.

Stephanie had sworn to him on that first occasion that she would never reject him. She told him that if she did not want to make love, she would tell him openly, without pretence, without pretending to be asleep, or to have a headache or a stomach-ache. And she would always hold him. That, she discovered very quickly, was what he really wanted: to be held gently and quietly.

She spread herself naked on the table and watched in amusement as he hopped around on one leg, pulling off his socks. When he was completely naked, she opened her arms and lifted her legs. "Now, where were we?" she whispered.

She turned around in the tiny shower and allowed the trickle of tepid water to roll off her body. He really should get the plumbing fixed in this building. It was the only drawback to making love in his office. But at least she wasn't heading back to her office. The last time they'd made love here, she'd had to go back for a meeting which lasted for the rest of the afternoon. She could smell him off her body for the rest of the day and imagined that the rest of the attendees could also.

She dried herself while Robert stepped into the shower. She was pleased to see that he'd started to take care of himself. When they'd first become an item, he'd been heading towards flab, with the beginnings of a paunch and with skin the colour of old marble. She'd encouraged him to exercise and he'd even joined the same gym she attended and now they exercised together. She'd booked him in for a session in a tanning salon and convinced him to colour his hair and have his teeth fixed. She'd been working on him over the past couple of months to have botox in the deep worry lines in his forehead.

The shower died down and Robert pushed the door open and stepped out.

Stephanie walked back into the tiny bathroom. "Will I see you tonight?" she asked. She was only wearing her white lace-trimmed bra.

"I'm not sure. Do me a favour," he added, reaching for a towel, "get dressed, please."

"Why?" she said innocently.

"Because, if you don't I'll just have to have you again."

"Promises, promises." She stepped away from the door and started to dress. If she gave him any encouragement, he would make love to her again, and she loved that passion, that need he had for her. "What about tonight?" she asked again. She couldn't find her . . . oh, there they were, hanging off the table lamp. How had they got there?

"Tonight is all screwed up. You know Jimmy and I were supposed to have dinner in Shanahan's? Well, I got Illona to phone to confirm the reservation. And it turns out there was none."

"What happened?"

Robert was standing beside her. He suddenly reached out and

stroked the swell of her breast with the back of his hand. The touch sent an electric ripple straight through to the centre of her groin and she felt her nipples harden. She caught his hand and pressed it against her skin; his flesh felt hot against her cool breasts. Then she lifted his fingertips to her lips and kissed them. She loved this man. Loved him.

And that thrilled her and terrified her in equal measure.

"I'm not sure whose problem it is, Illona's or Maureen's." For a moment, she had no idea what he was talking about, then she realised he was continuing the conversation. It took a deliberate effort of will to come back on track. "Maureen's, I think. But that's not the point. I've got a good client meeting me here in just over an hour, and I've no place to take him to dinner."

"It'll be difficult finding a place to eat this close to Christmas." She was still aroused and there was a perceptible tremble in her voice, but she didn't think he noticed.

"I know. And Jimmy won't want to go out of the city: he was talking about spending the night in his apartment in Temple Bar."

Stephanie returned to the bathroom to repair her make-up. "Be upfront with him," she advised. It was the advice she tried to live her life by: be truthful and honest with people.

And was her current situation with Robert truthful or honest, she was forced to ask herself. It was, she decided fiercely, because she loved him.

"You never know, maybe all he wants are drinks. If you get out relatively early, you might check out the Market Bar. You'll get drinks and nibbles there."

"Great idea."

"But that doesn't answer the question I asked earlier: are you going to spend the night with me? Should I wait up?"

Robert popped his head around the door and grinned. "If I do spend the night, I'll be sleeping. You exhaust me."

Staring intently at the fogged-up mirror, she reapplied her lipstick. "Well, look, I've an early start in the morning. If you can get to me before one in the morning, then come on over, but if you are going to be any later, forget about it. Send me a text when you've got an idea what's happening."

"Good plan."

Robert stood back to examine her as she stepped out of the bathroom. "There is no way you would guess that less than half an hour ago you were lying on this table making passionate love."

"I've no idea what you are talking about, Mr Walker. I was closing a very important business deal." She leaned over and kissed him, brushing her lips against his, leaving the tiniest thread of coral-red lipstick on his upper lip. "And I do like the way you close a deal," she added.

She checked her phone when she returned to the car. She had one missed call on her phone; it was from Sally.

"Here's the plan," Sally's chirpy voice said without preamble, voice dipping and crackling. "I got your message and understand that you are now unexpectedly free tonight. So am I. We can get dressed up and go out for drinks in a loud noisy bar filled with people we'd just want to smack, or I can arrive at your place with food. The menu for tonight is pizza with extra chillies, Chinese with extra chillies or sizzling prawns in a hot and spicy sauce. The luxurious repast is my treat but the wine is up to you. And I promise not to smoke, either inside or outside the house."

Stephanie hit the second speed dial which connected her with her friend. "Where are you?"

"I'm in the Shelbourne, waiting for the traffic to thin out."

Stephanie could hear the tinkling of glasses around her friend, and what sounded like a piano struggling to be heard over the noise. "I'm in Mount Street. I'll leave the car here and walk around. We'll get a quick drink, then some food. How does that grab you?"

"Sounds like a better plan."

Chapter 37

The moment she stepped into the Shelbourne, Stephanie knew it was a mistake. The bar was heaving with people and she recognised half a dozen faces immediately. Naturally, most of the men in the bar had turned when she'd entered, so she had no chance now of slipping out unnoticed. She smiled, nodded and waved at a few of the faces she knew, then lifted her phone to her face in an effort to discourage them from coming over to join her. She hit the speed dial.

"Where are you?" she asked in a sing-song voice.

"Right beside you," came the immediate reply and Stephanie jumped as Sally Wilson materialised out of the crowd.

Stephanie leaned down to kiss her friend's cheek. Sally Wilson was a year younger than her friend, and at least six inches shorter. She was blonde where Stephanie was dark, her features all angles and planes whereas Stephanie was more rounded. They were the exact opposites in just about every way possible and they were closer than sisters.

"This might have been a mistake," Stephanie suggested.

"It might," Sally agreed lightly, "but probably not the worst mistake we've ever made. We'll stay an hour, then head back to your place, and pick up some food on the way back."

Stephanie knew that the chances of escaping within the hour were very slim indeed and while the last thing she wanted to do was to spend an evening in a noisy pre-Christmas bar, the boisterous, happy atmosphere was already lifting her spirits. Although she loved being with Robert, sometimes – particularly of late, when he'd been so panicked and under so much pressure – she came away from him feeling depressed and worn down, as if she had absorbed his negative mood.

"What are you having?"

"Glass of white wine is perfect." She positioned herself beside the door and watched in admiration as Sally battled her way, with a combination of charm and elbows, to the bar. Whereas a throng of men were standing at the bar with their money in their hand, desperately attempting to catch the barman's eye, Sally was served immediately. Stephanie thought it might have something to do with the remarkably low-cut LBD she was wearing. Sally returned within minutes and handed Stephanie her glass. The two women silently toasted one another.

"I wasn't expecting you to be around with – with R&K after the conversation you had with Charles."

Stephanie shrugged uncomfortably. "Well, I did give Robert the contract for the pop video, so I've got to see that to its conclusion. But it will be the last job they get from us."

Sally sipped her wine, leaving a bright pink lipstick mark on the rim of the glass. "Does he know?"

"Not yet. I was going to tell him this afternoon, but I decided not to ruin his Christmas. Besides," she added with a cheeky grin, "we got distracted."

"Distracted?"

"Distracted."

"Oh." Sally stared at her friend. "You didn't … you haven't?" she asked in a horrified, yet fascinated, whisper.

Stephanie nodded happily. "In his office. This afternoon. It was fabulous. It's always great."

"Always? You mean you've done it more than once in the office? You never told me."

"We've done it a couple of times. Besides, I don't ask you how often you make out with Dave."

"Not often enough is the answer. Jesus; no wonder you're dizzy this evening. And I'm supposed to be the blonde, remember?" She sipped a little of her wine. "I've always wanted to do that with Dave in my office, but it's open plan, and I'm not sure the rest of the girls would approve." Sally worked as a secretary in Beaumont Hospital and earned pin money as an "extra" on TV. She'd recently picked up quite a bit of extra money working on some of the big-budget movies which shot in Ireland, and was talking – yet again – about becoming a full-time actress.

"I thought you were out with Dave this evening."

"He's working. He got a call this afternoon – one of the lads came down with this flu bug that's going around. He was grateful for the overtime, to be truthful." Dave was a hospital porter in the same hospital, a huge hulking bear of a man who stood six three to Sally's five-three. He earned more money at the weekend, by working the doors of some of Dublin's toughest clubs than he did as a porter, but he loved the work in the hospital. He took no shit from anyone, except Sally, who bullied him unmercifully.

Sally waved at a spike-haired young man at the bar who smiled and nodded back. "We were in that crowd scene in *Fair City* together," she explained to Stephanie's raised eyebrow. "And we were corpses together in *King Arthur.*" Then she added casually, not looking at Stephanie, scanning the crowd. "You know, I think he's going to propose this Christmas."

It took a couple of seconds for the words to sink in. For a moment Stephanie thought she was talking about the young man at the bar. "Who'll propose? Dave? How do you know?" Stephanie asked delightedly. Sally and Dave had been an item for three years now, and had lived together for the past nine months.

Sally turned away from the crowd and lifted her glass.

Stephanie toasted her. "Congratulations!"

"Oh, you know Dave. He's a big old ox. Likes to think he's being very subtle and casual; he kept taking off one of my rings a couple of weeks ago and trying it on his little finger. Thought I wouldn't notice or cop to what he was doing. And he's being very secretive lately, and if he's asked me once, he's asked me a dozen times what time I'll be home on Christmas Eve."

"And what'll you do if he asks you?"

"Say yes, I suppose."

"You *suppose*. I thought you loved him."

"I do love him. But is he the *one?*" Then she shrugged. "How can you be sure if any of them are the *one*. I'll say 'yes' of course. I could do a lot worse."

"That sounds very enthusiastic," Stephanie said sarcastically. This was rich – coming from the woman who gave her relationship advice!

"I'm happy," Sally admitted. "He's a good man, and will make a good husband and a great father. Sure, he's still a kid himself. His mother will be thrilled; mine will be pleased; we'll have a fabulous wedding. What more can you expect these days?"

Stephanie shook her head. There should be more, shouldn't there?

A group of young women were gathering up their bags at one of the corner tables. One glanced at Stephanie and nodded towards the seat she was vacating, with a raised eyebrow. Stephanie raised her glass in reply, then caught Sally's arm and began to manoeuvre her through the crowd towards the seats. "Thanks," she said as they swapped places with the girls, who swayed out into the night, trailing five distinct perfumes in their wake.

"Now you see, blokes would never do that," Sally said. "That's one of the major differences between the sexes; women look out for one another."

Stephanie wasn't so sure, but she didn't want to argue with her friend. "When do you think Dave will propose?" she asked.

"My money's on Christmas Eve, at midnight."

"Very romantic," Stephanie murmured, and it was very romantic. She wondered if she would ever be proposed to in such a romantic fashion.

"If he does propose – I'd like you to be my bridesmaid."

Suddenly Stephanie's eyes were full of tears. The two women had always promised that they would be bridesmaids to each other. She nodded, then, blinking furiously, she attempted a smile. "That means you'll have to be my Matron of Honour. If I ever get married," she added, surprised at the note of bitterness in her voice.

Sally's face remained an expressionless mask and she concentrated on her drink.

"You don't believe that he'll ever marry me, do you?"

"I could lie to you and say yes. But I won't do that. No, I don't believe he will. I think if you even push him for some sort of commitment, he's going to run a mile."

The crowd surged and swirled around them. In one corner someone attempted to sing "Jingle Bell Rock", but was quickly drowned out by the groans of the other drinkers.

"Why do you hate him so?"

"Because he's going to hurt you. Because I've been hurt by men just like him, and I know what it's like."

"Robert is different to other men."

"Robert is a man. And all men are after one thing."

"He's not like that."

But Sally was nodding. "He is. Look, we both know the real problem here is that you've fallen for him. That means you're not thinking straight."

"He loves me too," Stephanie said quickly.

"And how does he show that?"

"Oh, please don't start that again," Stephanie pleaded.

"Start what?" Sally demanded. "I'm your oldest friend in Ireland. Your closest friend. The first friend you made when you came over here," she reminded her. "Friends look out for one another. I'm merely telling you what I see. I see an older man getting his leg over with a younger woman, who happens to be able to bring him in some extra business to his ailing company. I'm not saying that's the only reason he's with you, but I'm sure it's certainly an added bonus as far as he's concerned."

Stephanie bit the inside of her cheek to stop herself from snapping out a response that would bring the evening crashing into an argument. She also knew that Sally was right; she was only saying what she'd been thinking herself.

"I don't see a good outcome to this. I know you didn't set out to trap him, or lure him away from the bosom of his family – from what you've told me he was already drifting. I know you love him, and it's all wonderful and magical and you think you're rescuing him from an uncaring, unthinking cruel wife . . . but you know something: consider the source. Remember, all you know about Kathy, you've learned from him."

"Well, some I picked up from the time I worked there," Stephanie said quickly, almost defensively.

"You saw one tiny aspect of their relationship for a very brief period of time. You cannot base your understanding of their marriage on that. No-one truly knows what goes on in a marriage, except the couple themselves."

This was part of the on-going argument the two women had over one another's boyfriends. Stephanie had very nearly persuaded Sally to drop Dave, and now here he was, about to propose to her.

"What do you think I should do?" she asked miserably, because, deep in her heart and soul, she knew that her friend was right.

"You've been going together for eighteen months; it's time for him to put up or shut up. Force him to make a decision. Make him choose. You or the wife. And you know something, you're really asking him to be fair to both of you, because right now, he's being neither fair, nor truthful with either of you. You're looking for commitment now, not vague promises for the future. Stephanie, the best commitment he can give you now is to be with you on Christmas Day." She paused and put down her drink. Then she took both of Stephanie's hands in hers and stared deep into her troubled eyes. "And is that unreasonable? No, it's not. And is it unfair? He may tell you it is, but you know something – it's not. What's unfair is leaving you dangling. What's unfair is lying to you."

Deep in her handbag, Stephanie's phone started to ring. She was almost grateful for the opportunity for the break away from Sally's savage intensity. It took her a few moments to locate the phone and snap it open.

"Hello?"

"Hello. Is that Becky?"

"No, you have the wrong number." She hung up, then sat for a moment looking around the bar, watching the couples especially, laughing, enjoying themselves, touching one another, holding hands, being close and intimate with one another, unafraid who was watching, not caring who saw them.

She wasn't able to do that with Robert. Not in Dublin anyway. He was afraid that people would see. Afraid that they would tell Kathy, and then . . .

And then what?

What would happen if Kathy knew? What would she do?

"What are you thinking?" Sally asked quietly.

"I'm thinking you're right." She shook her head and her smile was touched with pain. "I know you're right. All you've done is put words on what I've been trying to articulate." She leaned forward and kissed Sally's cheek. "Thank you."

"What are you going to do?"

"Ask a question. And demand an answer."

"And if you don't get one you like?"

"Then we're done."

CHAPTER 38

The phone buzzed as she turned onto the canal. She glanced at the screen and was surprised to see the XXX's across the screen. "I wasn't expecting to hear from you for ages," she began.

"Where are you?" Wind whipped away some of Robert's words.

"In the car, heading home. I met Sally for a drink in the Shelbourne. Is everything all right?"

"I'm not sure. I'll meet you at home. I'm just heading down Nassau Street; I left the car outside the office. It'll take me forty-five minutes to get to you."

"Rober . . ." Stephanie began, but the call ended and she wasn't sure if it she'd lost the call or he'd deliberately ended it. He sounded – strange. Not drunk; Robert drank very little and although she'd seen him tipsy, she'd never known him to be falling-down drunk.

Stephanie pulled the car in in front of the house and climbed out. She didn't need to be a genius to realise that something must have happened during dinner with Jimmy.

"There you are, dear."

Stephanie jumped with fright as Mrs Moore materialised out of the shadows. "You nearly gave me a heart attack."

"That's no joking matter," Mrs Moore said sternly. "A heart attack took my Frank."

"I wasn't joking," Stephanie said seriously.

Mrs Moore looked over the bags in Stephanie's hands, then glanced into the car.

"Can I help you, Mrs Moore?"

"Did the lady not catch up with you then?"

"What lady?"

"The lady with the Christmas hamper. She said she had to deliver it to you personally."

"And she had this address?"

"Yes. She had it on a sheet of paper."

That was odd; very few people had her home address. She directed just about everything to the office address. Possibly something from Robert . . . no, he'd give it to her himself. Then, it could only be something from home. Maybe that was it: a care package from her mother.

"I didn't get it. I'm sure it'll arrive tomorrow. Good night, Mrs Moore," she said, moving past the older woman to put her key in the lock and push open the door. Nosy old bat: maybe she wouldn't get Mrs Moore a present after all.

She took a quick shower before Robert arrived. If the evening went anything like the other nights they'd spent together, he'd want a quick shower before they made love – and she'd no doubts, despite his earlier reservations and protestations – that they would make love. They simply couldn't help it when they were together. Then they'd probably share a bath before falling asleep in one another's arms. And wake early in the morning and do it all again, she grinned.

She had just climbed out of the shower and wrapped a towel around her head when she heard the doorbell. He had a key: why didn't he use it? She grabbed the first item out of the wardrobe, her peach-coloured silk dressing-gown, and pulled it on. The flimsy material immediately stuck to her damp body – but she didn't think that Robert would mind. She hurried downstairs and along the hall to open the door.

"I really wasn't expecting you." And she wasn't; she thought he'd end up spending the night with Jimmy.

"There was a change of plan." He kissed her quickly, casually, and brushed past her into the apartment, and she knew then that something was definitely amiss. She could almost feel the tension and something else – anger? – vibrating off him.

"You look like you need a drink." She headed into the small kitchen, wondering if she'd any whiskey in the apartment.

"Coffee, no alcohol." He came and stood in the door of the kitchen, arms folded across his chest, one foot in front of the other, ankles crossed. One didn't need to be an expert in body language to know that he was wound up as tight as a spring.

She pulled open the fridge. "I've got a nice white chilling . . ."

"I'd better not. I'm driving."

"You're not staying?" That shocked her; Robert usually took any excuse offered to spend the night with her.

"No, not tonight. I can't."

"That wasn't the initial plan," she smiled, trying to tease out what was wrong.

"The plan changed."

"I'll make some coffee." She turned back to the sink and poured water into the coffee-maker. Out of the corner of her eye, she saw him lean forward and she realised that the front of her robe had gaped open exposing her breasts. She suddenly smiled. She knew then that everything was going to be all right. "You've seen them before."

"The day I get tired of looking at them is the day I'm dead."

"Tell me what happened?" she said softly. "I presume it's something to do with Jimmy, since you were fine – more than fine – when I left you a couple of hours ago? He's OK, is he?"

"He's OK. His life's a mess, as usual."

"I think he thrives on it," Stephanie remarked. She despised Jimmy Moran and what he represented, with his extraordinary arrogance built on too little talent and damn few past glories.

"He's not getting any younger. And this time the mess is bigger than usual. His wife is finally giving him the divorce he's wanted."

"Well, that's good news . . ."

"And taking half of everything he owns into the bargain."

Stephanie looked at him sharply, surprised by the disapproving tone in his voice. "Good for her. That is her right," she reminded him.

"I know that. He's going to marry Frances so they can raise the child together."

"So he should." Again she was surprised, and just a little disappointed with his reaction. Surely, he accepted that Jimmy had treated his wife abominably, and had a duty to his girlfriend and her child? "You don't look so sure," she added, watching him closely.

"I just remember that Frances was the woman who sold her story to the press. She used him to get free publicity, hoping she'd get that movie part."

Coffee started to percolate and the rich aroma of Kenyan filled the small kitchen.

"That revelation was really the beginning of the end for him and Angela."

"But he's still with Frances though," Stephanie said, pulling open cupboard doors and lifting out two tiny coffee cups. "He went back to her, got her pregnant."

"Put it in a mug, would you?" Robert asked. "Something a bit more substantial than those thumbnails."

Without saying a word, Stephanie reached into the cupboard and brought out a mug emblazoned with a yellow smiley face.

"I gave you that."

"I know."

273

"Frances ruined his reputation in return for a few column inches."

Stephanie laughed, shocked with the bitter tone in Robert's voice. He seemed to be blaming Frances for Jimmy's problems. But wasn't that what men did: blame the woman? "She did not. He had no reputation to ruin. You know he was notorious around Dublin. One of the reasons he could never get female researchers to work with him on projects was because he always came on to them – and expected them to reciprocate." She poured coffee, thick and black, into the mug and then filled her own tiny cup with the dregs. "Everyone knew about him," she added.

Robert accepted the mug from her hand and sipped it, making a face at the bitter taste. "People know about us, Stephanie," he said quietly. "Jimmy told me tonight."

So he knew. That's what was behind his attitude. She walked past him into the sitting-room and curled up on the sofa, tucking her bare legs beneath her, pulling her dressing-gown tightly across her body.

Robert followed her into the room and sat down facing her. "Did you hear what I said?" he said almost accusingly. "People know about us."

Was that fear she was hearing in his voice? Anger?

Ghostly wind chimes coming from the disc in the CD player filled the silence between them.

"You knew." He looked as if he had been struck. "You knew and you never told me."

"Yes, I knew."

"How long . . . I mean, why didn't you . . . what about your office . . . ?"

"There have been rumours floating about us for the last couple of months," she said simply. "I ignored them. This business of ours thrives on rumour and gossip. And when two people are regularly seen together tongues will wag, even if there is no truth to the rumours. About a month ago, I was called into head office.

Charles Flintoff himself asked me outright if you and I were an item."

"You said no," Robert said immediately.

"I said yes."

Robert looked at her blankly.

"Having a relationship with you is one thing – he doesn't give a damn about that. Putting business your way is another. But so long as it's above board, well, that's still marginally OK. However, lying to him was out of the question. The very fact that he was asking me a question suggested that he already knew the answer. I told him the truth."

Robert's mouth was opening and closing, but no sound was coming out.

"And it was the right thing to do. He had contracts for the jobs I'd given you, plus the costings. He'd done some comparisons with the other bidders and had an independent assessment of the final result." She shrugged. "He could find no fault with it."

"So how many people know?"

Stephanie frowned. He was obsessed with trying to prevent people from finding out about them. Or was he obsessed with trying to prevent his wife from finding out about them? "Why? What's the problem?" she demanded.

"Because if people know, then it's only a matter of time before Kathy gets to hear."

She had her answer.

"I wanted to be in a position to tell her myself. When the time was right."

"And when would the time be right, Robert?"

"When it's right. When I get myself sorted out," he muttered.

"And when would that be? And what constitutes 'sorting out'?"

Robert concentrated on his coffee and would not look her in the eye.

"We've been lovers now for eighteen months, Robert. Where do we go from here? What's the future?"

He wrapped his hands around the mug and stared into it.

"You told me how unhappy you are at home. You suggested to me – no, more than suggested, you told me, that you would leave Kathy . . ."

"I'm sure I never said that."

"Maybe not in those words, but that was my clear understanding. I would never have got involved with you otherwise. You told me you would leave her when the time was right." She remembered the moment clearly. They'd been lying upstairs in her bed, exhausted after a bout of strenuous lovemaking. He'd made the announcement out of the blue, with no prompting from her. "I'll be with you," he said. "I'll sort things out and come to you when the time is right." The words were etched on her consciousness. He might have forgotten: she hadn't.

"Well, when is the right time? This month? No, it cannot be this month because it's Christmas, and you don't want to ruin Christmas for the family. But you've no problem ruining my Christmas." She was unable and unwilling now to disguise the bitterness in her voice. "OK then, next month, but that's the start of the New Year and you probably don't want to ruin that for them either. Maybe February, but that's Theresa's birthday and that's not a nice birthday present to give her. March? But you know something, there's bound to be a problem with that too." Stephanie stopped abruptly. Exhaustion, leaden bone-numbing exhaustion washed over her and suddenly she did not want to speak to him any more. "Look, I'm tired. I don't want to be having this conversation with you now."

Robert nodded. It was obvious that he didn't want to have it either.

"I had a drink with Sally earlier . . ."

"Does she know?"

Stephanie bit her tongue to prevent herself from swearing at him. "Of course, she knows. She knew from the very beginning. She warned me, right from the git-go not to get involved with a married man. She explained to me exactly what would happen, and you know what: so far, she's been right. Just spot on." The room fractured into rainbow crystals as tears filled her eyes. She was angry with herself; she always felt that tears were the cheap option and she was not going to give in to tears.

"Stephanie," Robert began, "maybe this isn't a good time. We're both tired. Let's get some sleep."

"I think that's a really good idea." She stood up smoothly, and picked up his coat. She wanted him out of the house. Right now.

"I'll see you tomorrow. We'll talk."

She nodded as she walked him to the door, then she laid a hand on his arm. "I don't want to think that you've been making a fool of me. I don't want to think that you've been using me." Then she leaned up and brushed her lips against his. "Tomorrow. Tell me the truth. Don't disappoint me."

"We'll talk tomorrow."

She closed the door behind him and then turned away, so he would not see the tears now rolling down her cheeks. Automatically, she turned out the lights and headed upstairs to bed. Without even brushing her teeth, she knocked off the lights, and then still wrapped in the dressing-gown, crawled under the covers.

She heard a car engine start in the courtyard outside and wondered if it was Robert's. And then she realised that she didn't care.

He had one last chance; Sally would say that it was one too many. Tomorrow night, she'd know for sure by tomorrow night.

The car drove away, a lonely fading sound.

CHAPTER 39

Saturday 21st December

She slept remarkably well. Considering.

When she'd crawled into bed, she'd felt as if she'd been beaten and almost physically bruised. Sitting across from Robert, watching him act and react, she'd gradually realised that he was never going to leave his wife, and that she'd been naive to even consider it. The alarm bells had gone off when she'd seen how he'd sympathised with Jimmy Moran – philandering, lying, cheating Jimmy Moran. She'd seen how he'd reacted to the news that Jimmy's wife was looking for her share of Jimmy's money and he'd been upset that Frances expected Jimmy to pay for the rearing of the child. If he couldn't accept or understand the woman's side of the story, then how could he ever comprehend what she was going through? What chance had she?

She felt him slipping from her, and there was nothing she could do about it.

He had to commit to her: she'd already committed to him. She didn't feel guilty asking him to choose her over his wife; according to him, he'd already done that. She wasn't asking him to do anything he hadn't already agreed to do.

But the man who had sat across from her the previous night, the man who had said little, had almost been like a stranger to her.

She'd not expected to sleep, but as soon as her head hit the pillow, she'd fallen into a deep and dreamless sleep and awoken surprisingly refreshed just after eight. She'd lain in bed for an hour, deliberately not thinking about the situation, not allowing him to enter her thoughts at all. There were a few things she needed to do today – including looking at the availability of tickets to the States – and there was an open-air carol service in Stephen's Green that she thought she might attend. She could leave the car and walk into the city. She needed the exercise.

She was just swinging her legs out of bed when the call came in. Caller ID identified Robert's mobile and she actually hesitated for a moment before picking up. Six rings, seven, eight . . . She snatched it up.

"Robert." No hello, no good morning, just an acknowledgment of his name. She wasn't sure how she felt about him this morning. But if he was distancing himself from her, then maybe she ought to be doing the same.

"How . . . how are you feeling?"

"I'm tired, Robert." Not physically tired; emotionally exhausted.

"Do you want to see me?"

"I always want to see you." And it was true. She did.

"I was going to call over. I don't know how long it will take me; traffic is sure to be appalling."

And was she supposed to feel guilty about that?

But she didn't want him in the house today. She wanted to meet him on neutral ground. "I'm actually heading into the city; there is an open-air carol service being held in Stephen's Green."

"What time?"

"Starts about two."

"Why don't I meet you there? We can listen to some carols, then go and get something to eat."

"OK," she said shortly, feeling something shift and move inside her. "Give me a call when you're in the city." She hung up. And then she realised that she was smiling. She hopped out of bed. OK, so maybe she had misjudged him. When she'd seen his name on the phone she'd half expected to hear an excuse why he could not see her today – and if he had, then that would have been that. She had a few items of his clothing in her closets: two shirts, some underwear, a pair of socks. She would have put them in a Jiffy bag and left it on his office doorstep.

He was full of surprises. It was one of the things which had first attracted her to him.

Stephanie was moving away from the carol singers, pushing her way through the crowded Green when she felt the phone buzz in her pocket. She scrambled to pull her gloves off with her teeth and finally got to the phone just before it went to her message machine. "Where are you?" she asked, without preamble.

"In the door to the shopping centre."

"Stay there. Don't move. I'll find you. It's chaos here."

This was the last Saturday before Christmas, traditionally the busiest shopping day of the year. People always thought Christmas Eve held that particular honour, but by Christmas Eve a lot of the shopping was complete and people either did not come into the city, or started heading out of town early. The carol service, just over the little bridge in the heart of the Green had attracted thousands of onlookers and the main arched entrance was jammed with bodies as people pushed in and out of the park to get to hear the singers. Hundreds were lining the ponds and stewards were trying to prevent people from congregating on the bridge.

Stephanie hurried over the bridge, turned off to the right and pushed and shoved her way through one of the side entrances which came out almost facing Dawson Street. There was an art exhibition taking place on the railings around the Green, and that had brought in even more crowds. She found she was forced out onto the street as she tried to make her way towards the entrance to the Stephen's Green shopping centre.

As she closed on the entrance, she could not see him. The circular foyer was jammed with bodies and not helped by the street vendors selling Christmas wrapping paper – "five sheets for a euro, love" – or those collecting for any one of a dozen needy charities gathered just outside the opening.

There he was.

He was standing a little to one side, peering out towards the park, frowning at the crowds, hands pushed deep into his pockets, collar turned up, head ducked. All he needed was a hat and cigarette and he'd look like a 40's detective. She managed to get right up in front of him before he noticed she was there. He blinked in surprise, then leaned forward to kiss her, a quick chaste peck on the cheek, before catching her arm and moving her away from the doorway. "Where did you leave your toboggan?" he asked, referring to her practical, though not entirely flattering, winter clothing.

"Parked it upstairs alongside the sleigh."

They crossed the road, heading back towards the Green. He nodded towards the park. "Do you want to go back in?"

She shook her head. "The choir are loud but not good and the park is jammed. Let's walk around and look at the art." She pointed with both hands, "Left or right?" she asked brightly, guessing that he would want to take her to the right, away from the crowds. She knew he hated being seen in the city with her, especially on a day like this, where they could not make a work-related excuse.

"Right," Robert said, linking her arm and leading her away towards the College of Surgeons and the Luas stop.

He was just so fucking predictable, she thought bitterly.

"I'm sorry about last night," he began.

"So am I," she said immediately. "I should have told you that our relationship had been discovered. But I knew you were under so much pressure, I simply didn't want to add to it." It was more or less the truth too. She had seriously thought about telling him about her conversation with Flintoff, but Robert was no fool: he would have put two and two together and guessed that she would no longer be able to put work his way. She couldn't afford to have him panicking and going out scrambling for more work; she wanted to keep him focussed on the DaBoyz project.

"It might have been better if you had. When Jimmy dropped it on me last night, I thought I was going to have a stroke."

Stephanie glanced at him curiously; was he such a coward? She stopped to look at a spectacularly abstract oil, vivid in green and gold, slashed across with daubs of red and violet. She loved the raw emotion and energy in the painting. This was a work of passion. Where was the man she had fallen in love with, the passionate man? What had happened to him? The early days of their relationship – even before they started to make love – had been passionate days, full of light and life and energy. But as time went by, the passion slowly seeped away. They no longer went places, they did less and less together, and he no longer had as much time for her as he had previously. He was driven by work, obsessed with the need to make money to keep the business going. If this was how he had behaved with Kathy, she was beginning to understand how the couple had drifted apart.

Leaning forward into the painting, inhaling the rich aroma of oil and linseed, she said, without looking at him. "Tell me . . ." she waited until he had bent his head to hers, "do you love me?"

When he didn't answer immediately, she glanced sidelong at him. "No answer?"

"I suppose I was just startled that you had to ask me."

"Because I want to know." She walked away, and he fell into step beside her. "I want to know how much."

"I've told you often enough."

"I know that. But have you shown me?"

"I've given you presents . . ."

She bit back a savage response, and instead asked. "What is love, Robert?"

"Love is. . ." he floundered, " . . . well love."

"Typical man!" she snapped. "Think about it: what is love? You tell me you love me. What does that mean?"

"It means . . . it means I want to be with you. That I love being with you."

Was he just saying the words automatically, a rote response, or did he really mean them? Was he just telling her what he thought she wanted to hear? "Would you be talking about commitment now?"

"Yes. Commitment," he agreed.

A tiny delicate watercolour of a single daffodil attracted her attention and she stopped to admire it. Constructed of individual sweeping brushstrokes, it had an oriental feel to it. It looked delicate, ephemeral, fragile: which was exactly how she would describe her relationship with Robert at that precise moment. "And are you committed to me?" she asked.

"Yes."

Stephanie straightened. "Committed? How do you show that commitment?"

Robert opened his mouth to answer, but the young female artist moved in to try and make a sale. "We're not interested," Robert snapped. He caught Stephanie by the arm and led her through a small side gate opposite the College of Surgeons into the Green. She could feel the tension vibrating through his hand, and he was squeezing hard enough to leave bruises. "If we're going to talk, then let's talk. Let's leave the art for another day. What do you want from me?"

"The truth," she said simply. "I told you that last night. Just tell me the truth."

"I've told you I love you. That's the truth."

"And I believe you."

He stopped, surprised or stunned or shocked by her statement. She walked away from him, then stopped and turned back.

She believed him, truly believed that he loved her in his own way, on his own terms.

But did he love her enough . . . enough to walk away from everything he had and start again, start afresh?

"If you have something to ask me, then ask me out straight," he said.

Love and commitment, well, they were two separate things. But they should be one. Stephanie dug her hands into the pockets of her jacket and turned to face him. She was aware that if she blinked then the tears pooling in her eyes would roll down her cheeks and she wasn't going to give him that satisfaction.

"You tell me you love me. You tell me you want to be with me. You seem to enjoy my company. You certainly enjoy my body." She stopped and drew in a deep breath. "I need to know if there is more. If there is going to be more."

"More?"

"More of us. Together. Not snatched half-hour lunches or one-hour dinners, not fumbles in your office or dirty weekends away. I need to know if we're going to be together. As a couple. Openly." She quickly looked away and brushed the tears from her cheeks before he could see them. "That's all."

Because in the end that's what it came down to.

Not what had happened in the past, not what was taking place in the present and all that it represented, but the future: that's all that mattered now. She needed a future, either with or without him.

She looked out across the Green. The brilliant weather had brought people to the park, bringing it alive with stark colour against the leafless trees. When she'd first fallen in love with him, it was as if everything was brilliantly coloured, but in the past few weeks and months of their relationship it seemed as if the colours were leaching away.

"I've had relationships before, Robert, you know that. I've never felt about anyone the way I feel about you. I love you. I need to know if you love me. I need to know if you love me enough to do something about it."

She turned and walked away. He hesitated, and for a moment she thought he was going to walk in the opposite direction, but then he fell into step beside her. She was not going to say any more. She'd said more than she'd intended to. She walked up Harcourt Street, heading for the canal. She was going home.

"You want me to commit to you."

She wasn't sure if he was asking her a question or making a statement. She was numb and tired. "I don't want to be your bit on the side any more. That was fine for a while, because I wasn't sure if you were the one."

"The one?"

"The one I loved. And I allowed myself to fall in love with you – even though you were a married man, because I believed that there might be a chance for us." She walked a dozen steps in silence, controlling her breathing. "Then it came home to me. My girlfriends have gone away for Christmas but I was going to be spending Christmas alone, because I wanted to be close to my lover. But my lover was spending time with his family. It was that way last year too; I don't want it to be that way next year."

"Stephanie, I –" he said quickly.

She held up her hand. She needed to finish this. "If there is no future for us, then just say so. I'm not going to be stupid about it. I'm a big girl. I won't make a scene. I won't tell Kathy, if that's what you're worried about," she added bitterly.

They walked another ten yards in silence, each step taking her back to the apartment, each step moving them further apart.

Then, abruptly, Robert moved around to stand in front of her, stopping her in the middle of the path, catching hold of her shoulders, looking down into eyes. She was suddenly conscious that his eyes were huge, magnified now by unshed tears and his breath was laboured, as if he had been running. She saw his tongue flick out to lick dry lips.

"I love you. I want to be with you. To marry you. Will you marry me?"

The city went away. The noise of the traffic and the trams faded and dulled and there was only Robert and his words echoing and re-echoing around in her head.

I love you.

I want to be with you.

To marry you.

Will you marry me?

She wrapped her arms around his shoulders and pulled his face down and kissed him and she was crying and trying to speak, but her heart was thumping so hard she was sure it was going to burst.

I love you.

I want to be with you.

To marry you.

Will you marry me?

The world shifted and settled and the doubts and fears were wiped away in those four simple sentences. Three statements and a question.

She loved him.

She wanted to be with him

She wanted to marry him.

And yes, was the answer.

"Yes, yes, yes."

CHAPTER 40

Sunday 22nd December

"So, what do you think of that!" Stephanie demanded triumphantly.

Sally barely made it in the door before Stephanie blurted out the news. "He's proposed to me. Told me he loved me, wanted to be with me, wanted to marry me." Even as she said the words, she could feel the combination of excitement and maybe even fear churning inside her stomach. And relief, don't forget relief too.

Sally's eyes and mouth were wide with shock. "He proposed to you. Proposed! Slow down, slow down, slow down. What's happened? Tell me."

"He asked me to marry him. Proposed. Right there in the street."

Will you marry me?

That was the phrase that had shocked her, surprised her, undone her. She was thirty-five years of age, she was a strong, independent, established, businesswoman. She'd never felt the need for a man on her arm or by her side to validate her. Never really needed a man before. Enjoyed them certainly, loved some of them, but not since she was a teen had she thought about marriage. Marriage was a young girl's dream and she'd stopped being a young girl on the day she got on the Greyhound bus for New York.

And yet . . .

With those four words, he'd made her a young girl again, with all those dreams and futures made possible again.

Sally was speaking to her and she had to concentrate on the words. "What did you do to bring out this dramatic change?" she demanded. "I want all the details."

Stephanie grabbed her coat off the back of a chair and gathered up her handbag. "I really do listen to you. Maybe I just needed you make me think about the questions I should be asking, maybe I was just too close to the situation, making excuses for him all the time. I got tired of waiting, Sally. "

She pulled the door closed, then linked her arm through her friend's. They strode across the courtyard towards the gates. They were going to walk into the city, to shop for one another's presents – a tradition that had grown up over the many years of their friendship.

"I asked myself what I wanted – not for now, but for next year. Then I asked him if he loved me."

"And, of course, he said yes," Sally answered. "Men always say yes, but that's because they don't really know the meaning of the word. 'Yes' is just a filler in a conversation."

"But he did it, Sally. He did it. Told me he would marry me. I wasn't expecting that: I would have been happy with him committing to living with me for the moment!"

They turned right on the canal, and crossed the road to stroll along the path. With the sun fracturing on the water, it looked like a summer's day. They walked a dozen steps, then Sally wondered aloud: "And did he say when he was going to break the good news to his wife?"

Stephanie felt her euphoric mood slip and shift. That same thought had crossed her mind, but she'd dismissed it. "Well, no . . .

we didn't get around to discussing that. We were going to meet today, but I wasn't going to cancel you for anything."

"Thanks."

"Besides, I haven't had a chance to get Robert his big present. I needed some time to do that today too."

They walked another dozen steps.

"And when do you think he'll be moving in with you?"

"Oh soon," Stephanie said confidently. "By New Year, I should imagine. We'll have a New Year's celebration dinner – and remember, you're paying."

"If he moves in with you, and commits in that way to you – I'll gladly pay."

But Stephanie wasn't sure if Sally was being sarcastic or not.

Sally linked her arm through her friend's. "Come on, let's go buy stuff and we'll make a promise now not think or talk about men for one whole day!"

"Will we be able to manage that?" Stephanie laughed.

"Depends on what we're buying, doesn't? We're only getting girly stuff today. That means no boy's stuff."

"What about Robert's present?"

"It can wait."

Chapter 41

Monday 23rd December

Robert was wheezing like an old man when Stephanie took up position on the treadmill alongside him. He grunted a greeting, but didn't let up the pace. When she'd convinced him to join the gym, she hadn't really imagined that he would stick with it, but he'd surprised her by keeping his twice-weekly appointments. Once he got over the initial shock to his system, he almost seemed to enjoy it. She'd seen some slight improvements to his body, especially around his stomach, but his pecs still needed a lot of work. After his first session, she'd convinced him to go for a tan, and that went a long way to disguising some of his flabby sins. She noted the last time they made love that he'd continued to top up the tan.

She started up the treadmill. "Sorry I'm late. The office is closing today and there were drinks in the boardroom."

"No problem," he panted. "I got your message. Any issues in work about . . . ?"

"About us? Nothing. No mentions. And I did hear on the grapevine that it looks as if you got the DaBoyz gig."

"That's great, I think! I was meaning to ask you about that. Theresa said that two of the lads are gay."

Stephanie shook her head. "I've not heard. Wouldn't surprise me. Is that a problem?"

"Not at all. But she also said she heard on MTV that they are thinking of breaking up."

She bit back a flicker of irritation. It should be of no interest to him if the band were straight, gay or on the verge of breaking up. All he had to do was to concentrate on the video. "They were. That's why this single is so important. There's been a lot of investment in this group, and the investors are unwilling to cut loose their investment without one last shot. That's you by the way. Do the pop video right and you will have saved a lot of people a lot of money. Screw it up however and you'll never work in this town again." She laughed to take the sting from her words.

"I'm not sure whether you're joking or serious."

"A bit of both, I think. You'll do a great job. Remember, I've staked my career on it."

"So, no pressure there then," he murmured.

"And I'm sorry about yesterday. I really wanted to see you, but I'd already agreed to go shopping with Sally before . . ."

Robert glanced sidelong at her and smiled. "Before?"

"Before us."

"It was probably just as well. It gave me a chance to get a lot done in the office. If you and I had got together, we would have . . ."

She glanced at him. "What would we have done?"

"Talked. Planned."

"I know. You've made me so happy. Even Sally is pleased."

"One of these days I'd like to meet this mysterious Sally."

"She's looking forward to meeting you too. I've told her a lot about you."

"I suppose she was surprised by the news."

"Surprised. She was stunned. I said we'd get together after Christmas and celebrate. She's paying."

"Good idea." Robert began to run faster. "Why is she paying?"

"Because she once bet me the best meal money could buy that you would never leave your wife for me."

"Well, let's make sure that's an expensive bet. I'll book Shanahan's on the Green myself for this one."

They ran in silence for a while, then Stephanie asked the question that had been troubling her ever since Sally had raised it the previous day. "Have you given any further thought to Christmas?"

"I've thought about nothing else," he said quickly.

"Will you spend Christmas Day with me?"

Before he answered he reached down to increase the speed of the machine and she had an inkling of the answer. He was now running hard, breath coming in great heaving gasps. "Ah no," he said eventually.

His answer chilled her, and something must have shown on her face, because Robert said immediately, "Be reasonable." Realising that he was shouting above the noise of the machine, he leaned closer to her. She could smell the heat and musk coming off his body, but there was no arousal this time.

"Be reasonable. I can hardly go to Kathy and the kids tonight or tomorrow and say, 'Guess what? I'm leaving. Happy Christmas.' Can I?"

Well, when he put it like that, is sounded perfectly reasonable. But, of course, his every excuse sounded reasonable. "No, of course not." She nodded, not sure what she was hearing. Was he backtracking on what he had said on Saturday, or was this perfectly genuine? She needed a few moments to think. But her initial reaction was the bastard was backing down.

And having built up her hopes like that!

If he walked away from her now, having proposed to her, having got her hopes up, having made her incredibly, unreasonably happy, then she would go to his wife and tell her. If he hurt her like that, then she would hurt him back!

"But I will see you tomorrow. And I'll get down on Christmas Day," he added.

"And when do you intend telling her?" she asked. His answer had helped a little, but she needed more, she needed something definite, something she could hold onto, something she could count on.

"I was thinking the twenty-seventh, which is Friday."

"Why not Thursday?"

"Well, we're committed to going down to her sister's for dinner. All the arrangements have been made."

Something like panic was beginning to creep in around her now. Panic and a terrible anger. When Robert had said on Saturday that he wanted to be with her, she's somehow imagined that meant Christmas Day, but when she reran the conversation again, she realised that he'd never actually committed to any timeframe. "So what do I do for Christmas Day: hang around until you appear?"

"I will tell her on Friday and I will spend New Year's Eve with you," he said, not exactly answering her question. "We will see in the New Year together. It will be the start of a new year for us too. Come on; meet me half-way on this. This is a big decision, a huge move for me to make. You've only got yourself to think of; I've got Kathy and the kids to consider."

OK, she had her dates and she'd swap a Christmas Eve or Christmas Day for a New Year's Eve and the New Year's Day. "You're right, of course. Absolutely right. Another couple of days is not going to make that much difference to us, is it? And Christmas Day is just another Wednesday."

They switched from the treadmills onto the bikes. She started pedalling. Robert tried to keep up with her for a few minutes, but couldn't and slowed back down to a reasonable pace. "I need a little advice, however," he said, when he'd got his breath back.

Stephanie continued cycling as she looked at him. She was still breathing evenly. "What sort of advice?"

"It's about the company. R&K Productions. You know the K stands for Kathy and that she has a fifty-per cent share in it?"

"I know that," Stephanie said cautiously. What was he talking about? Maybe he was thinking of selling the company.

"I was wondering if you would like to join with me in the company, take over Kathy's share. We could call it R&S Productions. That is, if I can buy Kathy out, of course."

She looked at him in blank surprise. Whatever she had been expecting him to ask her, it hadn't been this. She eased up on the bike, allowed the wheel to spin to a stop. There was no easy way to say this, unfortunately, but it had to be said, and better he hear it from her. She took a moment to try and phrase the response as diplomatically as possible.

"I'm not sure I'd want to give up my present position. I would think going to work in your company might be seen as a retrograde step, career wise."

Robert started to laugh, then she watched the laughter die on his lips as he realised she was serious.

And, since he had raised the issue of the businesses, she thought she might as well tell him the rest. If he was being totally honest with her – and she thought he was – then she owed it to him.

"The other thing we'll have to bear in mind is that I will not be able to put any more business your way. It would not look good for me to be seen to be pushing business to my partner's company."

He looked as if he has been struck. "No more business . . ."

"Not from me. But I'll keep my ear to the ground. I'll keep you well up to speed with what's happening; there'll be no problems. Anyway," she continued, "I was thinking you might close R&K."

"What?" Beneath his tan she could see that he'd actually paled. Had he been counting that much on the work she could get him?

"Get a job with one of the big companies," she continued.

He wouldn't look at her now, merely stared straight ahead with what looked like a defiant – or sullen – expression on his face.

"It would be easier on you mentally and physically," she

294

pressed on. "There would be a regular pay cheque, and you could walk out at five thirty or six and not have to think about the job again until the following morning. Your weekends would be yours again."

"I'd be working for someone. I've been my own boss for a long time."

"At the moment you're working for Kathy and the children and the bank. They're your boss. This way you end up with more free time; time to spend with me. Time to spend with your children," she added.

He started laughing, a dry rasp, which turned into a cough.

Stephanie climbed off the bike and thumped his back. "Are you all right?"

"I'm fine. I was just thinking . . ."

"Thinking what?"

"Thinking that you're some sort of catalyst. Change happens around you."

She leaned into him, deliberately pushing her breasts against his chest. "We make our own changes, but sometimes you just need someone or something to do a little nudging." Sally had nudged her; she had nudged Robert. "Now, I'm going to get changed."

"I think two children would be wonderful, a boy and girl," Robert said, as they walked across the foyer towards the door that led out onto the carpark.

"Well, I'd like children," she said as they came through the door of the gym and out into the bitter night air. She'd never thought about children before he'd proposed on Saturday. Too many of her friends had babies and toddlers and she recognised the extraordinary amount of work that went into rearing a child. She had nothing but admiration for women who managed to juggle a career and family, but the very nature of her job, which

involved travel and odd hours, made having a child simply out of
the question. Well, out of the question if she was alone. But if
she had a partner . . . that might be different. Maybe this was what
she had first recognised with Robert: the possibilities. She had
looked at the lonely, slightly desperate, trapped man and
recognised the possibilities, the potential, surrounding him.

When they were together, and when the time was right, she
would love to have a child. Boy or girl, it didn't matter: it would
be theirs.

"When would you like to have them?" he wondered.

"Not immediately of course," she said, just in case he had any
ideas of an instant family. She reached for his hand, relishing the
warmth and strength of it. "Well, it's a bit of a Catch-22. I'm
thirty-five now. I can't wait too long and yet, I need another two
years at least before I'm promoted. Then we could start trying for
the year after that."

But was thirty-eight too old to be thinking about conceiving a
first child? It was. Maybe she'd think about a career break, have
the baby then go back to work, possibly in a part-time capacity.

Stephanie smiled as she walked towards her car: her entire
world was shifting, changing, altering. She was looking at
possibilities that simply hadn't existed forty-eight hours ago.

The cars were parked alongside one another in the darkened
corner of the carpark. They hit the alarm toggles together and
both sets of lights blinked simultaneously.

Robert opened her car door and she threw her gym bag onto
the passenger seat, then turned to him. She loved this man. And
she would love to have his child. She reached up, pressed the palm
of her right hand against the back of his skull to bring his head
down to a level with hers. "Think of all the fun we'll have
practising to conceive children," she whispered. Then she kissed
him, passionately and deeply. Finally they broke apart, panting
slightly. Without saying another word, Stephanie climbed into
the car, waved once and drove away. She was thinking about baby

names as she glanced in the rear-view mirror and saw him still standing by his car, talking on the phone.

And would she keep her own name, or take his?

She quite liked Walker. She tried it out, saying it aloud, "Stephanie Burroughs-Walker." No, just Stephanie Walker. That's what she'd become.

Mrs Walker.

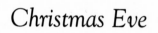

Christmas Eve

CHAPTER 42

Tuesday 24th December

When Stephanie Burroughs opened the hall door, she instantly recognised the woman standing on the doorstep. A dozen emotions flickered through her – shock, fear, anger – including, surprisingly, relief.

"Hello, Stephanie."

"Mrs Walker. Kathy."

On the drive over, Kathy Walker had rehearsed her conversation with Stephanie Burroughs a hundred different ways. She'd gone through every emotion – from anger to resignation, from disgust to horror, and what was left was . . . nothing. An emptiness. A hollow feeling inside.

She knew, right up to the moment she pressed the doorbell what she was going to say to Stephanie, how she was going to react. She would be polite, cool: if the bitch wanted Robert, she could have him!

But when Stephanie Burroughs opened the door and looked at her with instant recognition in her eyes, all her carefully laid plans, her nicely ordered words and phrases deserted her.

Kathy stepped forward and cracked Stephanie across the face with the flat of her hand.

The two women blinked at one another, each surprised, shocked, horrified by what had just taken place. Kathy felt herself start to shake: she'd never raised a hand to another person in her life.

Stephanie pressed her hand against her stinging cheek. She'd absolutely no intention of striking back. She bore the woman no animosity; Kathy had done nothing wrong. Almost from the very first moments of her relationship with Robert, Stephanie had been dreading – and expecting – an encounter with Robert's wife. She knew that once Robert told Kathy that he was leaving, she could expect a visit. And if she was visiting the home of her husband's mistress, she'd belt her one too.

"I'm sorry!" Kathy began, abruptly breathless. "I promised myself I wasn't going to do that. I'm sorry."

Stephanie hadn't been expecting a visit this soon; she didn't think Robert was going to tell his wife until after Christmas.

Kathy gathered herself. "We can . . ." she began, but her voice was trembling with emotion. She swallowed hard and tried again. "We can have this conversation here on your doorstep or you can let me in."

Stephanie looked at the woman. She didn't want to speak to her . . . but somewhere deep inside her, she felt a twinge of sympathy. Kathy deserved an answer. Mrs Moore's curtains twitched and that decided her. She moved aside. "Yes, you should come in."

The older woman hesitated a moment, then nodded and stepped into the hall. Stephanie directed her into the sitting-room then took a moment to compose herself. There were tears in her eyes, more from the fright than the slap across the face. She glanced at herself in the hall mirror: the imprint of Kathy's fingers was clear on her pale cheek.

Kathy looked at the room, and found that she liked it; it wasn't her taste, it was just a little too fussy, but it was homely and comfortable, not at all what she's imagined it was going to be. She'd somehow imagined that Robert's mistress would be classy and go for the old magazine favourites of blond wood and polished chrome. It was spotlessly neat, of course, but it was easy to keep a house clean if you didn't have two teens running about.

Stephanie hung back in the doorway, a hand pressed to her cheek, and watched Robert's wife. The woman was not entirely as she remembered her: older certainly, the skin on the face sagging a little, black bags under bloodshot eyes. She was simply dressed in a cream woollen polo neck over black pants, with simple jewellery, a gold necklace, a gold bracelet and gold wedding and engagement rings. Stephanie got the impression that Kathy Walker had taken some time dressing for this encounter.

Stephanie couldn't help but wonder how she would look if her lover had just said he was walking out. How would she feel? How was Kathy feeling now? In that moment, she felt an extraordinary rush of pity for the other woman. She folded her arms across her chest; she couldn't afford to feel pity for Kathy. This was the woman who had effectively driven her husband away.

Kathy turned a full circle. "It's very nice," she said eventually. She was relieved to find no pictures of Robert and Stephanie on the walls, no signs that he was already living there. "You know why I'm here."

Stephanie looked at her closely, spotting the remarkable resemblance between them, and realised with a frisson of horror that she was seeing herself as she would be in five years' time. Or at least as she would be if her husband had just left her for a younger woman. "So he's told you about us?" she asked coldly.

Kathy shook her head. "Robert didn't tell me."

Stephanie nodded. Trying to prevent her voice from trembling she said coolly, "So you found out."

"I found out," Kathy said, her voice as icy as Stephanie's. "I found out about you and him." Anger began to edge her words.

"I thought he'd told you. He said he was going to."

"Robert says he's going to do lots of things. Then he forgets," she added bitterly. "I just want some answers. That's all. I cannot ask him – I cannot ask him anything about you and him – because he'll lie. He'll lie to me," she added bitterly.

And although Stephanie did not want to speak to this woman, she found that she owed her that much. She nodded. "I was going to make some tea. Would you like some?

"Yes. Please." Kathy pulled off her coat and folded it over the back of a chair while Stephanie disappeared into the kitchen. Kathy hesitated a moment, then followed her, unconsciously taking up the same position and the same pose that Robert had adopted on Friday night.

"On the way over here I knew down to the last word everything I was going to say to you. Now that I'm here, I can't think of anything worthwhile to say. But I never intended to hit you," she added, curiously embarrassed by the action. "That was . . . unnecessary."

"I'd have done the same too, I think. If you want to shout at me, scream at me, I'd understand that too."

Kathy shook her head. "What's the point?"

Stephanie nodded.

"Why?" Kathy asked simply. "Why did you take my husband from me? Why would you do that?"

Stephanie concentrated on the kettle. "It just happened," she said, surprisingly softly. "It just happened."

"Things don't just happen," Kathy snapped. "People make things happen. You made this happen."

"And Robert too," Stephanie added.

Kathy nodded, forced to agree.

"And you." Stephanie rounded on Kathy. "You had a part in this too!"

Kathy was taken aback by the vehemence in the other woman's voice. "I did nothing –" she began.

"Exactly," Stephanie snapped. She was getting angry, terribly angry. She wasn't going to shoulder the entire blame for this. Kathy was responsible, Robert was responsible and she was responsible too. "I want you to know that I never – never! – set out to have an affair with him. I've never had a relationship with a married man before. I got together with Robert – I allowed myself to get close to Robert – because I understood that you and he had parted. Emotionally, I mean. That he was available. We're all responsible."

Kathy opened her mouth to snap a denial, but then she closed it again. Was it true? Could it be true? She watched the younger woman make tea in the rather sterile-looking kitchen. She'd recalled Stephanie as being much more glamorous than she was, slimmer, prettier. Maybe that was just her memory playing tricks: the Stephanie she was looking at now was rather ordinary-looking in a well-kept sort of way. Was this the woman Robert was thinking of leaving her for? She was only a couple of years younger; thank God she wasn't a twenty-year-old busty bimbo.

Kathy accepted the tea from Stephanie's hand, noting the slightest tremble on the surface of the tea. But maybe it was her own hands trembling.

Together the two women went back into the sitting-room, Stephanie taking up her usual place, Kathy settling into the chair usually occupied by her husband. They drank their tea in silence, not quite looking at one another.

"I saw you last night," Kathy said, breaking the long silence. "In the gym carpark. I was so angry then, but only for a moment. Just a single instant. Then I felt . . . nothing."

Stephanie nodded, not entirely sure what to say. She was trying to remember what they had said and done last night. They'd been talking about children and she'd kissed him. Had Kathy seen that? Probably. Stephanie found herself wondering how she would feel if she saw Robert kissing another woman.

"What do you want to know?" she asked eventually.

"I'm not sure," Kathy said truthfully. "When I set out to come here, I was going to fight for him. I was going to plead with you to let him go, to ask you not to take him away from me, from his children. But I'm not sure I want to do that any more."

"Why not?" Stephanie whispered.

"I want my husband back . . . but I don't want him to come back to something he doesn't want to commit to."

Stephanie nodded. She could understand that all too clearly.

"Tell me something . . ." Kathy continued.

Watching this woman, Stephanie tried to analyse the emotions that were churning through her at this moment. She'd never really thought too much about Kathy. Sally had been right: all she knew about this woman had been filtered through Robert. She supposed she'd deliberately avoided dwelling on her. If she'd had any strong feelings about her in the past, they would have been ones of disgust perhaps or even anger at the way she treated Robert . . . but she had to remember that Robert no doubt had shaped and twisted the story to make it his version of the truth. It worried her now that she was beginning to feel a deep sympathy for Kathy.

"Six years ago, when you first joined the company, did you have a relationship with Robert? And tell me the truth, please," she added sharply. "The time for lies is over."

"I agree, no more lies. No," Stephanie said simply, "no, I didn't. I was an employee, nothing more. I swear to you that there was absolutely nothing between us."

Kathy took a moment to absorb the answer. Was it the truth? She looked at the woman sitting across from her. They were strangers, with nothing in common – except the one man. Her man. That Stephanie Burroughs had tried to take from her. But that feeling was changing, that emotion was altering. Stephanie was right. She was not entirely to blame. Stephanie may have made herself available to Robert, but he, in turn, had responded.

"Do you believe me?" Stephanie asked.

Kathy nodded. Her eyes filled with tears. "I was wrong then. I was wrong."

"Wrong?"

"I made a mistake back then – about you and him."

"Yes, you did. I didn't realise until very recently that you'd made the accusation. Have you accused him again?"

"Not yet. This time I wanted to speak to you first."

"Maybe you should have done that before," Stephanie snapped.

"Maybe I should have," Kathy agreed.

"When did you realise about us?"

"Thursday evening. By accident. I needed an address for a Christmas card, and I discovered your name in Robert's phone. There was a little red flag beside it. I jumped to a conclusion: the same conclusion I jumped to six years ago. Then I was wrong; this time, I discovered I was right. When I went looking I discovered that the pieces weren't that hard to find. Sometimes I think he wanted me to find out and save him the trouble of having to face me and tell me himself."

"My experience of him would be different. As far as I can see, he's done everything in his power to keep this a secret from you. He didn't want to hurt you." Stephanie was unable to keep the trace of bitterness from her voice.

"I've been trying to analyse over the past few days when exactly the rot began in our marriage. I think I can pinpoint back to that moment, six years ago, when I accused him of having an affair with you. I made a mistake then; am I paying for it now?"

"I've told you: we weren't involved then."

"I believe you," Kathy said. And she did, she realised.

"Why did you accuse him in the first place?" Stephanie had the sudden urge to reach out and touch Kathy's hand. It was almost as if they were discussing a bereavement.

"He was always with you, always talking about you, spending time away with you. You were young, pretty, vivacious. I was jealous, I suppose. I thought it was inevitable that he'd sleep with you."

"But it wasn't. He certainly never made any advances towards me. Remember, we were working on that huge project. He couldn't afford to get in a new researcher, and you'd backed away from the business to raise the children. That's how we were thrown together."

"But I made the accusation. He denied it, of course. I called him a liar, doubted him, and you know something, once you doubt someone, then there's no way to come back from that. It taints everything."

Stephanie nodded. She's spent weeks doubting Robert's intention of committing to her. And even now, even with the words said, she still had the vaguest of niggling reservations.

They drank their tea in silence.

"I've been thinking about this a lot over the past few days," Kathy continued, "and there were times when I hated you. Just despised you. How dare you seduce my husband? I wanted to know if you were taking him just because you could, or as some sort of game, or –"

"It wasn't like that," Stephanie said urgently.

"Then what was it like? What gave you the right?"

"You did. You gave me the right," Stephanie snapped.

Kathy looked at her blankly.

"When you pushed him away, pushed him out of your life. Then I allowed myself to be interested in him."

Kathy opened her mouth to respond, but Stephanie held up a hand.

"And then I fell in love with him." She took a deep shuddering breath. "And that changed everything."

Kathy felt her stomach churn. It was hard to sit here and listen to this woman talk about loving her – *her* – husband. "Maureen said she'd seen you together. She told me that she thought you were in love with him. I thought a lot about that. I wondered how that could be."

Stephanie shrugged. "It just happened. I didn't plan it."

Kathy pressed on as if she hadn't heard her. "And I remembered why I had fallen in love with him. He was very kind."

Stephanie nodded.

"And he was gentle, and hapless and he made me laugh. And he was passionate. So passionate about his work. He had such dreams."

"He still has," Stephanie whispered.

"He doesn't tell me those any more."

"Why not?" Stephanie asked, and she was genuinely curious now.

"When I left R&K to concentrate on the children, he assumed that I'd no further interest in the business, I think. He no longer saw me as a business partner, and only as a wife and mother. He stopped telling me what he was doing, stopped asking my advice. I was rearing two young children. He had no idea how exhausting that is. He was leaving early in the morning, coming home later and later at night. I had the sole responsibility for rearing the children twenty-four hours a day. By the time he got home, all I wanted to do was sleep."

Stephanie stood up and took Kathy's empty cup and her own. She returned to the kitchen to fill them. Was it only last night she'd been thinking about having a child with Robert? How would that affect their relationship? How would he regard her once the child was born?

Robert had never really discussed his relationship with his children, Brendan and Theresa. He'd spoken about them in a general way, but she'd never realised just how much of their rearing had fallen to Kathy. When she was together with Robert, their relationship was entirely a selfish one: they concentrated on one another. She'd never really thought about his children . . . what would happen to them when he left? What would they think, not only of him and her, but of Kathy too?

She returned to the sitting-room with two fresh cups.

"I see you use proper cups, with saucers," Kathy remarked.

"Robert prefers mugs," Stephanie said. "I hate them."

"I know," Kathy said coldly. Every time Stephanie spoke about Robert in a personal way, she had to bite back her temper. "I visited here the other night; I needed to see where you lived."

"You were the woman with the mysterious Christmas hamper."

"That was me."

"What were you looking for?"

"Proof. Plus, I wanted – needed – to see you together."

"And when you did . . ."

"You reminded me of how we used to look. Happy. Holding hands, kissing, content with one another, relaxed together."

"I'm sorry about what's happened . . ." Stephanie began, and she was genuinely sorry.

"You didn't destroy our marriage," Kathy said, bitterly. "We just drifted. It there's blame to be laid, then it can be laid at both doors."

"Although you didn't find yourself a lover," Stephanie said with a wry smile.

"Not with two children hanging out of me, I didn't. An affair needs lots of free time, opportunity and commitment to make it work. I had precious little of any of those. I've gone beyond blaming you personally: I think that if he hadn't had an affair with you, then it would have happened with someone else."

Stephanie blinked in shock and drew back a little. She recalled her own flickering fears about Illona and the way she looked at Robert. "You mean . . ."

"I mean if he was withdrawing from me and wanted comfort or companionship, then he would have taken it anywhere he could." She was unable to resist adding, "You just happened to be convenient. The mistake Robert made was placing the job before his family; the mistake I made was allowing him. But there were always good reasons: there was never quite enough money. And I'm not using that as an excuse either."

"I know," Stephanie said numbly. Was what Kathy saying true? Was there the possibility that Robert would have had a relationship with anyone, or rather, any available person?

"When I discovered that you were putting business his way, I even began to rationalise his relationship with you, saying it was purely business. Then I hated myself for thinking that he'd sleep with you just to get some work for the company."

Stephanie opened her mouth to reply, but said nothing. That thought – that bitter foul thought – had crossed her mind on too many occasions. She licked dry lips and her voice was husky when she spoke. "Well, that's not going to happen any more. My boss has given me orders that R&K is not to get any more contracts from us."

Kathy sat back into the chair, absorbing the news. "Does Robert know?" she asked eventually.

"I told him last night."

"What are the implications of that decision?"

"If he doesn't get his act together and get more work real soon, then the company might go under."

"It might be a good thing if it did," Kathy said, surprising Stephanie with her vehemence. "Maybe if he could get a simple nine-to-five job, it would simplify things. He works too hard. In many ways, that's at the root of all this."

"I suggested the very same thing to him last night."

"I bet he wasn't pleased."

Stephanie shook her head, a ghost of a smile curling her lips. "He looked like I'd just hit him."

"I've seen that expression," Kathy agreed. "I've even suggested I'd go back into the business with him now that the children are a little older."

Stephanie said nothing; she didn't want to tell this woman that only the previous night – probably only moments before Kathy had spotted them kissing – they had been talking about having children together.

There was a long moment of uneasy silence. What do you say to your husband's mistress, or your lover's wife?

"When was he going to tell me?" Kathy wondered eventually.

"After Christmas," Stephanie said shortly. She was becoming increasingly uncomfortable with Kathy's presence in the house. She wanted her out, she wanted time to think.

"Was he going to move out?" Kathy wondered.

"He said he was going to spend New Year's Eve and New Year's Day with me."

"That's not quite the same thing as moving out." Kathy got up and stood by the window, staring out across the courtyard.

"No, it's not." Stephanie stood and folded her arms across her chest. "Kathy, I want you to know that I forced him to come to a decision about us on Friday night. We've been involved for eighteen months, and serious for about six of those – or at least, I've been serious. I wasn't so sure of Robert. I was tired of the uncertainty and the insecurity. I told him to choose. I'd a feeling that, left to his own devices, he'd have allowed things to drift on and on."

"He always did have a hard job making the tough calls. And you'd a perfect right to look for an answer." Kathy looked over her shoulder, a peculiar expression on her face. "You love him, don't you?"

"Yes. I do." She was unable to resist snapping back with, "Do you?"

Kathy turned back to the window. She could see Stephanie reflected in the glass. She thought about this question long and hard, asked it again and again, because, in the end it came back to this one simple question: did she love him? Even after all he'd done, even after the pain of the last few days?

"Yes."

The word hung on the air between the two women.

"Would I be here if I didn't?"

There were tears in both their eyes now and they were staring

312

at one another with intensity. This conversation should not have gone this way: Kathy should have shouted at Stephanie, called her names and walked away. Stephanie should have watched the wife drive away and felt victorious. Right now, both women were experiencing the same emotion: fear.

Stephanie felt her heart begin to trip. Her mouth turned to cotton. Kathy couldn't . . . didn't . . . Robert had told her that Kathy didn't . . . but was that what Robert believed, or what he wanted her to believe. She unfolded her arms and reached down to touch the back to the chair, feeling that if she didn't grip onto something she was going to fall.

"You know something: I still love him. Despite what he's done. He is my husband. My children's father." She swung back from the window. "Do you believe me?" she whispered.

Stephanie was standing frozen in the chair, staring intently at her, horrified by what she was hearing. She was listening to a woman in love. In love with the same man she herself loved.

"He's betrayed me, betrayed my love, betrayed eighteen years of marriage, betrayed his children who idolise him. I don't want to keep him out of spite, like Jimmy Moran's wife. If he wants to go, if he truly wants to go, if he is so desperately unhappy with me, then I love him enough to let him go and he's yours. There's no point in asking Robert what he wants to do. He'll only tell me what he thinks I want to hear . . ."

Stephanie was nodding.

"Or I can ask you. Do you want him? Do you want him so badly that you want to take him from me?"

Stephanie felt the room shift and sway around her. Kathy wasn't supposed to love him. That's what she'd always believed right from the very beginning, from six years ago: Kathy didn't care for him. Didn't love him.

But Kathy did.

And Stephanie did.

Loved him with all her heart, loved him because he was kind

and gentle, made her laugh, cared for her, looked after her, was thoughtful, considerate . . . and had asked her to marry him.

Because he believed his wife no longer loved him.

Would he have made the same offer if he believed otherwise? Would he have had an affair with her if he thought that Kathy still had feelings for him?

Would he?

She didn't want to think he would.

It was easier – much easier – to believe that Robert had betrayed Kathy almost by accident, than to accept that he'd gone out to have an affair with someone who might be able to put extra business his way.

She took a deep breath, trying to steady her nerves. How would Kathy react if she knew that Robert had asked her to marry him? *He'll only tell me what he thinks I want to hear.* Was that what had happened on Saturday? Had Robert been lying to her?

As he'd lied to Kathy?

No, he hadn't, he couldn't. This was the man she loved, the man who said he loved her. The man who wanted to marry her.

A shape moved in the courtyard over Kathy's shoulder. Stephanie tilted her head, thinking it was Mrs Moore snooping again. Then she suddenly turned and walked from the room. "Hang on a moment."

The door opened even before he hit the bell. Behind the brightly wrapped Christmas presents, the helium balloon and the bunch of flowers, Robert Walker brushed past Stephanie with a cheery "Happy Christmas!" and manoeuvred his way through the door into the sitting-room.

Where Kathy was waiting.

CHAPTER 43

There are moments etched in the memory.

Moments of passion, of pain, victory and terror. Especially terror. When all else fades, the fear remains. When Robert Walker strode into Stephanie Burroughs' sitting-room and found his wife waiting for him, he experienced one of those moments that he knew, instantly and instinctively, he would carry with him to his grave.

His mouth opened and closed, but he couldn't draw breath. It was as if he had been punched in the stomach and his heart started beating so hard he was sure it was going to burst. Acid indigestion boiled in his stomach and burned the back of his throat. He looked from Kathy to Stephanie and back again, trying to make sense of what he was seeing. A score of reasons, excuses and stupid possibilities flashed through his head in a single moment.

Until only the truth remained,

Kathy knew.

And that brought with it an extraordinary sense of relief.

No more sneaking around, no more furtive phone calls, no more clandestine meetings. No more lies.

Kathy stepped up to him, and slapped him hard enough across the face to rock his head back, chipping one of his brand new caps. She'd never intended to hit Stephanie, but she'd always known she was going to strike him. That was never in doubt. Her hand stung and she relished the blow.

Robert backed away from Kathy, and turned to Stephanie for support, but the strange look on her face kept him away from her also. "You – you told her," he finally said to Stephanie.

"You see," Kathy said conversationally, not looking at him, "he never accepts responsibility. It's always someone else's fault."

Stephanie folded her arms across her chest and nodded. She'd noticed that in Robert before. Abruptly, with the two of them here in the same room, she felt like an outsider.

Robert looked from one woman to the other. "Well, she must have phoned you, brought you here, how else –"

"How else, Robert?" Kathy snapped. "Because I'm not as stupid as you seem to think I am. And you're not as clever as you believe you are."

"I think . . . I think . . ." Robert looked around desperately, "I think I should go."

"No!" both women said simultaneously.

"Maybe not, then." He put down the Christmas present, and rested the bouquet of flowers on top of it. The balloon floated unnoticed to the ceiling.

Kathy resumed her position on the sofa, and Stephanie almost collapsed into her usual seat. He stood for a moment, unsure what to do, then sat down on the sofa, as far away from Kathy as possible. He looked from woman to woman, noticed that their expressions were identical.

"You owe us an explanation," Kathy said. "Both of us."

"I'm not sure what to say," Robert said miserably.

And it was true. He'd tried, over the past couple of days, to work out a scenario whereby he could tell Kathy that he was leaving her. He wanted to break it to her gently, though he knew there was no easy way to tell his wife that he was cheating on her, so what it came down to now was timing: choosing the right time. And even that was turning out to be impossibly difficult. If only Christmas wasn't in the way; that created such problems. He'd thought about speaking to Stephanie again, asking her to give him a little more time, just a couple of weeks to sort things out, but he knew she wouldn't believe him.

"Why don't you start with the truth, Robert," Stephanie said.

"The truth?" he looked at her blankly, and suddenly wondered how long the two women had been chatting before he arrived, how much they knew about one another. He was hunting for a formula of words which would not offend Stephanie or hurt Kathy too much when Stephanie spoke.

"I've always believed that Kathy didn't love you."

He looked at her blankly.

"You told me – more than once – that she didn't love you."

Unsure where this was going, he nodded. "That's right. She doesn't."

Kathy looked as if she had been slapped. "I've never said that! Never once." She turned from Robert to Stephanie. "I never said that to him." Then she rounded on Robert. She lunged down the couch and struck at him again, catching him on the side of the head. "You bastard! Is that what you've been saying: is that how you've been justifying your lousy affair: saying I didn't love you!" There were tears in her eyes now, tears of rage. "I do love you!"

Robert was taken aback by the vehemence of her response. He backed away from her, ear ringing. Kathy didn't love him, couldn't love him, hadn't loved him for ages. "But . . . but . . . you never said anything . . . I just assumed . . ."

"Well, you assumed wrong!" she snapped.

Robert drew in a deep shuddering breath. "You don't talk to me. You ignored me. You're not interested in me, not interested in the business."

"And were you interested in Kathy?" Stephanie wondered aloud, surprising them both.

Kathy looked at her in surprise.

Robert looked at her blankly. Whose side was she on?

"Did you ever ask about her day? Did you ever stop to realise just who kept the house going while you were running the business?"

"Hang on a sec . . ." he began, anger touching his voice. "I won't take that from –"

"From whom?" she demanded.

"From you," he finished lamely.

"I never stopped loving you," Kathy said into the silence that followed. "When I discovered that you were having an affair with Stephanie, I hated you, I, despised you. But it made me re-evaluate our eighteen years together, showed me some of the mistakes we've both made. It's not gone, Robert. It's still salvageable. If you want to salvage it. And there's one other thing you need to remember: I still love you enough to come here and fight for you."

There were many answers Robert expected, but not this one. And this answer terrified him. It had been easy to justify what he was doing with the understanding that Kathy no longer cared for him and even if she did find out, it was not going to be such a big deal. There would be a fight, sure, but then they'd separate and ultimately divorce. But it would all be fairly amicable he thought because Kathy had no strong feelings for him any more; there were times he thought she would actually be better off without him.

But she loved him.

Loved him enough to fight for him.

Stephanie watched the couple, saw the fear on Robert's face, the determination on Kathy's. In that moment, she discovered that she actually admired Robert's wife. It was every woman's nightmare, to face the mistress, and Kathy had the courage to do it. Stephanie found that she wasn't listening to a couple who hated one another.

She knew Kathy still loved Robert.

And Robert . . . did he still love Kathy? In fact, he had never said that he didn't or that he'd stopped loving her.

She was looking at a couple who still loved one another but who'd lost their way – both of them. They'd become distracted by house and home and children and job and forgotten what had created all of those things in the first place: their love, their relationship, their commitment.

And where did that leave her? Where did that leave Robert's promise to her?

"Do you love me, Robert?" Kathy asked finally.

Even before he answered, Stephanie knew the truth. She saw it in the way he had looked at her, saw it in his face. She knew how he would answer, though whether that was the absolute truth was open to question. She remembered how he'd been so desperate to keep the news of their relationship from Kathy. Once she thought it was cowardice – and it might be that too – but it was also love. He didn't want his wife to know because he didn't want to hurt her. Was that also why he'd kept from her how badly the business was doing? They were mistakes: he should have shared with her. Stephanie knew that Kathy was far tougher than Robert imagined.

"Yes," he said simply, "I love you."

"And Stephanie, do you love her also?" Kathy asked, surprising them both.

There was a moment – no more than a handful of seconds – but it seemed to extend for an eternity before Robert nodded and answered. "Yes, yes, I do."

The two women looked at one another. Their emotions were in turmoil. They loved the same man; he had slept with both of them. But they both knew that he had drifted from Kathy through ignorance – because he thought she no longer loved him. He had allowed himself to enter into a relationship with Stephanie for the same reason and she, in turn, had agreed to a relationship with him because she believed him to be emotionally separated from his wife.

"It's possible to love more than one person," Robert said slowly.

"I know that," said Kathy. "We know that," she added, glancing at Stephanie, who nodded in agreement. "But you have to make a choice now, because, Robert, you cannot have us both."

She could end it here and now, Stephanie thought. She could make him hers.

If Kathy knew that Robert had proposed to her, had offered to marry her, then Kathy would get up and walk out of the room. The relationship might survive the affair, but it could not survive that ultimate betrayal. And if she did walk out, what would that achieve? It would leave Stephanie with Robert. But Stephanie had been afforded a glimpse of her future with Robert and it was not what she'd imagined it was going to be.

But this was her chance to be happy.

From the moment Robert had proposed she'd been walking on air. She'd never imagined that such a simple sentence could make her so unreasonably excited. She'd spent the last few hours bubbling with excitement, planning for a future that was now – suddenly – under threat.

Kathy had come here to fight for her man.

What was Stephanie going to do in return? How was she going to fight? Or was she?

The single sentence, "*Robert proposed to me*," would send Kathy home, devastated, and Robert would be hers. But looking at him now, his eyes wide and locked onto Kathy's face, suddenly made her wonder how he would feel if she managed to drive his wife off. She'd watched him when he told Kathy that he loved her. He meant it. Would he be able to forgive her if she drove away his wife?

But she loved him.

And sometimes you have to let go those you love.

"I've made a mistake," Stephanie said suddenly. "A terrible mistake."

Robert and Kathy looked at her blankly.

Stephanie had the sudden urge to reach out and touch Kathy's hand. "I swear to you that I did not know he was still in love with you. I understood that he was going to leave you. I was wrong." She stood up, and the other two automatically rose to their feet with her. She stepped forward and placed the palm of her hand flat on Robert's chest. Kathy's eyes flared, but she remained still and unmoving. "I love you, Robert, as much as Kathy loves you. But I cannot have you. Go back to your wife. If she'll take you, that is." She felt something break inside her as the future she'd been planning shattered and twisted away. What was left was a deep bitterness – not directed towards Robert, not towards Kathy, but towards herself. How could she have been so stupid?

Because she loved him.

Kathy looked from Stephanie to Robert. She was missing something, she knew, some nuance that she hadn't picked up. She was also sensing something that sounded almost like relief in Stephanie's voice. Then Stephanie turned and walked from the room, leaving Robert and Kathy alone.

Kathy turned to look at her husband. "Well?"

"Well?" His voice was shaking, and he felt hungover. He'd run the full gamut of emotions in the last half hour. He'd got his wife back and lost Stephanie. On Saturday he'd been thinking about starting again; well, here he'd just been given another opportunity to do just that. To go back to the beginning and start again, but with Kathy this time.

"I'll take you back, but there will be conditions," she said. "Things will change. You know that?"

He nodded. He wasn't sure what had just happened. One minute Stephanie loved him, the next she was claiming she'd made a mistake.

"And I will change too," she promised. "We'll start again,

have counselling, try and rebuild our marriage, our relationship. But there's one question you have to ask yourself: do you want to come back to me?"

"I never really left," he laughed shakily.

Kathy slapped him again. "You left me a long time ago! You say I withdrew from you, but that cuts both ways. Give me an answer!"

Where had this Kathy come from, this feisty, strong-willed and determined woman? This was the woman he'd married a long time ago, the woman he'd thought had gone. And why had Stephanie rejected him? When he'd proposed to her . . . if Kathy knew he'd proposed to her . . .

And he understood then.

He nodded. "Yes. Yes, I do want to come back. If you'll have me. Start again. Start afresh."

"It may not work and we may end up going our separate ways, but I think we owe it to one another to give it a try."

"Yes, yes, we do." He spread his arms. "About this –"

Kathy raised a hand, silencing him. "You told me you loved me. Do you mean it?"

"Yes."

"Then that's all I need to know at the moment." She pushed him towards the door. "Go home now. I'll follow shortly."

Robert allowed himself to be ushered out into the hallway, then he hesitated. "Stephanie. . ." he began, but the look in his wife's eyes silenced him and he left the house. He thought he might make a detour on the way and pick up his wife's Christmas present, and maybe call into Maureen's with that Christmas bonus cheque.

Kathy went to stand by the bottom of the stairs. "We're going now," she called.

Stephanie appeared at the top of the stairs. Her eyes were bright, but she was not crying. Not yet. She came down the stairs slowly and close to the bottom step, she shrugged and said, "I thought he was the one."

"So did I," Kathy whispered, looking past the open hall door to where Robert was pulling away in the car, "and he was, once. Thank you," she said finally.

"For what?"

"For not telling me the promises he made." She leaned forward quickly and hugged Stephanie. "Take care – but, and I don't want you to take this the wrong way, I don't want to see you again."

"You won't," Stephanie said with feeling.

The two women walked to the door together. Mrs Moore across the courtyard thought they were sisters, which was strange because she knew that Stephanie had no relations in Ireland, but probably one had come home for the holiday. She waved and both women waved back. Americans were so friendly.

"What are you going to do for the holidays?" Kathy asked as she stepped out into the bitter December sunshine.

"Go home to my family," Stephanie said. "And you?"

"The same."

Also available from Poolbeg

SEASONS

ANNA DILLON

Dublin in 1900 is seething with discontent; poverty, disease and prostitution are rife, fuelling the flames of nationalist rebellion. Amidst this turmoil, a young fresh-faced English girl arrives to take up her new position as maid in the family of the cruel but magnetically handsome Englishman, Captain Lewis...

Katherine is instantly attracted to the charismatic officer, but she soon realises he is not quite what he pretends to be. She is wracked with further agonising doubts when she meets Dermot Corcoran, a patriotic young journalist, and discovers he is also hot on the captain's trail. And as the nationalist rebellion gathers pace, Katherine finds herself desperately trying to escape from an ever-tightening noose of conspiracy and deception. But, in Captain Lewis, she may have met her match - not only in love but in the deadly game of life itself...

"Racy, pacy blockbuster... A delicious read."
RTÉ GUIDE

ISBN 1-84223-126-X

Also available from Poolbeg

ANOTHER SEASON

ANNA DILLON

There are two things Katherine Lundy will never speak of – Ireland and her past...

But Ireland draws her son Patrick like a magnet. Fiercely nationalist, he leaves his family to follow his destiny and ignite the burning hatred he feels for England – and his mother...

Senga, his sister, is to be launched as a débutante, a glittering social butterfly in fashionable London. But her discovery of her mother's hidden past propels her into a completely different world – a murky world of deception and international intrigue...

From London to Dublin and Paris, Patrick and Senga are swept into the future by the changing winds of fortune. But they can never escape the past...

The heart-breaking sequel to the bestselling *Seasons*

ISBN 1-84223-127-8

Also available from Poolbeg

SEASONS' END

ANNA DILLON

Senga Lundy, on the brink of womanhood, has no reason to love her domineering mother. Yet Katherine's disappearance from glittering 1930's London plunges Senga reluctantly into her affairs – and into dangerous conflict with the law and ruthless villains alike – as the secrets of Katherine's past emerge to threaten Senga's life.

Frightened and confused, Senga flees to Montmartre and then to the uneasy dazzle of pre-war Berlin, her pursuers ever closer on her heels as she draws nearer to the very heart of the mystery. But which of her protectors – Scotswoman Billy, enigmatic policeman Colin Holdstock, adoring Rutgar von Mann, comfortable Aunt Tilly, or even her beloved brother Patrick and Katherine herself – can she truly trust?

In a violent denouement in the heart of Paris, Senga discovers the unexpected truth...

The triumphant conclusion to the bestselling *Seasons* saga.

ISBN 1-84223-128-6